MURDER
at
CLEVE
COLLEGE

BOOKS BY MERRYN ALLINGHAM

MURDER
at
CLEVE
COLLEGE

Merryn Allingham

bookouture

Published by Bookouture in 2024

An imprint of Storyfire Ltd.
Carmelite House
50 Victoria Embankment
London EC4Y 0DZ

www.bookouture.com

ISBN: 978-1-83525-856-9
eBook ISBN: 978-1-83525-855-2

This book is a work of fiction. Names, characters, businesses, organizations,
places and events other than those clearly in the public domain, are either the
product of the author's imagination or are used fictitiously. Any resemblance
to actual persons, living or dead, events or locales is entirely coincidental.

PROLOGUE

ABBEYMEAD, SUSSEX, OCTOBER 1958

He'd been foolish to come. He'd known that ever since the bus had dropped him in what appeared to be the main street of the village. A wild goose chase, he muttered to himself. Yet, despite the difficulties ahead, he knew he wouldn't give up. His father deserved no less.

After the letter, he'd visited his childhood home, what was left of it, spoken to a neighbour and been given the name of a boy. The lad had done odd jobs for him, the neighbour said, a nice boy who'd made good, working now in a local college. But when he'd managed to track him down, the boy, turned man, had been flustered, evasive – sly even. The encounter had made him more certain than ever that something was being hidden. But what? And who was hiding it?

A delivery van was the only other clue he had. He'd learned that from the neighbour, too. Every Friday like clockwork the vehicle had driven past his house, the chap had said, and on to the old home. It had the word Abbeymead plastered across its side. If you ask me – and the man had pulled a face – a bit of a flashy effort.

That was why he was here, knowing no one in this village

but hoping to find information. Just one snippet would make the journey worthwhile. He'd walked up the main street to the church, thinking he might talk to the vicar, a man steeped in village affairs and likely to be a valuable source. On the way, he'd seen a café and, for a moment, his spirits had risen high. Could the delivery van have belonged to the Nook? Would the café owners know something? But when he tried the door, the place was shut and he'd had to walk on.

The church had been open when he arrived, but the vicar busy. There'd been a group at the altar and he'd realised almost immediately that he was intruding on a wedding rehearsal and walked quickly out. For a while, he'd loitered in the churchyard, then decided to follow the group when they left. They were evidently local and seemed a cheerful bunch, people who might be willing to talk to him if he knocked on their door. They were ahead of him now but he could just glimpse the house they were walking into. A little scruffy around the edges but homely enough. They were decent people, he was sure. They would help him if they could.

With a new energy, he stepped up his pace, until the clank of an engine coming from behind had him slow. A large vehicle, a farm vehicle maybe, was filling the narrow lane. Might the driver prove more help than the group he'd been following? They must come from a local business, one perhaps that had delivered to the orphanage all those years ago.

Walking into the middle of the lane, he waved at the driver, a blurred image behind the windscreen. But they weren't slowing. The engine was churning, its growl getting louder. The vehicle was accelerating! Surely... surely not...

1

'I don't know who made these cheese straws, Jack, but I reckon they must have mice in their kitchen. If you can spot the cheese, you'll be lucky.' Alice Jenner's wiry grey curls bounced a reproof. Alice was head chef at the Priory Hotel and very few cooks in the county could meet her high standards.

'Try a sandwich instead.' Jack held out the large platter, before taking a third ham and pickle himself from the ever diminishing mound. As a crime writer, ham sandwiches had seen him through a fair number of author crises.

A stack of food – soufflés, pies and patties, and a variety of salads – had been set out on a Dutch blanket spread across Jack's sitting room floor, the kitchen having been judged too small to accommodate seven people.

'Or try one of Kate's soufflés,' Flora suggested. 'They're delicious.'

The all-important wedding rehearsal had passed off earlier without a hitch and she wanted this afternoon's party for Jack's birthday to go as smoothly.

'They're a special.' Kate Farraday's pale blue eyes were smiling. 'Very special, actually. Double-baked and I added a mystery ingredient. It's a shame they're too exotic for the tearoom, but the Nook has to keep to basics.'

Kate and Tony ran the village café, a popular meeting place for the Abbeymead regulars.

Taking a bite of the offered soufflé, Alice was mollified. 'Now you're talkin'. But then it's Kate's cookin'. You must have made them this mornin'. They're lookin' perky still.'

'We decided to close the Nook for the day.' She looked across at her almost new husband and smiled. 'It was such a treat. A whole morning cooking with Tony and not a customer to serve.'

'There's enough food here to feed an army.' Sally Jenner had been excused contributing to the party herself – as sole proprietor of the Priory Hotel, she was currently run off her feet. 'Perhaps we should keep some for next week. What do you think, Auntie?' she teased.

'Next Saturday we *will* have an army to feed,' Flora said a trifle wearily.

The whole of Abbeymead, it seemed, had expected and received an invitation to her and Jack Carrington's wedding. It was only fair, she supposed; most of the villagers had known her from childhood and the wedding would be a big occasion. An unexpected occasion. It had taken Flora time to relinquish the single life she valued, and give up, as she saw it, a prized independence. But her love for Jack, deep and strong, had finally had her say 'yes'.

'Keep some for next week!' Alice repeated, outraged by her niece's slander. 'We may be feeding the five thousand but... you leave it to me and Jessie.' She looked briskly around the group gathered in Jack's sitting room. Jessie Bolitho had been Flora's and Jack's housekeeper during their stay in Cornwall and was as excellent a cook as Alice. 'I heard from her last night. We had a long talk over the phone and everythin's under control. The menu's been decided and we both know exactly what we'll be doin'.'

'It's going to be a wonderful day.' Kate looked dreamily around the circle of friends. 'Flora will look beautiful – I've seen her in the dress. And I love my maid-of-honour outfit.'

'Mine, too.' Sally sounded wistful. 'The material is heavenly.'

'Don't you go gettin' any ideas about weddings just yet,' her aunt said sternly. 'You've a business to run. And now that no-good partner of yours has up and gone, that's what you need to concentrate on.'

'I'm very glad Dominic has left. It was more of a strain than I realised, working with him after we... parted. And right now, I couldn't be concentrating more, but I have to have some fun.'

'Mixing business with pleasure never works.' Alice wagged her finger. 'That Hector now...' Hector Lansdale was the dashing new sous chef at the Priory.

'Hector and I are just friends,' Sally said defiantly.

'Hmm,' was her aunt's doubting response.

'How's it going with your new staff?' Flora was anxious to avoid any argument over Hector Lansdale.

'I've had to do a lot of training, of course, but overall it's going pretty well.' Sally ran a hand through spiky blonde hair. 'A few bad mistakes – coffee spilt on a guest's silk shirt, the wrong bottle offered to the president of the local wine society! – but our hard work seems to be paying off and the hotel is three quarters full, right up to Christmas.'

'Sounds good.' Tony gave an encouraging nod. 'Though I'm not surprised you're booked out. The rain doesn't seem to have put people off coming to Sussex. Several times last week we had a café of drowned rats.'

'Be grateful it's been rain and not snow,' Alice said gloomily. 'We'll have to hope it holds off with Jack doin' that long journey to the college.'

'It's only twenty miles, Alice,' he protested. 'And it doesn't usually snow until January.'

Jack had recently agreed, along with writing his books, to become a student mentor at Cleve, an arts college some distance from the village.

'You can never tell—' Alice began when Sally interrupted, clearly irritated by her aunt's pessimism. 'How *is* the job?' she asked. 'You've been there now, what, two weeks?'

'Just over two,' he agreed. 'Not really long enough for me to decide. I like most of the students I've met and that's a bonus. They're certainly an interesting bunch. One chap I'm supposedly mentoring is retelling the story of the Battle of Hastings in blank verse, which is ambitious, to say the least, but he seems to have got his teeth into it.'

'And the staff? Any other crime writers to hobnob with?'

'No, I'm the prize exhibit. They're friendly enough, I guess. A bit distant maybe.'

Flora glanced across at him, noticing how uncomfortable he looked. He had reservations about Cleve, she knew, but he wouldn't want to speak of them openly.

'Time for the cake, don't you think?' she said quickly.

'And the champagne,' Kate put in. 'It was our turn to bring a bottle.'

Jack blew out his candles, thirty-eight reduced to eight, and the cake was cut. A clink of glasses and shouts of 'happy birthday' sounded around the room. Echoed around the room, Flora thought. Through the open doorway, she could see the cluster of packing cases in the hall, stacked one upon the other, and realised for the first time how many of Jack's possessions had filled this space: curtains, pictures, bookcases, an easy chair and several straightbacks. No wonder the house felt so abandoned today.

'And happy new job!' Sally said, already halfway down her glass of champagne.

'That dratted work of Jack's!' Alice declared, beginning to pack away what was left of the picnic. 'If it wasn't for that, you could both have been going on honeymoon next week.'

'But think what they have to look forward to, Auntie.' Sally beamed. 'Venice in June. Who wouldn't wait?'

'Alice was hard work,' Flora remarked as she and Jack began clearing up from the party.

'She'll be OK when things are more settled – when the wedding is over, Sally has stopped flirting with Hector, and we've come and gone to Venice.'

'That's a tall order. Are we going to suffer until then?'

'Probably. She's still a very kind woman.'

Flora sighed. 'Yes, she is, and Violet loved her.'

Flora's aunt Violet, dead for several years now, had fled London to make her home in Abbeymead and been a favourite with her fellow villagers. Alice had been a particular friend. The bookshop she'd established, the All's Well, was still running all these years later, owned and managed now by her niece.

'So... how does it feel to be thirty-eight? Or is that a daft question?'

'It is.' He turned away from the sink, hands covered in soapy water, and gave her a long hug. 'I'm feeling good, but not because I'm thirty-eight.'

'And the job? You were a bit... circumspect... when Sally asked you.'

'I guess I'm still finding my feet. Like I said, the students are delightful but the staff don't know me yet and I get the feeling it will take a while before I'm fully accepted. Maybe I've replaced someone they liked and, if he was sacked, they might be feeling resentful of the newcomer who's taken his place. I've no idea what happened to him.'

'Have you asked anyone?'

'Not yet. I'm expecting someone to dish the dirt any day now. Not the dean, though – there was no mention of my predecessor when he welcomed me to the college. Professor Dalloway seems to live on a different planet to everyone else. He has this indeterminate manner, so you're never quite sure what he's actually said. One of the art teachers, though, Jocelyn – I think her specialism is watercolour – has been friendly. She's come to talk to me over tea in the staffroom several times. I've no doubt she'll be filling me in with the gory details any time soon.'

'And the new novel?' Flora had always been concerned at how Jack would manage to write while working at the college. 'We've both been so busy lately, I haven't dared ask how the book is progressing!'

'Progressing is probably not the right word. Writing is slow. A lot slower, I have to admit. At the moment, my mind is constantly skipping between what I should be doing for the students and what for myself. But given time, I'll adjust to the new rhythm.'

Flora put down the tea towel she'd been wielding and clasped his arm. 'You know you can walk away from this job any time. We'll manage fine without the money it brings in.'

'I know I can, but I hate to be defeated. And it's early days.' He gave her chin a gentle pinch. 'Come on, let's get this stuff done. I'd no idea we'd used so many plates. They can't all belong to me, can they?'

'I'll shift the rest of my belongings mid-week,' he said, as they walked back along Greenway Lane to the cottage Flora had inherited from her aunt.

'Typewriter and all?'

'Remington and all,' he confirmed. 'The final push! I'll need to clean the place before I leave, I guess, and sort the garden as best I can – mow the lawn one last time or ask Charlie to do it.'

Young Charlie Teague had been Jack's mainstay in transforming what had once been a wilderness into a beautiful and productive garden.

'Charlie's looking forward to the wedding,' she said, smiling. 'I saw him yesterday when he collected the books for his delivery round, and he seems to be counting the days.'

'Counting the days to another feast, you mean. He could have come to the tea party, I guess, but he wasn't part of the rehearsal and, in any case, he'll have been off with his mates playing football this afternoon.'

'The thought of being a page boy revolted him. Not that I ever suggested it seriously. But Tony did a grand job today, didn't he? Standing in for your friend.' Jack's journalist buddy, Ross Sadler, had been delighted when asked to take on best man duties, but hadn't been able to travel down from London until the day itself. 'Tony's also promised to meet Jessie from the train on Thursday.'

'He's been a brick. Did you know he offered to nip out of the church just before we walk back down the aisle and gallop over to the green to make sure the marquee is still standing – you can't trust October weather! – and the catering has arrived?'

Flora frowned. 'I hope he didn't say that in front of Alice. Throwing doubt on her organising skills will have her up in arms. Mind you, I'll be doing my own double checking. Rose has agreed to cover my Saturday morning, but I'll need to make sure she's still happy to do it. I don't want to be haring from the All's Well in a wedding dress!'

'Is it working well? Having an assistant in the shop parttime? You've not said much.'

'Early days, but it seems to be. Rose Lawson is a natural at selling books – my sales definitely increase on the days she works!'

'Here, let me take that basket. You're drooping a bit and we're only halfway home.'

'*Our* home now! It will be strange no longer coming to Overlay House. It's not exactly a comfortable place but still...'

'It's been one of the most uncomfortable houses I've ever lived in,' Jack said with feeling. 'I'll really only miss the garden, but at least the landlord has agreed that while it remains unlet I can pick any produce that's ready. He was reluctant, of course. I never met a meaner man!'

'I'll miss the garden as much as you,' she said, and he could hear the regret in her voice. 'I did a small tour while you were in the kitchen helping Alice. Your veg patch is stunning and even the flowers are looking good – it's been so mild for the time of the year. I love those purple asters. All the rain we've had has kept them blooming and the veg growing. And look at *these* hedges! Such a brilliant green, it's positively technicolour... but ... what's that?'

'What?'

'A splash. Something red – there – sticking out of the ditch.'

He followed where she was pointing. 'You're right. That's odd. Something lost maybe?'

Jack clambered up the grass bank and peered down into the gully. When he turned, his expression was grave. 'It's a sock.'

She gave a small shrug. 'Someone will get cold feet.'

'Very cold.' He felt slightly sick. 'The sock is on a foot and the foot is attached to a leg.'

'A body? It can't be.' She was staring at him in disbelief.

'I'm afraid it is, and half drowned in water. I'll try to get to him. There's a small chance he may still be alive.'

Edging his way down the very steep ditch, he gradually made out a second foot, a second leg, and a few inches of white skin. Most of the man – it was certainly a man – was obscured by greenery, but his body appeared to be sprawled lengthways along the mud-strewn channel.

Jack was at the bottom now, slushing through a foot of water. Tentatively, he bent down and held his fingers to the man's throat. Then, looking up at Flora, feet above, he shook his head.

'Who is he? Do you recognise him?'

'No one I know.'

He reached into the man's jacket pocket, wholly submerged beneath the water, and found a wallet. But, after flipping it open and checking its contents, it took him only seconds to replace it. A dig into the man's trouser pocket was equally unsuccessful.

'There's nothing to suggest who he is,' he called up to her. 'His pockets are empty, apart from a wallet, and that contains only a few banknotes.'

'You're soaked, Jack.' Flora had climbed onto the grass bank and was looking down on him with concern. 'Come out before you get pneumonia.'

It was with some difficulty that he scaled the slippery bank, having to take hold of Flora's hand to haul himself finally over the edge and onto the lane.

'He's definitely dead?' she asked, as he stood dripping pools of water on the tarmac.

'Quite dead.'

'And he's a complete stranger? You've never seen him before?'

He shook his head but refused to meet her eyes.

A pair of hazel eyes, narrowing in suspicion, were trained on him. 'Are you certain?'

He wasn't. In truth, he was fairly sure the man in the ditch was the same chap who had walked into St Saviour's during the rehearsal. Flora had been talking to Kate, standing at her side as maid-of-honour, while Reverend Hopkirk riffled through his bible to find the place he wanted. She hadn't heard the squeak of the church door but Jack had and, looking over his shoulder, he'd spotted the intruder. The man, seeming to realise at that moment that he was interrupting a private ceremony, had ducked back into the porch and presumably walked away.

Except Jack was certain he'd seen him again, sensed him at least, loitering in the churchyard behind one of the huge lichen-covered gravestones, as though he were waiting for them. But then, with the rehearsal safely over and a birthday party ahead, he'd forgotten about the chap. And that was for the best. If Flora knew the man had been hanging around the village for some time, she would want to discover why, and a new mystery disturbing their lives was the last thing Jack wanted.

'I'm sure,' he said, slightly ashamed at the brazen lie.

'What on earth was he doing in Abbeymead?' Flora seemed unconvinced by his response. 'And how did he fall into that ditch? He can't have been there long. It was only a few hours ago that we walked past this spot and there was no sign of him then.'

'It's a puzzle, but we need to report it. I'll telephone Constable Tring from the cottage. The police will have to find out who he is and contact his family.'

For a while, they walked on in silence. A day that had held nothing but bright promise seemed to have darkened. For both of them.

'I don't like it,' Flora burst out suddenly. 'Who is he? Why was he in the village and how did he die in a ditch? It's horrible. And it's suspicious.'

Jack came to an abrupt halt. Taking her by the shoulders, he looked directly into her face. 'Flora, in less than a week we're getting married. That's what we need to focus on. It's most likely a terrible accident. Tring will be the one to sort out the mess.'

'Tring sort something out?' She gave a small puff of derision. 'That's a joke, yes?'

2

Alice's kitchen was warm with baking when Flora walked in unannounced late the following Friday. Her friend was rescuing yet another tray of sausage rolls from an oven that had hummed for most of the day, while Jessie Bolitho was icing an array of small cakes. Tomorrow was the big day.

'What do you think of these, Jessie?' Alice was saying, as Flora poked her head around the kitchen door.

'They look handsome enough.' Jessie nodded approval. 'I'll mebbe try one – just to make sure!' She gave a deep-throated laugh, then noticed Flora hovering in the doorway.

'Well, if it isn't Miss Flora,' she said, looking delighted.

'I'm so pleased to see you.' Flora bounded forward and clasped her in a big hug.

Jessie hadn't changed a bit, a sprightly sparrow of a woman with a spare frame and a pair of sharp brown eyes. But why would she have changed? It was only two years ago that she and Jack had bid the housekeeper goodbye after a momentous stay in Jessie's Cornish village, though it felt much longer with everything that had happened since.

'How is everything back home?' she asked.

'Not much different than when you saw it last, my lover. I'm not workin' so much – Mr Roger leavin' me that money has helped a lot. A bit more time on my hands now.'

'Time to cook for a wedding.' Alice beamed.

'Tha's right. It's goin' to be quite a feast!'

'We thought,' Alice began, 'if it's all right with you, Flora, that we'd include a few Cornish treats like the mini crab cakes Jessie made this morning. Take a look.' She pointed to several covered plates.

'That sounds a splendid idea.' Flora lifted the lid on a dish of golden patties. 'I remember when you cooked them in Treleggan. Delicious!'

Jessie pulled out a chair. 'Sit yourself down,' she ordered, 'and I'll make a pot. You're looking a bit wan, I must say.'

Flora tried hard to suppress her surprise. It was clear that Jessie had made herself at home in the cottage, but it was more than that. Alice's kitchen now seemed to belong to her as much as to Alice which, knowing her friend's insistence on being in charge, was extraordinary. The two women must have found common cause in providing what was destined to be Abbeymead's most extravagant wedding breakfast.

Alice stopped scrubbing baking trays and scrutinised her closely. 'Yes, you're lookin' peaky,' she confirmed. 'Give her one of my scones, Jessie. Loads of butter and jam. That will build her up.'

It wasn't building up she needed, Flora thought, just a few days of doing nothing. Despite Rose covering the shop as usual this Friday, and agreeing in addition to work tomorrow morning, she'd still felt the need to call at the All's Well to make sure there'd be no problem on her wedding day. That was before she'd rushed home and found Ross Sadler on her doorstep. He'd arrived earlier than she'd thought and with an unexpected request to stay over. The spare room had quickly to be made ready, including moving Jack's Remington and a stack of his paperwork. Then more hours spent finding places for as many of his possessions – mostly still in packing cases – as she could. For a man who travelled light, Jack seemed to have a surprising amount. And then there'd been the trying decision as to what to pack for the few days they'd booked away in Eastbourne. The Grand Hotel had a formidable ring to it.

'That Tony's a lovely lad,' Jessie said, presenting Flora with a buttered scone and a cup of tea. 'He couldn't have been kinder yesterday, meetin' me from Brighton, and with all that luggage I was carryin'. Not so much my stuff, I don' have that many clothes to bring, but two baskets of food and a whole box of ingredients. And he's promised to take me to the station when I'm ready to leave.'

'That won't be for a while.' Alice wiped a pair of floury hands on her pinafore.

'Alice has invited me to stay on for a few days, and I think I will.' Jessie wore a wide smile. 'It's a nice village. Bigger than Treleggan, o'course, and there's no river, but Alice tells me the coast is nearby and we're plannin' a day out once the weddin's over.'

Flora was surprised again. 'The two of you sound as though you'll be having fun.'

'And so will you, by all accounts,' Alice put in. 'Three days at the Grand Hotel!'

'Ooh la-la,' Jessie said unexpectedly, making Flora laugh.

They had made their vows, kissed at the altar, and were walking down the aisle and out into the sunshine of a calm October day, the tulle and lace of Flora's dress swishing against the ancient wooden pews. Jack glanced down at the woman by his side. Kate had been right. Flora was always beautiful, but today she looked ethereal, her face a pale glow and her red-brown hair piled high on her head and laced with small pearls. She'd refused to wear a veil and he was glad. Why would you want to hide a face that lovely?

At the lychgate, they turned to wave at what, in Jack's calculation, was at least half the village. Laughingly, Flora raised an arm and tossed her bouquet high into the air. A bunch of white and pink roses, nestled in silver foliage, flew over the crowd and it was Sally who caught it, in her eagerness almost toppling Elsie Flowers who'd made a similar grab for the bouquet.

Neither he nor Flora said a word, but he saw her pull a small face. They were thinking much the same. Was Elsie, a confirmed spinster in her sixties, hoping to be the next to marry – unlikely – or was it Sally, ignoring her aunt's advice on mixing business with pleasure, and thinking of making Hector her husband?

'We're straight off to the village green? No photographs?' Ross Sadler, looking particularly handsome in smart grey suit and a shirt as dazzling white as Jack's, had caught them up, with Mr Houseman, the greengrocer, several paces behind. He had been Flora's choice to give her away, a dear man who had been part of her life since childhood.

'Flora didn't want an official photographer – and neither did I,' Jack confessed. 'I asked Hector Lansdale to take some and his photographs should be good. He has a new camera. But there was Dilys, too, I saw, snapping away with her Kodak.'

'Say no more.' Ross gave him a gentle nudge on the shoulder. 'Pictures from the Brownie should give you a laugh, if nothing else. I'll go ahead with Mr Houseman. I can see people already milling on the pavement and they'll want to chat to you on the way.'

Despite the chatting that accompanied them along the high street, he and Flora were at the green in a matter of minutes. Some of the congregation had walked ahead and faces, familiar to Jack from his eight years in Abbeymead, greeted them as they walked through the marquee entrance: the vicar's housekeeper,

Amy, clutching a handkerchief to her face and sniffing slightly; Evelyn Barnes, her sour expression for once absent as she made a minute inspection of the two long trestles groaning with food, and Dilys, the postmistress, in a blinding ensemble of tangerine and lime, a plate already in her hand, waiting for the signal to eat.

'All's well.' Tony materialised from behind a clutch of tables and chairs. 'The food's magnificent and already causing a stir.'

The marquee felt huge, though it was the most modest Jack had been able to book, but not too huge, he decided, when, within minutes of their arrival, the rest of the congregation joined them. He caught sight of Charlie, washed and brushed and looking uncomfortably different from the boy he knew, except for the fact that he'd made a beeline for the trestles at the far end of the tent and was loitering hopefully.

There would be speeches, it was inevitable, but Jack had asked his best man to keep it brief and his friend had been happy to comply. As for his own, that was even briefer and, without either set of parents present – Flora was an orphan and his were spread across the globe – and with Mr Houseman declining an invitation to contribute, the formalities were at an end within a very short time and a genteel stampede to the food was soon under way.

Hector, having packed away his camera, had taken on the role of barman and was kept busy for the first half hour, dispensing glasses of beer – most of Abbeymead had little patience with sparkling wine – and soft drinks for the children.

'Hector Lansdale is looking rather smart,' Flora whispered. 'I think he's had a new haircut. Sally can't take her eyes off him. Have you noticed?'

'Let's hope eyeing him is all she does – until we've made our escape.'

'Don't worry. Alice is too busy monitoring the food to

notice. I've just seen her retrieve a full plate of crab cakes from Elsie's greedy little hand!'

'It's a brilliant spread. They've done us proud—' Jack was saying, when Evelyn Barnes appeared at their side, her lips forming their usual tight circle.

'Who did the catering?' she demanded.

'There's not a problem, I hope.' Flora's voice had the slightest edge and Jack didn't blame her. Couldn't this woman manage even a mumbled congratulation?

'Just the opposite,' Evelyn said brusquely. 'The food is damn good. I expect it's Alice Jenner's work, but that other woman, over there, she seems to know what she's doing as well.'

'That other woman is Jessie Bolitho,' Flora replied, still with an edge to her voice. 'She's a friend from Cornwall.'

'Dismal place. Always raining. She might like a change. I could have a word with her, eh, Harry?' She turned to the stolid figure by her side, digging him in the ribs to grab his attention.

Her husband, his plump face glistening from a third glass of bubbles, tried to look as if he'd been listening.

'We need a cook,' Evelyn went on. 'Mariella does all right but she's unimaginative. I need variety. And *he* needs a decent diet.' She pointed to Harry's rounded stomach. 'Too many pies. They're Mariella's speciality.'

'The music has just started, Mrs Barnes,' Jack murmured, as the first notes of 'Dream a Little Dream of Me' filled the marquee. 'I'm sure you'll excuse us.'

He hoped very much that Jessie, resplendent in a deep blue brocade and, for once, minus her pinafore, could enjoy the rest of her day and be spared Evelyn's bullying. No doubt Alice would ride to her rescue.

'Would you excuse us?' he repeated and, without waiting for an answer, swept Flora away to the small circle that had been marked out for dancing to one side of the tables.

'Good move.' Flora was laughing as she walked into his arms.

'I'm not great at this,' he confided, pulling her close. 'How about you?'

'Who cares how good we are? We're dancing, Jack. Actually dancing. For the first time ever!'

And dance they did. The band Ross had persuaded to travel from the capital didn't disappoint, the Rollers' bass drum and two guitars swinging from one favourite song to another. The singer, in a glamorous red satin sheath, her voice swooping from the boisterous to the honey-laced, filled the marquee with sound, enticing people to leave their tables and join the fun. At one point, the whole of the village seemed to be dancing, faces pink and jackets, and even shoes, abandoned.

It was as the band began on a final song, 'Love Me Tender', that Inspector Ridley walked through the entrance of the marquee and, taking no notice of the band or the dancers, strode up to Jack and tapped him on the shoulder.

'Sorry to crash the party, Jack, but I was desperate to catch you – before you leave for wherever you're going. I've been phoning your home this last week but never got an answer.'

Jack tried to make sense of the inspector's words, while Flora slipped from his arms and was staring in amazement at the intruder. Ridley wouldn't have got an answer, not this last week. He'd hardly been at home. But what was the man doing here? At their wedding! He'd been adamant in declining their invitation, citing the pressure of work.

'You're on duty? Is it that important?' he managed to ask, noticing that people around them had stopped dancing and were staring, too.

'Getting to be, old chap. You'll be away for a while – I don't know how long – and I needed to see you. I knew I could nab you here. Just a word in your ear, that's all, then you can carry on dancing.'

'Thanks,' Jack said drily and, holding Flora's hand, led the way to the side of the marquee.

'That man you found – the one in the ditch,' Ridley began, once they were clear of the dancers. 'We've not been able to identify him. My chaps have spent hours looking for a lead, but nothing. Now the local press have got hold of the story, splashed it across their front pages. Headlines I don't need. "What are the police doing?" "Somewhere a widow is desperate to find her husband." "Somewhere a mother is grieving for her son." That kind of rubbish. The truth is we'd love a widow to contact us, love a mother to come forward, but nobody has. The chap's still anonymous and cluttering up the morgue.'

Flora, who had stayed uncharacteristically silent, raised her eyebrows at this.

'Beg pardon, Miss Steele – Mrs Carrington,' the inspector floundered. 'Tring never interviewed either of you properly – why aren't I surprised? – but you might have noticed something, anything, that can give us a clue as to who this bloke is.'

Jack stared at him for several seconds, still reeling from having his wedding day interrupted so unceremoniously.

'Why pin us down today of all days?' he asked, certain there must be more to it than appeared. 'This is our wedding, Alan!'

The inspector looked sheepish. 'I realise that – it's why I knew where to find you. And I'll come clean. The super hauled me into his office this morning. He'd seen the newspapers and demanded I *do* something. But what the hell am I supposed to do? The pathologist has confirmed the chap was run over by a large vehicle, possibly from a farm, though none of the farmers my men have questioned say they were working in that area. And that's it. So, what am I looking at? Dangerous driving? Manslaughter? Maybe murder if the man was targeted, but how am I even to start investigating without an identity? Can either of you tell me anything – anything at all – that might help?'

Jack had forgotten the incident, forgotten the man. There'd

been too much else to fill his mind. 'I can't say any more than I said to Constable Tring. I climbed into the ditch, checked the man wasn't still breathing, found his wallet – it contained money but nothing else – and climbed out again, before ringing the police house. There's nothing else I can add. Nor Flora.'

He looked at her for confirmation and she shook her head. 'Nothing,' she said. 'And, really, is this the time to be questioning us?'

There wasn't the glimmer of a smile on her face. Flora had prophesied trouble the afternoon they'd found the man, warned that his death was suspicious, and now the inspector had brought that trouble, that suspicion, into what had been the happiest day of both their lives.

'I wouldn't normally, of course, but...' The inspector was floundering again. Jack looked around and saw the dancing was coming to an end, with several of their guests looking decidedly uneasy.

'We'll contact you if we remember anything that might help,' he said, in a voice that brought the interview to a definite end.

'OK,' Ridley said awkwardly. 'Any clue that comes to light. And sorry again. I bought a present.' He smiled uncertainly, wanting, it seemed, to appease. 'It's in the car. A kettle – hope that's acceptable.'

Jack heard an almost imperceptible groan. It would be kettle number three and Flora was keeping count.

3

They'd had three blissful days by the sea together before Jack drove to Cleve College to begin another week of teaching. Today, he was finding it difficult to rouse enthusiasm, feeling frustrated at having again to leave his Remington idle. The current work-in-progress had turned sluggish, no more than limping along, he admitted, and while he'd willingly forgone writing for the wedding and their short break in Eastbourne – the Grand had been the most luxurious stay and the weather kind enough for a daily stroll on the promenade or more strenuous walks over the South Downs – it was more than time that he buckled down. Two thousand words a day was the target he'd set himself.

But not this day. Driving slowly through tall, wrought-iron gates, still bearing the crest of some long-dead nobleman, he thought that at least the college was looking its best this morning. This far into autumn, the trees were bathed in every shade of gold, their fallen leaves carpeting swathes of neat lawn while, in the distance, the mellow brick of a Queen Anne mansion, the main location for classes, basked in hazy sunshine.

Steering the Austin to his reserved parking space, Jack's

enjoyment of nature came to an abrupt halt. He was being watched. He was sure of it. A figure was skulking in the building's expansive porch, half concealed by a stone pillar. And the man's stare, fixed on Jack, never wavered.

Playing for time, he took a while to check the instrument dial, then leant across to the glove box in a pretence of searching, all the time managing brief glimpses of the figure in the porch. Brief but long enough for him to recognise the man standing motionless but intent. It would have been difficult not to.

Joe Miller, the college caretaker, lived on site and, from Jack's limited experience, made a habit of appearing at unexpected moments. He had felt the man hovering close several times in the weeks since he'd joined the college: on the stairway to his office, in the library, even in the refectory. Had Miller chosen to watch *him* in particular? Did he perhaps think Jack might damage college property or steal something precious? Perhaps he spied on all the staff, considering it part of his duties or simply a perk of the job. It would fit what Jack had seen of him. A surly man, he'd concluded, from their very first meeting.

Opening the car door, he picked up his briefcase and collected his overcoat from the passenger seat, looking across at the porch as he did so. The figure behind the pillar had disappeared, melted back into the red-brick building. For some reason, the man's scrutiny had unnerved Jack more than it should. Perhaps he should ask his fellow teachers whether they, too, suffered from Miller's surveillance – break time might offer the chance.

With that in mind, Jack made sure a few hours later that he walked into the staffroom as the grandfather clock in the foyer chimed eleven, and was immediately accosted by the art teacher who'd befriended him.

'Did the wedding go well?' Jocelyn Draper asked, a mug of tea in her hand. With the other, she fidgeted with the smock she habitually wore, a billowing garment so voluminous it seemed in danger of blowing away. An extremely clean smock for a painter, Jack noticed, but perhaps watercolours were less messy than vivid splashes of oil or the dust of pastels. 'I must say, you had a wonderful day for it.'

'We were lucky. The sun shone and most of the village turned out to wish us well, then ate the marquee empty!' Instinctively, he filtered out any mention of Ridley's appearance at the feast.

'And Eastbourne? You were planning to stay somewhere grand, if I remember.'

'Literally the Grand. Yes, brilliant, thank you.' He took the cup of tea she'd poured him. 'Life has been a little hectic, so it was wonderful to relax, if only for a few days.'

An expression of sympathy flitted across her face. 'Shall we find a chair?'

The staffroom had been extended by the simple expedient of tacking a former classroom onto what had years ago been the original owner's study, the division between the rooms still clearly visible: at one end the green tiles and shiny cream paint beloved of institutions and at the other, the mansion's old oak panelling. A portrait of one of its early owners hung above the gaping mouth of a large brick fireplace and looked down on the assembly in puzzlement. A variety of odd sofas and unmatched chairs spread haphazardly around the room with a somewhat rickety table – the hot water urn had found a permanent place there – bunched against one wall.

'This one's a bit less uncomfortable.' Jocelyn plumped herself down on a sofa of beige chenille, a trifle soiled around the edges and with a definite list to starboard.

Flora should sit on this one, Jack thought. He'd endured months of criticism for his own lumpy effort, now left behind at Overlay House – she had flatly refused to have it in the cottage.

'I can imagine how hectic,' Jocelyn said, cradling her mug. 'Not just moving house, getting married and writing a book, but starting work at the college as well. Cleve isn't always an easy place.'

'I'm enjoying my time here,' he reassured her. 'The setting is beautiful and the job is turning out more interesting than I'd realised, though I fear I'm not doing it too well. The variety of writing projects is tremendous and I'm not able to help every student as much as I'd like.'

'It doesn't matter. Not really. Do what you can. You're a figurehead more than anything else.'

Jack was surprised, unsure what to make of her remark. 'How does being a figurehead work?'

'It's simple. Dalloway gets a well-known artist or writer to join his staff, publishes their name with a great fanfare – in the school magazine, the local paper, wherever else he can – and the name attracts more students. More students pay more money and money is all that interests our dear professor.'

'Really?' Jack sounded as sceptical as he felt. 'What I've seen of Maurice Dalloway suggests he's pretty disengaged from the world – and that would include making money.'

'Don't be fooled, Jack. That's his façade. It's what he hides behind. He's a businessman and quite ruthless. Poor Greg found that out.'

'Greg?'

'Your predecessor, Gregory Gilmore. He was flavour of the month at first. You couldn't pick up an item of college literature without Greg's name being blazoned across it. He was well-known, of course, a crime writer like you who sold a lot of books, and it was his reputation that brought a good number of students into the college.'

'And?' His heart sank a little. Arthur Bellaby, his agent, had never disclosed details of the man Jack had succeeded. Perhaps Arthur hadn't known. Jack himself had only a vague memory of seeing Gilmore's name mentioned in the literary columns, but little else.

'And... everything was fine and dandy until Greg began to have problems, then Dalloway didn't want to know. In fact, quite the opposite. He started looking for ways to get rid of Greg, except Greg did it for him.'

'Gilmore had personal problems?'

'He must have, though he never confided in me. Not really. Nor anyone else, as far as I know. He was a good friend but a very private person.'

'Maybe it was simply the job was wrong for him?'

'Oh, no. He'd loved his job but...'

'Why did he leave then?' A growing uneasiness was taking hold of Jack.

'He didn't. He died.'

His eyes widened. He hadn't expected that. 'Gregory Gilmore was an older man? Funny, I'd imagined him to be young.'

Jocelyn carefully lowered her empty mug to sit on a swirl of the patterned carpet. 'He was young, possibly younger than you. It wasn't natural causes. He drowned – in the college lake.'

He felt a small shock wave run through him, though somehow the news wasn't a surprise. No one at the college had seemed keen to talk about his predecessor, even when he'd attempted once or twice to broach the subject, and he'd suspected there might be some mystery attached to the man – one that was likely to be bleak.

Jocelyn leaned forward, the thin curve of her eyebrows raised. 'They said it was an accident,' she murmured, making sure only Jack could hear, 'but I've never believed that. Greg was a very strong swimmer. I used to swim with him, you know, every few mornings down at the lake. There's no way he could have drowned by accident.'

She bent even closer. 'I reckoned it was suicide,' she said confidently.

Jack took the comment unblinkingly. 'The personal problems you mentioned – they were to blame?'

She nodded, the tight bun on top of her head bobbing against its constraints. 'He'd become depressed. I saw it happening though I never knew why. Like I say, Greg wouldn't confide, but day by day he seemed more downhearted. And it affected his work which was when Dalloway started moves to get him out of the college.'

'That couldn't have helped.' Jack straightened his back as best he could – by now, the sofa's lumpiness had become extremely uncomfortable – but this was a story whose end he needed to hear.

Jocelyn snorted. 'It was atrocious. Greg was always bubbly, the life and soul of any party. But that kind of person... they're often quite miserable inside, aren't they?'

He couldn't find an answer to that and she went on, 'I did think he was pulling out of it a little, but then suddenly he went downhill again. It took me by surprise, actually, it happened so quickly.'

'Was there anything in particular that could have revived his bad feelings?' Jack had begun to feel huge sympathy for the benighted Greg.

'Dalloway was harassing him, of course, otherwise ... but now I think of it, there was a man who came to the college. He asked especially for Greg. The caretaker – Joe Miller, what a horrible man he is – took the chap up to Greg's room. Your room now. I passed them on the stairs, wondering what was going on. We don't get that many visitors. Afterwards, I noticed that Gregory looked quite ill.'

'You don't know who the man was? What he looked like?' A chord was being struck. A nerve touched. Invisible and barely sensed, but present nevertheless. An unknown man, an unusual visit. But that man had been in Abbeymead, not at Cleve College, and what possible link could there be between them? Jack shook his head as though to free himself of meddlesome thoughts. There could be no connection.

'No idea who he was,' Jocelyn said cheerfully. 'And he looked – well, just ordinary. Brown hair, not sure about his eyes, medium height. Just ordinary. Afterwards, Greg was tight-lipped when I asked about his visitor, so I didn't ask again.'

'The day Gregory... the day he died... were you with him at the lake?'

Jocelyn made a show of thinking, which Jack thought odd. Surely she would know if she'd been there on the day the poor man drowned.

'No, I wasn't,' she said at last. Then seeing his puzzlement, tried to explain. 'We sometimes went down to the lake together, but we always swam in different parts. The water at the top end is far deeper and that's where Greg made for. There's a diving board set up there that he liked to use. I'm not a very experienced swimmer and made sure I always stayed at the shallow end. And I never swam for as long as Greg, but I'm sure I wasn't there that day.'

'If you had been, I imagine you'd have been aware of someone struggling in the water. The lake isn't that large.' Jack pictured it in his mind: a long, narrow sheet of water, lying at the very bottom of the college grounds and enclosed by a line of trees.

She nodded in agreement. 'If I'd gone that day and was still swimming, I would have heard... splashing? A shout maybe? Oh, there's the bell. End of break time. I'd best get going or I'll have them fighting over the Delft blue. We're nearly out of it and I've only just reordered.'

She jumped to her feet, her handbag falling to the floor and spilling half its contents across the carpet – tissues, comb, powder compact and several letters. Something glittering had fallen beneath the sofa and Jack bent to fish around until his hand fixed on a small object.

'A St Christopher,' he said, pulling out his trophy. 'Something you should never lose.'

'Thank you.' Jocelyn almost snatched the gold chain from his hand. 'Sorry, I have to go,' she repeated.

Back in his office, Jack sat for some while staring at the wall that faced him. Gregory Gilmore had decorated it with a cluster of framed Sussex landscapes, possibly places he'd loved, and Jack hadn't yet got round to changing the pictures. Now, he thought he wouldn't. Gregory was more than a victim and his life should be celebrated. He'd been a teacher, a writer, a unique individual, and his spirit was here in the office he'd occupied, in the college he'd loved. The pictures he'd chosen should remain to bear witness.

4

Jack arrived back from college earlier than Flora expected and it seemed sensible to use what was left of the afternoon for a visit to Overlay House. The landlord had not yet managed to re-let the place – in Flora's view, he'd be lucky to do so – but in the interim they'd make regular trips to harvest any fruit and vegetables that were ready.

Despite the sun making a brave attempt to cut through a white blanket of sky, they set off muffled in heavy coats and scarves – the weather had turned markedly chilly since they'd returned from Eastbourne – and carrying several baskets between them. They were hoping for a goodly amount of produce but, given the heavy frost of the last few nights, were unlikely to find flowers still in bloom.

Walking arm-in-arm with her husband – how strange that sounded – Flora was wondering how he must feel returning to the house that had been his home for so long. Had been his refuge for the years he'd buried himself away as a recluse. Until she'd winkled him out and into the world again. Her cottage was a good deal smaller than Overlay and they were having to adjust to sharing a relatively tiny space. Overall, it was working well, but Jack was already thinking aloud if, perhaps, they should look for somewhere else. Not sell the cottage, he'd been careful to say, but rent a larger property. With his new salary and Flora's inheritance, they could afford it. As long as it wasn't Overlay House they were planning to rent, was Flora's unspoken thought.

Greenway Lane today looked very different from the last time they had walked from Jack's house, the grass rimed white and the hedgerows no longer a verdant green but wilting beneath the onslaught of a newly arrived cold.

They were passing the spot where they'd found the dead man, she noticed, their footsteps ringing sharp in the clear air. The inspector hadn't been in touch again and since neither of them had thought of anything new to say, they hadn't contacted him. His intervention on their wedding day had been extraordinary and Flora found it difficult to forgive. All she could think was that Ridley's grilling by his superintendent that morning had sent the man into an unfamiliar spin, allowing him to think it fine to gatecrash such a huge occasion for them both.

It was a surprise when Jack untucked his arm and brought her to a halt. 'It was here,' he said.

'It was,' she agreed and watched him peer down into the ditch.

'No water now. Just mud, frozen hard,' he reported.

'Did Alan Ridley ever say how the man died? Did he drown?'

'I don't think so. From what I gathered, he was killed outright by a large vehicle. Probably from a farm.'

'Then how did he end in the ditch? We've never asked that question.'

'We've never asked because we've had far too much else to think about, but he could have been tossed there, I guess.'

'That would have been difficult, if not impossible.' Flora walked into the middle of the road. 'Imagine the scene. The tractor, or whatever vehicle, is trundling down the middle of the lane and—'

'Not trundling. It must have been speeding.'

'OK. The tractor is going as fast as it can, keeping to the side of the lane, with the man directly in its path. So, the driver hits Mr Unknown about here.' She moved to stand by the grass verge. 'If the man were up *here*' – she scrambled up onto the bank – 'he wouldn't have been hit.'

'Which means he was on the road and didn't try to escape.'

'Exactly. He wasn't expecting the tractor to knock him down.' She looked down at Jack. From this height, she was actually taller than him. She must try it more often. 'He would have seen a farm vehicle, hardly unusual in a village, bearing down on him and thought – what? – that the driver hadn't yet seen him, that the driver would stop. Yet he didn't stop. He hit the man fair and square. But that wouldn't have landed the body in the ditch, would it? At the most, the dead man would have ended halfway up the grass bank.'

'It could be murder then, as Ridley half suggested. The killer gets out of the vehicle, checks the man is nicely dead and throws him into the ditch. Unless it was a hit-and-run and the culprit was trying to hide the body.'

Flora shook her head. 'Hit-and-runs are just that. A driver panics at what they've done and flees the scene before anyone can take note of their number plate. I think it's evidence that our unknown victim was a target. He was meant to die. It's why he had no identification on him. The murderer stripped him of it before tipping him down there – as a way of protecting himself?'

'More than likely. People usually carry some form of identity. The man's wallet should have had a name at least, but it was empty except for the bank notes.'

'Then that's one thing we know! The murderer isn't a thief.'

'Not terribly useful. Come on down, we've baskets to fill and I do believe the sun is breaking through... just a smidgen.'

Flora turned to go, a last look into the dank channel below. Something winked at her. An object the rare shaft of sun had alighted on. 'There's something down there,' she said.

'Not another body, I hope.'

'Not unless it's a particularly shiny body. Whatever it is, it's glinting at me. I'm going to find out.'

'Don't! Let me.' Jack started towards the bank but she held up a hand.

'It's fine. The ground is like iron – I'm not going to slip – and it's my turn to have fun.'

Before he could stop her, she began climbing, crawling more like, down the steep ditch to the bottom and, walking forward a few yards, bent to extract the glittering object from where it had become tangled in a heap of wild briars.

'It's a cigarette case,' she shouted, her voice coming muffled to Jack.

Tucking it into her coat pocket, she began the climb back up the bank, a more difficult task than the downward journey.

Halfway up, she held out her hand. 'OK. I admit defeat.' Jack reached down and, with some effort, hauled her out of the ditch and onto the grass verge.

'Not easy going in that direction, is it?' He was grinning. 'You look like a demented bird's nest.' He picked a few twigs out of her hair and brushed the crumbs of earth from her coat.

'Demented or not, I've discovered what's possibly the only clue Inspector Ridley will have for Mr Anonymous. It must have fallen out of the man's pocket when he was thrown over the bank and was lost in all that water. Here, take a look.'

'No embossed initials,' Jack said, turning the case over in his hands. 'Not a good start. Let's see if we're luckier inside.'

Flora peered over his shoulders as he snapped open the

case. A huddle of ruined cigarettes were moulded together, still emitting a strong smell of tobacco.

'He was a Craven A man,' Jack remarked. 'I can just make the brand name out.'

'He was also a man who was sent letters. Look.'

There, squashed against the inner rim of one flap of the case was an envelope, the writing on it blotched and blurred.

'An envelope addressed to a flat. A flat... on a street... in a town,' he said, deciphering it with difficulty.

'Freshfield Road, Brighton,' Flora spelt out slowly. 'Number 82a. But still no name. I wonder why. Let's see if there's a letter that's survived.'

The envelope was soft and pulpy and it was with infinite care that Jack felt for the letter inside and brought out a single sheet of paper.

'Unaddressed and... unsigned,' he commented, his eyes skimming to the bottom of the page.

'But what does it say?'

Flora was wriggling beside him, trying to get a better view, when a sudden whirr of wings had her turn. A family of birds had erupted from the opposite hedge and, for a moment, she paused and looked around. 'The writing is so badly blotched,' she said, returning to the letter, 'I can hardly make it out.'

'You'll have to try. I've left my glasses at the cottage.' Jack's tortoiseshell reading glasses had provided endless fun for Flora – tortoiseshell was the mark of a *real* writer, she always contended.

Taking the letter from him, she held it pinched between her fingers.

'It's just about legible, but only just. It says that if the recipient wants to find out what happened to their father, they should investigate somewhere called Rillington Orphanage.'

They looked blankly at each other. 'Rillington Orphanage? Do you know it?'

Flora shook her head. 'I don't, but maybe someone like Alice might. What a strange message. What do you think it means?'

'I've no idea but perhaps someone at the orphanage will.'

'Or someone at 82a Freshfield Road.'

Holding hands, they walked on and it wasn't until they'd reached the front gate of Overlay House that Jack said, 'We have an address now – what do you think? Tell Ridley or go ourselves?'

Flora beamed, a sparkle in her eyes. Reaching up to give him a kiss, she murmured, 'Do you really need to ask?'

5

Pushing open the door of the All's Well, Flora breathed in the smell of bookshop, the spicy, woody smell that she'd lived with and loved for most of her life. Saturday morning and it was good to be home. Rose Lawson had proved a brilliant deputy this last week, what with the wedding, their stay in Eastbourne, and several days spent organising the cottage around two people rather than one, but today Flora was back where she belonged.

Confident that Rose would have been diligent with the feather duster, she decided to forgo the daily chore and instead took time to wander through the shop, zigzagging in and out of the angled bookshelves, stopping to stroke her favourite volumes, patting spines into place and pulling others forward to make them more noticeable. The building was old – parts of it from the fifteenth century, Flora had been told – and its walls twisted and turned in dizzying fashion, often culminating in a dead end. There had been times when dear Aunt Violet had been forced to ride to the rescue, discovering a customer in one of its hidden nooks, unable to find their way back to the front door.

Two large cardboard boxes had been stored beside her desk;

Rose must have taken delivery of new titles during the week and left them to be displayed on a front table that was set aside for the latest publications. It was a job Flora always enjoyed. Once more, it seemed, she was settling into the comfortable rhythm of a life that had changed only a little: Kate was at the Nook, Sally and Alice at the Priory, Jack now working at Cleve College or hunched over typewriter keys in the spare bedroom and she – here, of course, for most of the week. But what of the free time she'd gained? There would be two whole days when Rose would take over. How would she fill those days?

Flora felt suddenly adrift. Winter was on the horizon and, with it, rain, snow, ice, a whole gamut of weather that made gardening impossible. She could work indoors, clean and tidy the cottage, maybe redecorate here and there, but for how long? She could take to baking, though there were only so many cakes you could eat.

The letter! She mustn't forget the letter. It was the promise of a new investigation, but only a promise. An unknown man, even dead in a ditch, wasn't much to go on. Jack had suggested they drive to Brighton this afternoon, once she closed the shop, and find 82a Freshfield Road. They were likely to discover the man's identity when they called, but after that? Maybe there'd be something more, she thought hopefully, an excuse to play sleuth again before they handed the letter to the inspector. Jack was insistent on that.

Wrapping herself in a thick cardigan, she set to work opening the new boxes. If anything, it had become colder since leaving home this morning, though there'd been a thick frost on the ground when she'd wheeled a reluctant Betty from her overnight shelter. She was halfway through one of the boxes, enjoying her first sight of so many new covers – she'd picked up *A Bear Called Paddington* for a closer look – when Alice Jenner walked through the door, breathing hard. Her friend unsmiling, her colour high and her forehead creased.

'Something's wrong?' was Flora's immediate response. 'What's happened, Alice?'

She hadn't seen her friend since the day of the wedding, but there'd been no hint of trouble when she'd telephoned a few days ago to say that she and Jack were home again.

'It's that Hector.' Alice emitted what was close to a wail. 'He's asked her out. Sally,' she said loudly, as though Flora could be in any doubt. 'He's asked her out.'

'But—' Flora began and was interrupted.

'He's been a help I won't deny, 'specially with all the extra work for Charlie's party, but it's right. He's takin' advantage. I've warned Sally over and over but the girl won't listen. Won't learn her lesson – and after Dominic Lister turned out the liar I always suspected and let her down so badly! Can you talk to her? She might listen to you.'

'Hector seems a decent chap,' Flora managed to get in.

'He's a good sous chef, I'll give him that, and that's what he should stay. Angling to take over the Priory, I reckon, get in with Sally and then—'

'Surely not. I think he really likes Sally,' she dared to say.

Alice plumped herself down on the window seat beneath one of the bookshop's latticed windows.

'There's likin' and likin',' she said mysteriously, her breath still coming short. 'If she's desperate to get married, Sally should look elsewhere. She's a pretty girl, a clever girl. There's plenty of fish – that Ross, what's his name, Jack's friend?'

'Ross Sadler?'

'That's him. Handsome chap. He talked to Sally plenty at the wedding and she seemed to like him, but then Hector interferes and asks her out. I was wonderin' – do you have the man's phone number?'

'Surely you wouldn't...' Flora began to say, then changed tack. 'You know, Alice, I'm not sure Ross would be a good idea.

He's a newspaper man and they don't make the best of husbands, according to Jack.'

'Jack was a journalist hisself,' Alice said a little pettishly. 'I don't notice it's been a problem for you.'

'He wasn't a journalist when we met,' she pointed out. 'Crime writers are a much better bet.'

'You best find me one then,' she retorted. 'Or find Sally one before she does something stupid – again.'

'Charlie's party?' Flora asked, desperate to change the subject and avoid having to divulge Ross Sadler's number. She felt herself grow hot at the thought of what Alice might be planning.

'It's Charlie's big day today or had you forgotten?'

Flora's hand went to her mouth. She had forgotten. Last month, Charlie Teague had won a competition run by *Tasty Bites*, a popular food magazine, by inventing a new cake recipe – a chocolate-and-orange rolled sponge – and, as a reward, Alice had promised him a party with the schoolfriends he'd said goodbye to at the end of the summer term. Charlie would have been the first to remind Flora but she hadn't seen him since the wedding. He called at the All's Well every Friday to collect any books the shop needed delivering, but it was Rose who would have seen him yesterday.

'Are we supposed to have bought a present? But will Charlie even want one? He was scathing when the *Tasty Bites* prize was free magazines for the year. I think he might prefer money. I'll have to rob the till and pay it back later!'

Alice shook her head but then softened. 'You've had a lot to deal with these last few weeks,' she conceded, 'and he'll be happy enough with money. But there's still the party this afternoon at the Priory.'

Flora blinked. Concentrate, she told herself. She'd forgotten the party – again.

'I've Tony hangin' a Congratulations banner,' Alice went

on, 'Kate's helpin' with the cookin' and I suppose Hector did come good with the balloons. Sally is givin' us one of her small sitting rooms and, by the look of the party list, it's goin' to be full. You *are* comin', I take it?'

'Yes. Yes, of course. We'll be at the Priory – around half past two?'

They couldn't let Charlie down. He was sure to have invited a host of friends, but he'd want them in the background and Alice would need help: carrying in plates of food – and knowing Charlie, there'd be an unending stream – pouring lemonade, overseeing games and generally making sure the party went smoothly.

A question flashed suddenly into Flora's mind and the party once more faded. 'Have you heard of Rillington Orphanage, Alice?'

Her friend stared at her. 'Everyone's heard of the orphanage.'

'I hadn't.'

'I s'pose not. You'd be a child when it happened and Violet wouldn't have wanted to tell you, not with other children being involved.'

This was intriguing. 'Have you ever been there – to the orphanage?'

'Never seen the place, but heard plenty about it. There was a lot of trouble way back. It got a bad reputation and closed.'

'The council closed it?' There would have to be a very serious reason for that, she thought.

'Not the council. For once, it wasn't them that was the problem. It was owned by some private company. Mebbe the council used it for kids they needed places for, but mostly families paid – if they were left with children they couldn't look after. Grandparents too old to be parents again, that kind of thing. Or mebbe because families couldn't control the little tinkers,' she said darkly.

'How did it get a bad reputation?' Rillington Orphanage had assumed a new level of interest.

'There was a gang of boys causin' trouble, that's what I heard. Bad trouble. The owners wanted to sell, but couldn't find anyone to take the place on, even when they reduced the price, not with the reputation it had. So... they closed it down.'

'And the boys? It only took boys?'

'Part of the trouble, I reckon.' Alice nodded wisely. 'I dunno what happened to the children when it closed. I don't think the building ever sold – it was a big place, too. As far as I know, they just left it.'

'Whatever happened there must have been pretty dreadful for no one to want to buy at a knockdown price.'

'I reckon so. There was a lot of talk, but... I've got to get goin'. There's still the jellies to sort out. I'll see you and Jack later.'

Flora waved her goodbye, grateful that Ross Sadler hadn't been mentioned again, but reluctant to do as her friend had asked and 'talk to Sally' who Flora felt sure would tell her, and rightly so, to mind her own business. It was Alice with the bee in her bonnet buzzing ever louder – and Alice who'd have to solve the problem.

Picking up the telephone, she dialled the cottage. Jack, she hoped, hadn't decided to go for a long walk. The current novel wasn't progressing as quickly as he'd hoped and walking, he'd told her, cleared his mind and often allowed the intricacies of the plot to fall into place. Plot or no plot, she needed to warn him he was on party duties this afternoon – hopefully, they might still manage a visit to Freshfield Road.

6

Jack and his car were outside the All's Well as the bookshop's Victorian station clock, one of Violet's treasured auction buys, struck twelve thirty.

'Sorry I didn't come in,' he said, as Flora climbed into the passenger seat. 'If I'd switched off the ignition, Harriet might not have started again. She doesn't like this cold.'

'Harriet?'

Jack patted the steering wheel, his face breaking into a grin he couldn't quite suppress. 'If you can have a bicycle called Betty, I can have an Austin called Harriet.'

'Really? It's a bit late in the day for a name, isn't it? You've had the car for nearly three years.'

'It takes time. I've been getting to know her.' The grin became wider.

'Stop teasing and tell me – if you can't switch the engine off, how are we going to leave the car when we get to Brighton?'

'Harriet will be fine by the time she's had a long run.'

It was said with confidence, but Flora mentally crossed her fingers. The Austin was temperamental at the best of times and now it had a name it could well become a fully fledged diva.

In the event, the car drove the fifteen miles to Brighton without mishap and it took them little time to find Freshfield Road. As expected, number 82a was a flat, on the top floor of a tall, terraced house.

Jack rang the apartment's bell, though he wasn't expecting a response. If their unknown victim had shared a home with someone, then that someone would surely have reported him missing by now.

A second ring was followed by further silence.

'I'll try 82b,' he said. 'A fellow tenant might know the chap.' But, once again, they were met with a blank.

He was about to try the final bell when the front door opened and a harassed-looking man poked his head out.

'It's no good you ringing for Miss Dalrymple. She goes to her elderly aunt every Saturday afternoon.'

'We've not actually come to see Miss Dalrymple.' Flora smiled encouragingly at the man, noticing his unbrushed hair and the shirt half out of his trousers. 'I'm sorry we've disturbed you.'

'It's Dad,' he said, making an unsuccessful job of rescuing his shirt. 'He's playing up today. Doesn't like all the bell ringing. So, who *did* you want?'

'Are you the landlord, by any chance?'

'Yes,' he said brusquely. 'I live downstairs, in the basement flat. Well, Dad and I do.'

'And your tenant upstairs – on the top floor?'

'You know Mr Farr? Do you know where he is? I haven't seen him for days.'

At last, they had a name.

'Is that unusual?' Flora asked, going for caution.

The landlord considered the idea for a moment and then agreed that it was. His harassed expression had turned to one of mild suspicion. 'What do you want with him anyway?'

'We've come from Abbeymead—' Jack began.

'The village over Steyning way?'

'Yes. I'm afraid that a man was found dead there a couple of weeks ago and the police have been unable to discover his identity. The only clue we have is the letter that was found on him.'

Jack delved into his jacket pocket for the precious envelope. 'You'll see it has this address but no name. We were discussing the case with the policeman in charge, mentioned we were coming to Brighton this afternoon and promised to call – to see if anyone living here could help.'

Inspired, Flora thought. Invoking the police with just the slightest suggestion they were working alongside them.

The landlord took the envelope from Jack's outstretched hand. 'That's his address, but why doesn't it have Russell's name? Who'd want to send a letter like that?'

'Perhaps if we took a look at Mr Farr's flat, it might offer a clue.' Flora tried another smile. 'We could take any information we gather to the police and then you wouldn't be bothered by a visit. Your father might be happier if a policeman wasn't ringing your bell.'

The man still looked doubtful, but reluctantly agreed. Flora's mention of his father's likely reaction to a constable on the door had evidently decided him. Turning to run down the stairs to the basement, he left them on the doorstep, huddled together from the cold, but was back within a few minutes, a large brass key in his hand.

Two flights of stairs led to what was little more than an attic. A very clean and neat attic, Flora thought, as the landlord threw the door wide, while continuing to hover close. There was no way, it seemed, that they'd be left alone to explore Russell's small domain.

There wasn't, in fact, much to explore. A bright main room, unexpectedly spacious, but with little furniture; a much smaller second room with a single bed, a single wardrobe and a chest of drawers; and a narrow galley kitchen with a window that overlooked a scrubby and poorly maintained garden. There was no sign of a bathroom and Flora presumed it was elsewhere in the property and the inhabitants of 82 Freshfield Road must share. It was a modest life that Russell Farr lived, austere even.

In silent agreement, she and Jack moved together to the one piece of furniture that exuded authority: a grand Edwardian desk made of solid oak. What the drawers contained was likely to remain a mystery – Flora's surreptitious tug on a handle confirmed they were locked – but the surface of the desk presented a picture as neat as the rest of the flat: a small stack of papers sat primly on one side, a pen rack and unmarked blotter filled the centre, and on the far side another neat stack, smaller this time, of photographs.

She went straight to them, flicking swiftly through the pile. They appeared to be pictures of a rambling mansion, Victorian by the look of it, taken from various angles at what seemed different times of the day and in different weather conditions. Whatever the changed situation, the house remained the same: a dark sprawl of old brick, its windows small and pinched – some, she thought, looking as though iron-barred – a high sloping roof with sharply pointed gables and a central spire that split the sky. It was a house from which you'd want to escape.

'Mr Farr seems to have liked Victoriana,' she said, tapping the photographs.

The landlord came to stand by her shoulder, a crease between his eyebrows. 'I dunno why Russell would want to photograph that building. It was a bad place.'

'You know it?'

'Doesn't everyone? Rillington, that's where that is. It was an orphanage till they moved the kids out. Like I say, not a good place. Least, that was the rumour.'

'Does anyone live there now, do you know?'

'No idea. It's over by Chiddingly and I haven't been that way for years. It was a large building, though, one of those rambling piles the nobs used to build – when they had the money and the power – plenty of ground, too. Probably one of them developers bought it.'

'I wonder, Mr...' He didn't offer a name. 'Could we perhaps take one of these photographs? For the police,' Flora was swift to add.

'I s'pose,' he agreed warily. 'But I dunno when they were taken. It's likely the place doesn't look like that now. Turned it into more apartments, I reckon. That's what developers do.'

Alice had thought otherwise but, whatever the truth, Rillington Orphanage was in definite need of a visit. Jack must have thought so too and, sharing a look with her, he turned to walk back down the stairs, on the way thanking the landlord for his time.

'You'll tell the police then?' the man said at the front door. 'They won't come bothering us?'

'We certainly will,' Jack reassured him when once more they were back on the street. 'They'll be relieved to have an identity. It means they can begin to contact relatives.'

That was unlikely, Flora thought. No one had reported Russell Farr missing, though he'd disappeared over two weeks ago, and not one word of sympathy or even regret had passed the landlord's lips.

'They won't find any,' the man prophesied, as though listening in to Flora's thoughts. 'No relatives, as far as I know. No friends either. A few letters came for him, a handful, really. Oh, and there was one telephone call. That was all he had the whole time he lived here.'

'When was the telephone call, do you remember?'

'Yeah. A few weeks ago. Why?'

'It might have been a relative or a friend,' Flora suggested, while not believing her own words.

The landlord shook his head. 'I asked him – it was that unusual to knock on his door to tell him he had a call. He did go to the phone, a few minutes that was all, and afterwards told me it was "nobody that matters". Those were his very words. Doesn't sound like a relative or friend to me. I didn't ask any more. With someone like Russell, it'd be daft. A waste of time. Russell's life was pretty empty. He went to work at Steadfast and came home again and that was it.'

'Steadfast?'

'It's an insurance company near Hove Park. He worked there since he was a lad. Lived here since he was a lad. Russell was a loner, you see. Private like. No trouble, though. Usually.'

'Usually?' The word stuck in Flora's consciousness.

'Owed me rent, didn't he? I'll not get that back.'

It was past three before they walked into the panelled foyer of the Priory, once the baronial hall of local aristocrats. Evidence that the party was already well under way was everywhere. Outdoor shoes had been kicked off and strewn across the polished wood, coats in various stages of destruction had been thrown over the pair of easy chairs and a stack of wrapping paper lay crumpled and torn on the reception desk. The valuable Chinese vases, Flora noticed, brought to England as trophies by a past Lord Templeton, had been removed to a safe distance, while the portraits of those very Templetons looked down on the scene with disdain.

From somewhere nearby came the yells and loud laughter of a group of boys determined to enjoy themselves. Alice came bustling out of a side room as they were shrugging off their winter coats, her cheeks pinker than ever.

She looked down at the serviceable watch she wore – they'd arrived nearly an hour late, Flora realised – but it was Sally, following close on her aunt's tail, who was the one to speak.

'Why did I ever agree to this?' She pulled a face but was laughing at the same time.

At that moment, Kate and Tony appeared from the staircase that led down to the kitchen, one carrying an enormous tray filled with sandwiches, sausage rolls and potato crisps and the other a tray of jellies, tarts and iced cakes.

'The pièce de resistance is still in the kitchen.' Sally took the tray from Kate who had begun to wobble slightly. 'Auntie has done a cracker. A cake in the shape of a football. Wait till those urchins see it!'

'I know the party's going strong, but what can we do?' To Flora's eyes, Alice was looking exceptionally tired.

'You can help organise the games.' Her voice was as weary as she looked. 'Tony's tried but they're gettin' out of hand by the sound of it. Jack, you'll be good at that.'

'I will?'

'Yes.' Alice was definite. 'But why are you so late? Where have you been?'

'Brighton. We had some chores to do,' Flora said airily.

Her friend looked suspicious. 'What kind of chores? Not more of that sleuthin'. You don't need that – neither of you. You're married now.'

How the two were connected was beyond Flora, but she took Alice's arm and had begun to steer her towards the noise when her friend stopped suddenly and pointed to Jack's hand. 'What's that you've got?'

She had spotted the photograph they'd taken from Fresh-field Road. Why hadn't Jack left it in the car? There would be questions now, Flora thought. And there were.

'That place – I've seen it before.'

How could that be? Alice had never been to Rillington. She'd told them that all she knew of the place was by hearsay.

They looked at her, both instantly alert. 'You've seen it before?' Jack asked.

Alice nodded. 'At Harry Barnes's place. On a wall of that palace he owns.' Pelham Lodge, a sprawling but ugly house, was the largest property in the district and had grounds to match. 'It was in the scullery. Nice painting, I thought, but a bit too gloomy for me. Still, hanging it in the scullery...'

She looked at them, her eyes sharp, her gaze narrowed. 'You *are* sleuthin' again!'

'The games?' Jack reminded her, as an even louder burst of noise came barrelling through the open doorway.

7

After the rigours of Charlie's party – it had stretched well into the evening – they slept late the next day. Jack uttered a few silent curses when his bleary gaze fixed on the bedroom clock. He'd meant to be up bright and early, sitting at the Remington for most of the day and adding at least a chapter to a book that was proving troublesome. Now, he would manage two hours at the most tucked away in the second bedroom. Flora had planned a roast dinner for Sunday lunch and he felt guilty at dipping out of kitchen duties but, when she bounced out of bed full of energy – did being ten years older make that much difference? he wondered – it was to insist that he write all morning while she cooked.

'And maybe,' she said a trifle slyly, 'if you get on well this morning, we could take a trip to Rillington this afternoon.'

He might have known she was planning something, but it was with good grace that he agreed, spurred on to get down to serious work while he could. He was at that sticky point of a book, the dreaded sagging middle, wondering if he was on the right track or had allowed himself to stray. Wondering if the plot was finally going to work or whether he should throw the whole thing in the bin and start again. But no, he couldn't do that – he didn't have the luxury of time.

Three hours later, when Flora called to say the roast beef needed carving, he'd more or less surmounted the sticky patch and was feeling a good deal more cheerful. Cheerful enough to contemplate a drive to Rillington once they'd eaten their way through crispy potatoes, buttered carrots and fresh peas, plus a large helping of a Yorkshire pudding that had puffed to enormous proportions. By this time, feeling full and sleepy as he did, a doze in the chair had begun to look enticing. But mindful of his promise, as soon as the last plate was washed and dried, Jack collected his wallet from the bedroom, shrugged on his overcoat and grabbed his keys from the kitchen counter. Flora, of course, was already out of the house and waiting by the Austin.

They made a single stop in Chiddingly and, outside the parish church, nabbed a passing church warden going about his Sunday business for instructions of how to get to the orphanage. They proved necessary. Driving slowly along the surrounding lanes, turning this way and that, the journey seemed endless but then, quite suddenly, they came upon the place. A large pair of gates, badly rusted and with hinges missing, had been left wide open, an invitation to anyone who wished to trespass. Jack drove through the gap and onto a rutted driveway that ran a mile or so into the distance, the grounds stretching as far ahead as he could see.

'It's wild,' Flora murmured.

Wild and unkempt it was. Trees that had once been magnificent had here and there lost limbs in the storms of twenty years, their branches scattered through grass that had grown thigh-high. Painful-looking clumps of brambles were everywhere, the wilderness slowly colonising what was left of the gravel driveway. Fortunately, it was still possible for a car to pass

– just – the Austin making slow progress along the winding ribbon of road.

'Alice was right,' Flora remarked, as they rounded a final bend and a derelict mansion came into view. 'No one could have lived here for a very long time.'

'What a waste.'

'Is it?' Jack looked down and saw her doubtful expression. 'Would you have wanted to live here even when it was whole?'

'Maybe not,' he said thoughtfully, staring through the windscreen at Russell Farr's Gothic pile. Weeds were sprouting from the roof, he noticed – they hadn't been obvious in the photographs – and the masonry was crumbling just about everywhere: window sills, balconies, even the four walls of the house.

'Come on. Now we're here, we should look around, though maybe keep a distance from the building. I'm not too sure how safe it is.'

Flora nodded and climbed out of the car, hugging her coat tight to herself. It was cold but not as cold as it had been. Something else, he thought, was making her shiver.

As they made a slow circuit of the building, he could see the damage was considerable. At the rear, several windows had been broken and there'd been no attempt to board them up.

'Over the years, rain will have penetrated,' he remarked. 'Rotted every piece of wood in there. The floors won't be safe.'

'It's a horrible place.' Flora had been unusually quiet as they'd orbited the house.

'It doesn't look too good,' he agreed lightly. Rillington was having a bad effect on her and he could understand why. Watching as a faint sun dipped out of sight, silhouetting the sharp gables, the cruel spire black against the sky, he imagined it had been just such a horrible place twenty years ago.

'What on earth made Farr want to photograph it?' he asked, as they made their way back to the car.

'It must have meant something to him, something important, or what happened here did. It's what we need to find out.' Flora tucked her arm in his, happier now they were leaving. 'If we knew that, we'd know why he was so interested in the place that he came here over and over again. And he must have done. Every one of his photographs was taken at a different time... a different day...'

She tailed off, coming to an abrupt standstill.

'What is it?'

For a moment she didn't answer, but turned full circle, scanning first the house and then the grounds. 'I thought I heard something.'

'From the house?'

'Maybe.'

'I doubt it. It looks too dangerous for anyone to venture there. Unless it's children playing somewhere they shouldn't. Look, why don't I ring Ross? See what he's able to find out.'

'Would he help, do you think?'

'He will if he can. Perhaps rummage through some of the local papers at the time the orphanage closed. Although when that was, we don't know with any certainty. About twenty years ago, but that could mean an awful lot of papers to rummage.'

'Ross is a good investigator,' she said, climbing back into the car. 'And we mustn't forget Harry Barnes. Why does he have a painting of this place? We should talk to him.'

She was desperate to take on the mystery, Jack could see, and wondered if he'd done the right thing in mentioning Ross. Would it have been better to hand the letter they'd found to the police and let them take over? He'd been feeling uneasy that they hadn't told Alan Ridley of their discovery. He should have passed the envelope to the inspector as soon as they'd found it, but the case had been too tempting – he admitted he'd been as tempted as Flora – and she, of course, had been eager to investigate. There would be a victory dance if she discovered information the police, with all their resources, had failed to find.

Look on the bright side, he told himself as they bumped their way back towards the ruined gates, the image of the desolate building gradually slipping from his rear mirror. If their enquiries led them into trouble, the inspector would be delighted to hear from them.

Monday was not a day Jack would have chosen for his lectures at Cleve College. For one thing, it was a day Flora was at home and, though he would have been writing most of the time, it would have been good to share lunch with her and maybe take a short walk together if the rain held off. The cold snap seemed to have disappeared overnight and in its place harsh winds and heavy rain were urging him to stay in Abbeymead.

Monday morning, however, was the time designated for lectures or workshops – the college timetable possessed little flexibility – and Jack had foolishly arranged to give a talk to a small group of would-be novelists. So it was that he climbed into the Austin at nine o'clock that morning and drove to meet what he hoped would be a circle of interested students.

Passing through Cleve's imposing gates, he saw a line of windswept pedestrians ahead, stomping soggily through the college's now ragged grounds. Jack had brought an umbrella – it was a fair distance from his parking space to the safety of the house – but in this wind, he'd be lucky to keep it intact. Leaving it on the front seat, he scrambled from the car, locked it quickly, and beetled, head down, towards the shelter of the porch. He shook the rain from his shoulders before making for the stairs to his office, still with his head down, but was brought up sharply by almost cannoning into someone on the top step. Had the man come out of Jack's office? His locked office.

It was Joe Miller – naturally.

'Were you in my office?' Angered by the possibility, Jack challenged him without pausing to think.

'Good morning, Mr Carrington.' The man gave him a sly look. 'Just checking.'

'Checking what?'

'Water leak reported from the upstairs room. I'm the caretaker here,' he announced, knowing that Jack was fully aware of the fact. 'Have to check that everything's OK. Make sure your office isn't flooded.'

A lie, he was certain, but what was the man after and why? He remembered Jocelyn Draper's warning, although he hadn't needed it.

'I'll let you know if something isn't OK,' Jack snapped, pushing past the intruder. Then, on the spur of the moment, turned to ask, 'Have you seen Miss Draper this morning?' Jack wasn't sure why he'd posed the question, but Miller's reaction to Jocelyn might be interesting.

The caretaker shook his head, then walked back to stand close to Jack. Too close. 'A word of warning, Mr Carrington. Be careful! A bit of a man-eater, our Miss Draper, and you just married! Had her claws into Mr Gilmore but now he's gone...'

Was that the pot calling the kettle black? Or was there anything of substance there?

Jack turned back to his room, feeling his anger build. It seemed the man wasn't content with watching him covertly but was now trespassing in what should be private space.

For an instant, Miller had looked surprised, slightly shocked, at seeing him on the stairs. But then the familiar smugness had taken over. The caretaker must have thought himself safe from discovery – previously Jack had chosen mid-week to be at the college – and but for the talk he was giving, he would never have known of the intrusion.

Or would he? He looked around the office, trying to remember how he'd left it. Nothing seemed out of place and yet... his eyes fixed on a tiny scrap of white poking from what should have been a locked drawer. It was there he kept the pieces of work students had given him to read. Several were handwritten while one had been laboriously typed and none would be easy to replicate. Students had invested time and energy – and hope – in their work, and it was up to him to keep it safe.

For Joe Miller, though, that would be of no interest. Jack looked more closely at the drawer and saw that the lock had been depressed. What Miller had used to trigger it, he didn't know, but his anger was mixed now with unease. If the man had been able to ransack a locked compartment, he could access anything he wanted.

Jack bent down to the open drawer. The number of scripts he'd been given appeared to be correct and, as far as he could see, undamaged. Still mentally checking them, his attention was caught by a scrap of blue lined paper that had become lodged in a crack of the wood, behind the stack of students' work. Bending down further, he managed to extricate it.

An address. He grabbed at his glasses. And not any address, he could see now, but Russell Farr's, the very place he and Flora had visited on Saturday. Jack stood for some time, staring at the slip of paper in his hand. An address – but why? Surely, it couldn't be what Miller had been after? Why would the man be interested in Russell Farr? – there was no connection between them that Jack could see. And if, by chance, there had been in the past and the connection was waiting to be unearthed, Russell was already dead. If Miller had hoped to use this address for his own purposes, whatever they might be, the information was useless.

He tucked the sliver of blue paper into his pocket. Was it then that Miller had known the address, had been aware it was in Gilmore's desk, or suspected it was, and wanted to prevent Jack finding it? Too bad, if he had. That ship had already sailed.

His satisfaction, though, was short-lived, as more and more questions crowded in. Why would Miller worry that Jack might find it? Why, in any case, was the man continually dogging his footsteps? Why the unhealthy interest in him? Jack shut the desk drawer. The answers didn't lie there.

8

Flora had been planning to use her free Monday to finish sowing the spinach that would grow through winter, but the changed weather had made it impossible and, left alone in the cottage on a thoroughly miserable day, she was feeling fretful. Everyone was busy: Jessie was back in Treleggan, Alice in the Priory kitchen, hands-deep in flour, and Kate at the Nook cooking yet another full English. And she was here, doing nothing.

She could go to the All's Well and catch up with paper-work, she supposed, but Rose might not like it. *She* wouldn't like it if she was in Rose's shoes – the discomfort of feeling watched over, of suspecting you weren't trusted to do a good job. No, she couldn't go to her beloved bookshop.

Walking to the kitchen window for the umpteenth time that morning, she looked out on a bedraggled garden. She should have begged a lift with Jack, she realised, as soon as she'd pulled back the curtains and seen the sky grey and the windows splashed with rain.

But she could still go to Lewes! Surprise Jack on campus, perhaps, once he'd finished the talk he hadn't wanted to give.

He wasn't comfortable at the college, Flora could tell. He'd said very little but she knew him well enough to know that the job wasn't working out as he'd thought.

It would mean taking two different buses and she'd probably end up soaked, but what else was she to do today? Glancing at the kitchen clock, she reckoned she could just make the mid-morning bus to Brighton and from there change to one travelling eastwards. She ran up the stairs to the bedroom, pulled her trusty raincoat and bright yellow wellingtons from their shared wardrobe, and grabbed her handbag from the chair. Within minutes, she was out of the front door and splashing a path along Greenway Lane.

It was nearly two hours later that the Tunbridge Wells service dropped her in Lewes High Street. The college campus, Flora knew, lay to the south of the town. Grateful that at last the rain had abated – she'd dried out from her previous soaking as she'd travelled – she set off along one of the many roads that led downhill.

There were bookshops aplenty in the town, as she'd told Jack, and she'd passed two already. But just before turning into a lane that would take her to the bottom of the hill, she came across a large second-hand bookshop. Play It Again, it was called. That made her smile – someone had a sense of humour – and, on impulse, she pushed open the door, nodding to the assistant behind the counter, and involuntarily began to browse the nearest shelves.

The shop specialised in historical works, mainly factual books with some autobiographies and biographies included, but with a much smaller selection of fiction. It was the fiction section that Flora was studying when a fellow customer emerged from around the other side of the bookcase.

'Have you found anything?' the woman asked her. She was

smartly dressed, her long hair coiled elegantly at her nape. 'There's not a great selection, is there?'

Flora nodded. 'It's a little thin,' she agreed, 'but the non-fiction is impressive.'

'I can never get on with history as history, whereas when it's part of a good story, an imaginative walk through the past as it were, I love it.'

'Me too. But there are other bookshops in the town.' Flora lowered her voice, mindful of the assistant.

'Plenty, but I went through those last week. I'm Roberta Raffles.' She held out her hand. 'It's good to meet a fellow bookworm.'

'Flora Stee— Carrington.'

'You don't sound too certain,' the woman joked.

'I'm only just married,' Flora confessed, 'and I'm still getting used to a new name.'

'Congratulations, my dear. Look, why don't we go for a cup of tea somewhere and you can tell me all about it.'

Flora was unsure what there was to tell. She'd met Jack three years ago and, despite her misgivings, had fallen in love. Now he was her husband and that was it, but she sensed Roberta might be lonely and in need of company.

'I'd love a cup of tea,' she said cordially.

Over drinks at a small teashop a few doors along the high street, she was encouraged by her companion to describe her wedding day, her cottage and, finally, the All's Well.

'My goodness, you actually own a bookshop! How wonderful. Are you on a mission today – to gauge the competition?'

'Nothing like that.' Flora laughed. 'I've found an excellent assistant and I'm taking a few days off every week.'

'Perfect. I don't work,' Roberta confided. 'Not any more.' She sounded a little regretful. 'Looking after Paul takes most of my time.'

'Paul is your husband?'

'A dear man but one wedded to his job. He has a punishing schedule and needs looking after. He works in London, in the City. High finance. Don't ask me what he does, I don't understand a thing about it except that he leaves the house at dawn and I don't see him again until late evening.'

It sounded exhausting. Marrying a writer had its benefits – she was glad to have Jack's company for much of the week.

'Are you planning to use your free days to travel around all the Sussex bookshops?' Roberta asked, pouring them both a second cup of tea.

'I hadn't thought of it, but it's a fun idea. I came to Lewes today because Jack has a new job here. At Cleve College. Do you know it?'

Flora wasn't sure, but she thought she saw a slight shadow pass over her companion's face. 'He's a writer,' she went on, 'but for a few days a week he's mentoring students at the college.'

'But you live in Abbeymead?'

'Yes. Jack has moved into my cottage – his house was rented. I think the principal offered him a small flat on campus and I did think about moving there a few days a week – to save Jack the journey – but if I'm honest, I don't really want to.'

Roberta's frown was deep. 'Don't take it, my dear. Stay in your village.'

'Is there something wrong with the college?'

'No, not at all.' Her companion brushed away the suggestion. 'It's simply that you seem so happy with your life in the village, why would you change it? Why move out for a job that you say is part-time and may only be temporary? Best to stay where you love, but come to Lewes whenever you can. I've lived here for over ten years and I'm only just beginning to know all its nooks and crannies. It's a very old town, Anglo Saxon at least, and the twittens – those funny little lanes – pop up everywhere and you're never sure where they'll lead. Come over another day and I'll be happy to show you what I've discovered.'

'I'd like that,' Flora said dutifully, though unsure whether she actually did.

Roberta was amiable and good-natured – the invitation to tea, the interest in Flora's life – but, at the same time, appeared a little distant, a trifle guarded in what she said of herself. Something of a puzzle then. Nevertheless, it seemed to Flora that she'd made a friend and, in this new life she was beginning, that could be nothing but helpful.

'Are you going to tell me the problem?' Flora stopped peeling potatoes, her gaze fixed on Jack who was setting the table for the evening meal.

They had travelled home from Cleve College together, Jack fortuitously driving through the college gates as Flora had arrived to see him. She'd been eager to hear about his day, but a few mumbled phrases was all he'd vouchsafed before retreating into silence. She'd been the one to make conversation, telling him of her journey to Lewes, the meeting with Roberta Raffles and her plans for visiting the town more often. Now, preparing their supper together, she was faced with silence once more. It was very unlike Jack and it worried her.

'Problem?' He adopted a blank expression, but she wasn't deceived.

'Yes.' She walked over to him, the potato peeler still in her hand. 'You're not happy and it's Cleve College to blame. Am I right?'

Taking the peeler from her, he led her to a chair and sat down opposite, her hands cradled in his. 'I'm uneasy, Flora, that's all. There's something not right at the college but I can't work out what.'

'Tell me what bothers you.'

'First off, there's Joe Miller. He's the college caretaker and he seems to have an uncomfortable interest in me.'

She was mystified and must have looked it.

'What I mean,' he tried to explain, 'is that he's always around. I know you'll say that if he's a caretaker he needs always to be around, but every so often I'll feel someone close to me, or feel I'm being shadowed or stared at, and it will be Joe Miller a few paces away. Today, I caught him coming out of my office. He'd unlocked the door – he has keys to all the college rooms, of course – but it was more than that. He'd found his way into my desk, into a locked drawer.'

'What was in the drawer?' It was a practical question.

'Nothing much. Well, yes, students' work. And a scrap of paper with an address – believe it or not, Russell Farr's.'

'What?' Flora stared at him.

'I don't understand it either. Gilmore must have made a note of the address but what the connection is between them, I've no idea.'

'Farr's address was what this Joe Miller was after?'

'At first, I thought so, but it couldn't be. Russell died over two weeks' ago – why would Miller want it now? But there was nothing else in the drawer that could possibly interest him. Maybe it was to stop me from finding it. It's as if Miller thinks I have something to hide, that I need constantly watching, and now I have to be searched.'

Flora disentangled her hands, giving his a small squeeze as she did so. 'And he's said nothing to give you a clue?'

'He's a man of few words. But... ever since I spoke to Jocelyn Draper, I've been wondering... and now I've discovered this connection... I'm wondering if it's to do with what happened to my predecessor.'

That wasn't what Flora expected. Jack had said he knew nothing of the man who'd filled his job before him. 'You've learnt something?'

'I have and it's not pleasant. He didn't just leave the college, he died – by drowning in the college lake.'

More unexpected news and Flora was shocked. 'He was a young man?'

'Younger than me, apparently, and a very strong swimmer.'

Her eyes widened. 'Was it foul play?'

'Another murder? I don't think so, at least not from what Jocelyn said. She believes it was suicide, that Gregory Gilmore was depressed and took his own life at a particularly bad moment.'

'What was causing his depression?' That seemed crucial. 'Was somebody threatening him?'

'Jocelyn doesn't know how it started – from what she said, the chap was pretty buttoned up. The quality of his work tailed off and Dalloway, the principal, was keen to get rid of him and, to that end, made his life even more of a misery.'

'Well, he did get rid of him.'

'Jocelyn's very words. It was brutal, according to her.'

Flora got up and started back on the potatoes. 'I don't see any connection, Jack. I don't see how this Miller following you and searching your office could have anything to do with Gilmore's death.'

'Neither do I,' he confessed. 'Not really. I snatched at it – it was all I could think of. Maybe the principal is worried I'm likely to go the same way. One of the creative types, you know, and he's asked the caretaker to keep an eye on me.'

She turned, her face breaking into a grin. 'That's too much of a fantasy, even for me!'

'You're right. Let's forget it. Hopefully, Miller will soon find someone else to focus on. Can I do anything to help?'

'Coal from the bunker?'

Jack groaned. 'I knew I shouldn't have asked.'

9

They'd eaten the last mouthfuls of a beef casserole when the telephone rang. Jack got up to answer it, saying over his shoulder, 'Leave the dishes, Flora. My turn.'

It was Ross Sadler. Jack had telephoned his friend the night before, as soon as they'd returned from their visit to Rillington. He'd felt awkward bothering Ross on a Sunday evening, but his friend had been happy to hear from him and glad to help if he could. 'I'm between stories,' he'd told Jack. 'I'll start digging tomorrow.'

Could he have dug already? It seemed unlikely.

'Got some news for you,' Ross began. 'Fascinating place, Rillington. Not somewhere you'd really want to end up. It took a bit of time to get the right year – twenty years ago was a trifle vague – but newspapers in the summer of 1937 couldn't get enough of the topic. The local rags were full of it. You were interested in why the orphanage had closed?' Jack nodded silently at the telephone. 'Now, I can see why. It appears that the last director had a fatal accident.' Ross paused for a moment. 'The chap took over the orphanage in 1934 and seems to have run the place like a military institution. An article I uncovered from one of the local papers reported on a summer fair held there. The boys, and they were all boys, were dressed in what looked like a uniform and lined up in a platoon to greet visitors, then barked at – they were the reporter's own words – to take up their various duties, and quickly.'

'And the accident?'

'The director fell from an upstairs balcony onto the terrace below. Granite flagstones – made a nasty mess by all accounts.'

Was the stonework crumbling even then? Jack wondered. Or was the man ill, a stroke, a heart attack perhaps? Or even drunk.

'The post-mortem could find no obvious reason for the fall,' Ross continued. 'The chap's vital organs were OK and he hadn't consumed any alcohol.'

That was one theory to bite the dust.

'No suspected medical emergency either. All the doctor who attended could say was that perhaps the man had suffered a dizzy spell – a pretty weak conclusion for a man not fifty and in good health.'

'Any suggestion it wasn't an accident?'

'No sigh of a struggle, no sign of anyone else in the vicinity.'

'I think the place must have closed fairly soon after that. I wonder why they didn't appoint a new director.'

'You're right. It closed two months after the chap met his death. There was a lot of talk – locally, and beyond, I imagine. Maybe that's why no one else took on the job.'

'What kind of talk?'

'In the articles I read there seemed very little sympathy for the man among people the journalists spoke to. That was common to staff as well as to boys. The main story that emerges is of a group of boys, older boys, who were at war with the director. God knows what the rights and wrongs of it were, but he'd been giving them a bad time and they seemed to have given him one back.'

'All this was in the paper?'

'It was common knowledge, apparently. Gossip travels and the journalists who reported it were careful to point out that it was hearsay only. But the police must have got wind of the trouble because they interviewed the boys. In the end, they must have decided the kids had nothing to do with it and went for a verdict of accidental death. Might be interesting, though, to see the police reports.'

Jack pushed back an annoying flop of hair – he really must find a barber in Lewes. It might be interesting, as Ross suggested, to have a copy of those reports. A meeting with Ridley: he could ask about them and about any interviews the police had conducted with the older boys.

'It's true there was talk,' he told Ross. 'One of our friends here, Alice Jenner, you met her at the wedding, knew about this gang of boys, though she didn't recall the details.'

'I remember her. Nice lady. Great cook, too! How's it going, Jack, married life? You didn't say much last night.'

'There's not much to say other than I like it!'

'Well, that's a relief,' he joked. 'Anyway, I'll let you get on with your evening, but give me a ring if there's anything more you think of. I might come down one weekend and pay you a visit.'

'That would be good and thanks, Ross. Oh, Ross...' he said quickly, 'who *was* the director?'

There was a rustle of paper at the other end of the line. 'Name of Farr. Benedict Farr.'

As soon as they'd taken a tray of tea into the sitting room, Flora fixed him with a look.

'Well, what did he say?'

'Ross?'

'Yes, of course Ross. Don't be irritating.'

All he'd told her over the washing up was that the call had come from his friend. He'd been prevaricating, Jack realised, because he knew what Ross's information would mean. Flora would be off almost before he'd finished speaking, her hunting instincts aroused.

He took a deep breath. 'Rillington closed because its director had a fatal accident. He fell from a top balcony. And his name was Benedict Farr.'

There, he'd made a full confession.

'Farr!' Flora grabbed the name as he knew she would, and a single beat later, 'Russell Farr's father?'

'It has to be.'

She began to pour the tea, but stopped every so often, distracted by thoughts that were crowding in. 'Russell received an anonymous note telling him to investigate Rillington,' she said slowly, putting the teapot down, the cups half empty. 'Maybe until then he'd believed his father's death was an accident, but the letter changed his mind. Started him asking questions. And that's what he was doing in Abbeymead, asking questions. Someone – someone with something to hide – had to prevent that happening, and killed him. So... Russell's father... it wasn't an accident! The coroner's verdict was wrong. The fall was deliberate. Benedict Farr was pushed off that balcony.'

'Hey, too fast, too fast. We don't know for sure that Russell *had* decided to investigate.'

'Then why keep the letter?' she retorted.

'He could have kept it for any number of reasons. And if he was killed because he was poking his nose in where it wasn't wanted, why did he come to Abbeymead?'

Flora chewed at her lip, seeming for a moment taken aback. 'Why travel from Brighton to a small village?' she asked, on the front foot again. 'He has to have had a reason and I don't think it was birdwatching. Did he come to see someone? Someone who lives in Greenway Lane? But who would he want to visit there, and why didn't they come forward when we found his body?'

'I don't know why he came here. I'm not even sure *he* really knew.' A picture of the man hovering in the churchyard, uncertain, tentative, melting into the background, flashed into Jack's mind.

He saw Flora's frown – she hated ambiguity – and decided he'd be best to make a full confession. 'I didn't mention it before, but Russell came into the church during our wedding rehearsal, although I had no idea at the time that he *was* Russell. He backed out when he saw what was going on, but I think I saw him loitering in the churchyard when we left. He didn't seem to know where he should be going and I've always wondered if he'd been following us down the lane when he was killed.'

'You never said a word!' She shot him an accusing look.

'I didn't think it would help identify him.'

'It didn't. It was finding the cigarette case that did. But from what you saw, it's clear that Russell came to Abbeymead looking for someone, a person who, in some way, is linked to Rillington. We should try to find that person, Jack.'

'Abbeymead must have been a long shot for him. I wonder how many weeks, months, Russell had been looking – there was no date on the letter. He must have tried other avenues first.'

'And must have drawn a blank. It's a long shot for us, too.'

For some time, they sat thinking, while the silence lengthened and the tea grew cold. Jack felt confused, unable to decide what best to do. He had a book to write that was proving a struggle, a job to do that made him uneasy, and beneath it all a fear that Flora was about to plunge them into trouble that he didn't want. It was unusual for him to feel this way. An investigation always added spice to a life spent inventing crime, but right now there was just too much going on. He was wishing they had never walked down the lane that afternoon.

'Farr kept the letter in his cigarette case.' Flora broke the

silence. 'And because of that, we've been assuming it was important to him, that he started on a quest to piece together the past.
But there is another possibility. What if he'd just kept the letter
– as a curiosity, say – and we're on the wrong track entirely?
What if he was in the village for a completely different reason?'

'What reason, though? From what I saw of him, he didn't
seem to know where he was going. He was looking for something, I'm sure, or someone, even though he didn't know who or
what.'

'But not necessarily connected to the letter,' she argued.
'We should try to find out more about him. We have only his
landlord's word that he had no friends or family. He must have
had colleagues – he might have confided in *them* – he'd worked
with them for years.'

'True.' Jack gave a slow nod. 'It was an insurance company,
wasn't it? In Hove.'

'Hove Park. Steadfast Insurance. What a splendid name for
Russell – it fits him perfectly. He seems to have been a thoroughly steadfast chap. So when do we go?'

Jack tried not to sigh too loudly. 'Wednesday afternoon, I
guess. It's early closing and I've no plans to go to college that
day.'

10

At half past eight the next morning, Jack watched as Flora wheeled Betty down the front path to the garden gate and out into Greenway Lane, giving him a cheerful wave before she disappeared. Through the window, he heard the bicycle clank into life, ready for the short journey to the high street, both of them, he was sure, glad to be following the familiar routine.

Making short work of clearing what breakfast dishes remained, he walked into the hall and picked up the telephone to dial Brighton police station. Inspector Ridley had just this minute walked in, he was told.

'Have you had any luck with your dead man?' Jack asked, once the usual courtesies were over.

If, by now, the inspector had discovered Russell for himself, Jack decided he'd keep silent on their visit to Brighton. He was always conscious that he might be stepping on toes and, in this case, he'd been privy to important information for some days without disclosing it.

'It's slow work, Jack. One of my chaps has turned up a bus conductor who thinks he remembers the man getting on in Brighton and off at Abbeymead. Only thinks, mind. All we had to show him was the photograph of a dead face. But we're pursuing it. The person the conductor remembers boarded his bus in the Hanover district and I've officers there going door-to-door this week, asking if anyone could be missing someone!'

Jack cleared his throat. 'I think we might save your men a few hours.'

There was an ominous silence at the end of the line.

'Oh yes,' the inspector said at last, his tone hardly inviting.

'We... um... found a letter.' Jack was careful to avoid saying when. 'In the ditch where the body was discovered. In a cigarette case,' he gabbled. 'The address was Freshfield Road and it's a Russell Farr who's gone missing. The landlord at number 82 is sure to identify him.'

The silence had grown even more ominous. 'So, when were you thinking of telling me this little lot?'

'It was complicated,' he muttered, unable to think of a single good excuse.

'I bet it was.' Alan Ridley was terse. Then, after another short silence. 'If this Russell Farr is our man, I owe you. I'll get a bloke round there straight away.'

The landlord would not be happy, Jack reflected, his promise that the police wouldn't be ringing doorbells well and truly broken.

'There's something more you should know.' How would Ross Sadler's news go down? 'The letter mentioned that Farr should visit Rillington if he wanted to know how his father died and I asked a journalist friend to find out what he could about the orphanage there. A Benedict Farr was its director for some years – we're guessing he was Russell's father.'

'Sounds reasonable.'

'The thing is, Farr senior came to a bad end – fell to his death from a balcony. The coroner judged it was an accident, the police, too, but... it's likely that Farr started to play detective to uncover the mystery surrounding his father's death and ended up dead as well. It looks suspicious... at least, *we* think it does,' he finished lamely.

There was another long silence.

'Someone doesn't want the truth to come out, Alan. Can you look at the police report on the accident? The man had no health problems and the balcony was judged sound. There should at least be questions.'

'You know what you've done, don't you?' the inspector demanded. 'You've landed me with another potential murder. Two of 'em, now. Unless Greenway Lane was a hit-and-run and the fall at Rillington really was an accident.'

'We think it might have been a revenge killing.'

'You and Miss Flora seem to have done a lot of thinking.'

'There were some boys, older boys, who seem to have been causing a great deal of trouble – trouble aimed at the director. The police interviewed them at the time so there must have been some suspicion they were behind the death, but nothing came of it.'

The inspector gave a small puff. 'That's probably because there *was* nothing to come of it. But... I'll get the files up... in case.'

'If you do, could you pass on anything interesting?' Jack waited.

'I might.' He could feel the inspector weighing his options. 'Pie and a beer at the Cross Keys – say, two o'clock? I should have had time by then to scan any reports we've kept.'

'That would be good.'

And, for once, a pie and a beer seemed bearable.

Jack cut through the smoke of the Cross Keys to find his way to the bar. The inspector was already at the counter, ordering his favourite beef pie with mashed potatoes and gravy.

'Got you a beer, Jack,' he said over the heads of fellow customers, 'but—'

'A packet of crisps,' Jack said quickly. 'They'll do fine. A late breakfast,' he lied.

Settled in Alan Ridley's favourite bench in his favourite corner, the inspector adopted a severe expression.

'I should be hauling you in front of the beak,' he said, 'keeping vital information from the police.'

'Except I've passed on what I know.'

'When you decided you would.'

'Well, yes,' Jack was forced to agree, 'but has it been useful?'

'I guess so.' It was a reluctant acknowledgement. 'Mind, we still have no relatives in the picture. No one to bury the poor bloke when we release the body.'

'That won't be for a time, I imagine. Maybe someone will pop up as your investigation goes on, though from what the landlord said, Russell Farr was something of a loner.'

The inspector took a leisurely sip of his pale ale. 'You can say that again. His father's dead, no one knows where his mother is and he doesn't appear to have had a single friend. According to the landlord – Norris was with him for an hour this morning – he worked in an insurance office in Hove. I telephoned the chap in charge but all he could tell me was that the company had taken Farr on straight from school and he'd been there ever since. Small promotions but nothing earth-shattering.'

Jack had been wondering if he should mention the visit he and Flora intended to make the following day. Now, though, he felt excused. If the inspector had found nothing of interest at Farr's workplace, they were unlikely to either. It would probably prove the frustrating afternoon he'd foreseen.

'They did produce his job application,' the inspector went on, 'which is something of a miracle since he started work in 1937.'

'He was young.'

'Sixteen? But that's the age most youngsters start, though in Farr's case – he was privately educated, went to a boarding school up in Yorkshire of all places – you'd think he'd have stayed on for longer. Found a better paying job than an insurance clerk. The school's my next port of call, though I'm not hopeful.'

'Did you have his father's post-mortem on file?'

Ridley nodded. 'Nothing untoward that I can see. His injuries were consistent with having fallen from a considerable height onto a terrace of paving stones. No signs of bruising or cuts that shouldn't have been there.'

He broke off to welcome his pie and mash and, unrolling cutlery from the paper napkin the barman had handed him, said decisively, 'An accident looks like it was the right verdict. The letter you mentioned – did you bring it?'

Jack produced the now crumpled sheet of paper from his jacket pocket.

'Anonymous.' The inspector's eyes had travelled down the page. He gave a dismissive sniff, then turned over the envelope. 'Not even addressed to Farr. Most likely a crank, Jack. Someone he got the wrong side of and who wanted to rile him.'

'If that's so, why was he killed?'

'He might not have been killed. I'm keeping an open mind. His death could have been a hit-and-run, even an accident like his father's. He comes to Abbeymead on a fool's errand and gets in the way of a tractor or some other farm vehicle where the driver doesn't see him.'

'But you haven't found the tractor, Alan. And you know as well as I do, there's no way he could have ended in that ditch unless someone picked his body up from the lane and tipped it over. Which rather suggests it was a deliberate killing.'

'So, who sent the note, Sherlock?' The inspector tossed the wrinkled sheet to one side.

'I've no idea, and no sense of how I might find out. But the boys I mentioned? Did you find the police interviews?'

'They were with the post-mortem – the investigation appears to have been efficient, wrapped up in a couple of weeks. The interviews made interesting reading, but in the end the team investigating decided there was nothing to pursue and, having read the file, I'm inclined to agree.'

'What was the interesting reading?' Jack wasn't giving up.

'There were three lads who seem to have formed a small gang. All of them around fourteen, fifteen years old. On the brink of leaving the orphanage and going out to work. From what the police gathered from the staff at the time, Benedict Farr was a hard taskmaster and, in particular, didn't much care for the older lads he was responsible for. Especially these three. They seemed always to be in trouble.'

'What form did being a hard taskmaster take?'

The inspector screwed up his face. 'One comment stood out for me, though there were plenty of others. It was the cook. She said that Farr had forbidden the boys any family visits and insisted he approved any applications they made for a job.'

'In other words, he wanted complete control over them.'

'Looks like it. And the boys kicked back.' Ridley bent down to pull from his briefcase a sheaf of papers, then flicked through several of the pages. 'This one – Joe Miller – comes over as a real hard nut.'

'Joe Miller?' Jack couldn't keep the incredulity from his voice.

'Yes, why?'

'Nothing,' he said quickly. 'The name seemed familiar for the moment.'

He should come clean with Ridley, he knew, but a small devil was tempting Jack to hold the information close. Every day, the Farr mystery had grown more complex, spreading its tentacles into unknown territory. And, despite his earlier qualms, the familiar desire to win through, to discover the truth, had returned. Strongly.

'His family, what there was of it, had given up on him. Seemed to have lacked any authority over what he got up to. Maybe that's why Farr senior had to come down hard. Joe's dad was an alcoholic and his mother, well, I'll leave you to guess. The council took him from a home that according to the report was chaotic and filthy and settled him at Rillington, though the orphanage doesn't seem to have made young Joe's life very much better. He wanted to go in the army, that's what the cook says, but the director refused him a reference and he was turned down. However' – the inspector's finger travelled down the page – 'he did eventually get his wish. He signed on as a private in the Royal Sussex regiment, but that didn't last long. A year, tops. I reckon something bad must have happened.'

Jack was trying to absorb this torrent of information. Miller had been at the orphanage and had hated the director. He'd served as a soldier but left the army under a cloud, yet here he was – a caretaker at Cleve College. Here he was, Jack thought, shadowing my footsteps, searching my office, constantly spying. All this against a backdrop of two men dead, a father and a son. More and more he was convinced that, despite Flora's desire to widen their scope, Rillington orphanage had to be the connecting thread.

He needed time to think. A mass of time. But Ridley had finished his pie and was draining the last of his beer, making ready to leave.

'Who were the other two boys?' Jack remembered to ask just in time.

The inspector went back to his paperwork. 'One was a Paolo Ruffini,' he said, mangling the Italian name. 'Now... he's an intriguing lad. His father was Italian, no guesses there, but a nasty bit of work by the look of it. Murdered Paolo's mother and was banged up for life.'

The revelations kept coming. 'Not hanged?'

'There were mitigating circumstances, apparently. The wife went for him, too, and the jury couldn't decide who'd started the barney. Neighbours testified that the couple were always rowing and it was often violent. Dad got life and not the rope while Paolo was sent to the orphanage.'

'No relatives?'

'His mother's parents had died and his grandparents in Italy said they were too old to care for him. And Paolo didn't want to go. When he was interviewed, he said he wanted to stay in England, go to night school, make something of himself. That's what I mean. An intriguing boy.'

'Admirable,' Jack agreed. 'And did he? Make something of himself?'

'No idea.'

'And the third boy?'

Ridley began collecting his papers together. 'He was a genuine orphan. Both parents killed in a train crash when he was a tiddler, though by some miracle he survived. But again, no relatives, no foster parents available, so it was off to Rillington at – what would it be? – the tender age of seven. He was part of the trio who were interviewed, but I get the impression from reading statements made by the staff that whereas the other two were tough lads, this one wasn't. It was more that he was dragged along with them. It can happen. I've seen it before.'

'Do you have a name for him?'

'I should have. Let's see.' Pages were once more shuffled. 'Yes, here he is. Gregory Gilmore.'

11

_____

The Steadfast Insurance company occupied the second floor of an impressively modern building in the road that ran opposite Hove Park. The park itself wore a sad air this afternoon, much of it shut for the season some weeks ago with tennis courts locked and the café closed. Despite a threateningly dark sky, a few brave people were taking their daily constitutional beneath trees bare of any leaf.

Jack had always been doubtful about making this visit and, after what he'd learned from the inspector yesterday, he was more certain than ever that it would prove a dead end, and hadn't held back in saying so. Flora could see why. The information they had was pointing solidly to a connection with the orphanage and that should be their focus, but it was best not to ignore the most trivial of leads. She felt that forcibly. Often, they were the ones that led to the final pieces of the jigsaw fitting together, and the more they knew of Russell Farr, a shadowy figure at the moment, the more useful it could be.

She'd walked ahead of Jack and, at the reception desk, asked to speak to the managing director. Aim high, she decided – at least to begin with.

The receptionist looked taken aback at the request. 'I'm afraid that's not possible. Our managing director has his office in Holborn,' adding with a simper that verged on the pitying, 'That's London, you know.'

'Yes, we are aware. So, who *can* we see? We need to talk to someone who knew Russell Farr.'

'Russell? But he's—'

'Dead? Yes, we know that, too. That's why we're here.'

'Helping the police,' Jack murmured, excusing himself the lie.

The woman hesitated, tucking long strands of mousy hair behind her ears, while seeming to decide. It looked as though she was about to send them on their way, but then changed her mind.

'Mr Harrison is the office manager.'

'Splendid,' Flora said. 'May we see Mr Harrison? We won't keep him more than a few minutes.'

She was truer to her word than she'd anticipated. Greeting them with a tepid smile, Mr Harrison ushered them into his office. A limp handshake followed and a gesture for them to take one of the Dralon-covered seats designed for visitors. Retreating behind his desk, he perched rather than sat on a large chair of black leather, clearly expecting to show them to the door as soon as he could.

'Russell Farr.' He pursed his lips when they mentioned the name. 'A police sergeant already called – yesterday. But a sad business. He worked here for years. For as long as I've been managing the office. Longer, in fact.'

'Can you tell us anything about him? His relatives, his friends – anyone he was close to in the office?'

Harrison shook his head. 'I don't ask employees for personal details.'

'Not even when they've been working with you for years?'

'No, certainly not.' He sounded scandalised at the suggestion.

'What about his colleagues?'

'I've no idea how friendly or otherwise he was with others in the office. I told the sergeant. Farr was a good worker. Reliable, punctual. He did his job well.'

'Did he always do the same job? We understand he worked here from a very young man.'

'He was given a small promotion a few years back. I made him a section leader. Apart from that, he never showed any wish to climb the ladder.'

Mr Harrison wriggled forward, almost tipping himself off his chair. 'I'm sorry I can't be more help. Now, if you...'

'We'll be off,' Jack said, Flora joining him in silently conceding defeat.

They walked out into a huge open space containing what seemed a hundred desks arranged in several separate squares, before making their way back to the main entrance. The receptionist had hurried them through this enormous room on their way to the manager's office, but on their return there was time to look around. And, looking around, Flora spied one desk that was conspicuously different from all the others. It was empty of files, empty of a ringing telephone, and missing a head bent over a stack of documents.

She paused to speak to the clerk sitting at the next desk, a young woman, fresh-faced and comfortably plump.

'I'm sorry to interrupt your work,' Flora began.

The girl looked up and grinned. 'Don't be. Interruptions are always welcome.'

'Is it so dull?' she asked sympathetically.

'Deadly,' the girl agreed. 'Was there something you needed?'

Flora pointed to the empty desk a few feet away. 'I was

wondering if you knew Russell Farr well. I imagine that was his desk.'

'It was, but no, I didn't know Russell that well. I don't think anyone did. He was a good section leader, though. Quiet but efficient. Not a taskmaster like—' She stopped herself. 'Why do you ask?'

'We're trying to find out as much about him as we can. Any details of his life. They're hard to come by.'

'I imagine they would be.' The girl pulled a face. 'I can tell you—' She broke off.

When Flora turned to look over her shoulder, she saw Mr Harrison's squat figure walking purposefully towards them.

'I'd better get on,' the girl said swiftly.

'Sorry to have bothered you.' Flora took hold of Jack's hand and whisked them out of the office, through the reception area, and into the street before saying, 'She would be worth talking to.'

'She didn't know Russell well,' Jack protested. 'She said so.'

'Maybe, but she was going to tell me something if that horrible Harrison hadn't appeared on the scene. Let's wait and talk to her.'

'Here?' Jack waved his hand at the windswept park opposite.

She didn't answer him directly. 'What's the time? I didn't wear my watch.'

'Just past four.'

'The Steadfast will close at five almost certainly. When the girl leaves for home, I'll nab her.'

'Meanwhile, we freeze beneath the trees.'

'Don't be a grump. There's a café I noticed on the main road, but we might miss her if we go there. We'll have to keep walking,' Flora decided. 'That way we'll stay warm and healthy at the same time.'

'Now, why didn't I think of that?'

'You're not practical, Jack,' she chided. 'Not like me.'

'The Lord save me from practicality.' He flicked the bobble on her woollen hat. 'Come on. Ten rounds of the park should do.'

In fact, they had completed only half a dozen circuits before a church clock somewhere in the distance struck five, causing Flora to race ahead and take up position at the entrance to the Steadfast office block.

The girl they'd spoken to drifted out five minutes later, chatting casually to one of her colleagues until she saw them waiting.

'Hello,' she said uncertainly.

'I'm afraid we're bothering you again.' Flora stepped forward. 'We were wondering if we could talk to you for a few minutes?' Jack had suggested that she be the one to approach the girl, one woman to another.

'OK,' she said, though sounding even less certain.

'There's a café around the corner. Shall we have a cup of tea? We've been walking in the park, hoping not to freeze.'

'And not been too successful,' Jack put in.

The girl glanced at Jack. She'd not seen him properly when Flora had stopped by her desk, but now his appearance seemed to reassure her. A tall, quiet man, with calm grey eyes rather than this bouncing, impulsive girl, Flora thought.

'This is Jack,' she said. 'And I'm Flora.'

'Elizabeth,' she introduced herself. 'Tea would be nice. Warm me up before I walk home.'

'You live in Brighton?' Jack asked.

The street she named had him look surprised. 'That's quite close to Freshfield Road, isn't it, where Russell Farr lived?'

'That's right. We used to walk home together sometimes. When my boyfriend wasn't meeting me.'

'You knew Russell outside of work?' Flora was quick to pursue a possible lead.

Elizabeth shook her head. 'Not really. But he was a nice man,' she said sadly. 'It's horrible knowing he'd died like that.'

'When you say not really' – Flora pushed open the café door – 'does that mean you did see him occasionally out of the office?'

There was a general flurry as coats were draped over chair backs and their order given to the waitress who'd appeared as soon as they'd walked in.

'There was just this once,' the girl said.

Flora sent her warmest smile across the table. 'Yes?'

'I felt sorry for Russell. He didn't seem to have many friends. Any friends,' she added thoughtfully. 'And he never spoke of anyone special in his life.'

'Like a girlfriend?' Flora prompted.

'I tried to do a bit of matchmaking, I suppose, but it didn't work out. It was several years ago now, when I was with my former boyfriend. One of my sisters – the one that's married – got talking to the girl who'd just moved in next door. She was at a loose end, a bit lonely, and my sister asked me if I could organise an evening out with her. I asked Russell if he'd come along.'

'And he did?' Flora was amazed.

'I don't think he was keen, but he said yes and actually the evening went off pretty well. They seemed to get on fine.'

'Did they carry on getting on fine?' Jack asked.

'For a while, but then something bad happened. I never knew what. When I asked Russell about it, he just said that he didn't see her any more. And said it in a way – well, you know – in a way that I didn't feel I could ask him for details.'

'Did your sister talk to the girl afterwards?'

'Daphne, that's my sister, said her neighbour was very upset. Distraught, she said, but I took that with a pinch of salt. Daph's always exaggerating, though I did find the girl very intense that evening. But then Daphne told me the girl was blaming *me* for the break-up.'

'Why on earth would she do that?' Flora was beginning to think this woman, whoever she was, was slightly unhinged.

'I've no idea, but she told Daphne she was sure I'd been trying to take Russell away from her which was ridiculous. I did break up with my boyfriend around that time, but then I met Craig. He's lovely.'

'And Daphne – does she still see this girl?'

'They lost touch. The girl was horrible to her, then refused to speak to her again. I think she moved house after that. Daph didn't care – she's got hundreds of friends.'

'So... you've no idea where she might be.'

'As far as I know, she's still living in Lewes.'

'She lived in Lewes?' Jack and she put their teacups down at the same time.

'Yes. My sister does, too. I think the girl worked in a college there. I remember she said she was a teacher. She taught art, I think.'

'Do you have her name?'

Elizabeth looked concerned. 'I only knew her first name and maybe it's best I don't say. She's someone I'd rather forget. My sister, too. Actually' – she stood up abruptly, grabbing her coat from the chair back – 'it's time I got home. The cat will need feeding,' she explained. 'But thanks for the cuppa.'

After she'd left, they sat in silence for a while, staring at three empty cups, until Jack said heavily, 'I wish Elizabeth had given us a name. Imagine if it was Jocelyn Draper!'

'What's the likelihood that the only girlfriend Russell ever had teaches at Cleve College?'

'To be fair, the college has a large staff and Lewes is only a small town. It's not implausible that she rented the house next to Daphne and, as a favour, Daphne asked her single sister to make up a foursome. Elizabeth probably thought she was doing Russell a favour, too.'

Flora tapped a teaspoon rhythmically against the saucer. 'For a moment, let's say it *was* her. Does that mean the two men who apparently rejected Jocelyn both died prematurely?'

'Elizabeth said that the Russell relationship was over in a few months and it happened two or three years ago. So ... if we're thinking that Jocelyn sought revenge and killed Russell for leaving her, why wait that long?'

There was another silence, until Flora crashed the teaspoon down onto the table, her face shining. 'I bet Russell Farr went to the college! He'd worked out the connection with the orphanage, found Miller and Gilmore. Jocelyn must have seen him when he visited.'

Jack's expression was intent. 'She mentioned that she saw Miller taking a man up to Gregory's office. But she said nothing about recognising him. In fact, she was adamant that she didn't know him. Couldn't even describe him very well – just an ordinary man, she said.'

'There you are then. There's her motive. Seeing Russell again brought it all back – the rejection she'd suffered. Don't forget that it was at precisely this time she was angling after Gilmore, and he wasn't having any of it.'

'We don't know that's true. It's a rumour, and one spread by Joe Miller. I wouldn't believe a word he said.'

'In this case, perhaps you should. Jocelyn went swimming with Gilmore most mornings, you said. She obviously valued his friendship and it may well have been more than that. Let's say she made overtures to him and he said no. Then she sees the man who'd rejected her a few years previously. At that point, I think she'd be burning with revenge.'

'Conjecture, Flora, conjecture, but I am thinking it odd that Farr went to the college seemingly without a second thought. He must have known Jocelyn was a teacher there and that he was likely to run into her. If their break-up was that bad, you'd think he'd find another way of speaking to Gilmore and Miller. A letter to both of them maybe suggesting a meeting place.'

'Except that he wouldn't be sure he'd get a reply. Neither Gilmore nor Miller would want to talk about the orphanage, would they? By turning up at Cleve unannounced, Farr was sure to pin them down. And perhaps Russell assumed that Jocelyn had moved on. If she was as unhappy at the break-up as Elizabeth suggested, she should have moved on. Perhaps he'd even forgotten her. It's possible,' she said, seeing Jack's doubtful expression. 'Russell Farr seems to me a very closed-in kind of man, the sort of person who would compartmentalise his life quite easily. The interlude with Jocelyn was over – he wouldn't think of her any more.'

'If that's the case, then she must have felt extremely agitated when she saw him with Miller. He'd come to the college, but it wasn't to see her.'

'And hadn't even bothered to seek her out. Maybe he saw her watching him climb the stairs with Miller and looked straight through her, as though she was someone he didn't know.'

'It's a theory.'

'A good one.' Flora turned to look around the café. 'Shall we go? I think they're wanting to shut up shop.' There had been a definite increase in the sounds of cups being stacked and cutlery being rattled.

Jack helped her on with her coat and they walked out into the cold night. The Austin was parked a street away and they didn't speak again until they were driving out of Brighton.

'Jocelyn talked a lot about Gilmore's depression,' Jack remarked. 'I thought it was because he'd been a good friend and she felt sad for him, but now I'm wondering if she used it to suggest a motive for his death. The more she emphasised his depression, the fewer questions there'd be over an accident or even a possible suicide. She was very keen, I noticed, to tell me how badly Gilmore had gone downhill after Farr's visit.'

'And she lied about the visit itself, pretending to you that she didn't know the man on the stairs.'

'Jocelyn's lying seems something of a habit.'

'And maybe the suggestion that Gilmore's death was suicide is another. I'm wondering... did Jocelyn get away with murder the morning Gilmore drowned? And Russell – has she got away with killing Russell Farr? On the surface, his death could be judged an accident, too. A driver hits him, panics and runs away.'

Jack turned off the main thoroughfare at the signpost that pointed to Abbeymead. 'Gilmore's death is definitely suspicious but there's one major problem with her killing Farr. How did Jocelyn know he'd be in Abbeymead that day?'

'She'd know his routine,' Flora said stubbornly. 'He was a man who had a schedule and stuck to it.'

'But that means she'd have had to be watching his house to know that he'd broken his routine and was on his way to Abbeymead. And that's impossible – Jocelyn has a full timetable at the college. And haven't we just argued that it was the shock of seeing Farr appear out of nowhere, the shock of an earlier rejection being replayed, that sent her off to murder? If she didn't know he was intending to visit the college, she couldn't have been watching his house.'

Flora thought about this for a while, but as the Austin was turning into Greenway Lane, a memory slid into her mind. 'There was a phone call. Remember the landlord telling us? For Russell to receive a phone call was so extraordinary that it stuck in his mind. What if that was Jocelyn on the line? Russell might have given her his telephone number when they were going out, in case she couldn't make a meeting, and she kept it.'

'So, she rings him up and says are you off to Abbeymead any time soon?'

Flora gave him a light smack as they pulled up outside the cottage. 'Of course she didn't. If the call was from her, and who else would be phoning him, it might have been in the hope of rekindling their friendship.'

'Do you really think that?'

'Gilmore was dead by that time,' she reminded him. 'And he'd been a disappointment. Jocelyn is lonely, wants someone of her own, no one else on the staff is a candidate, so she goes back to the boyfriend she used to have.'

'But he was the one who'd said goodbye.'

'I don't think we're talking here about a woman who is entirely stable.' Flora paused. 'But no, I think it's more likely that she was plotting. We can't know for sure exactly when the call came through but, by what the landlord said, it was after Farr's visit to the college.'

'After she'd decided she wanted revenge?'

Flora nodded. 'Russell's indifference made that certain. Remember what the landlord said of his response when he asked Russell who was phoning? "It was nobody that matters." That's how Russell thought of Jocelyn and she'd feel it.'

'OK. She's seen him at the college, been ignored, and she wants revenge. How does she get him to meet her?'

'It can only be supposition and we'll probably never know, but maybe she rang Russell to say she'd seen him at the college, and it had made her remember what good times they'd had together, and would he like to meet? She'd do it casually – even if she is a tad unhinged, she hasn't entirely lost sight of reality or she wouldn't be able to stay teaching. Perhaps she says, come to Lewes at the weekend or I'll come to Brighton, and he panics and says sorry, he's tied up. He's already arranged to go to this village. He has someone to meet there.'

'Tentative, Flora, very tentative.'

She climbed out of the car. 'I agree, but you know what they say about a woman scorned.'

12

The following day, Flora was back at the All's Well and enjoying her morning. She'd had a steady stream of customers, mostly villagers who hadn't called since the wedding and were keen to see how she was surviving marriage, but one or two had stopped to buy, and now she was facing Dilys who stood, solid and square, at the other side of her desk. The postmistress had dropped by in her lunch hour, ostensibly to buy a new gardening book, but really to ensure that Flora would not again trespass on post office terrain by selling calendars this coming Christmas.

'It's hard enough to make a living as it is,' she complained, the bobble on her woollen hat, canary yellow today, wobbling dangerously. 'And calendars do sell well.'

Flora was assuring her that this winter's calendars would be Dilys's very own, when Kate Farraday walked through the doorway.

'I won't stay,' she said quickly, looking from one to the other. 'Tony will have a queue otherwise – the Nook's pretty busy. I just wanted to make sure you're OK for supper tomorrow, Flora. Tony's been invited to a card party so it will be just us three.'

Just us three: Alice, Kate and Flora. Friday was the traditional evening for the three friends to take turns in hosting a meal, a chance to catch up with each other's news and share whatever titbit of village gossip was doing the rounds. The meal was so much part of all their lives that Flora wondered why her friend had come especially to remind her. Kate was beaming and Dilys was gazing at her with a knowing look. What was going on?

'Have you won a big, new order?' It must be why Kate's smile was as wide as the room.

'Well, yes, sort of... Mrs Barnes is having a lunch on Saturday for her women friends and we've been asked to cater.'

'She didn't get that Cornish woman to stay then?' Dilys asked her. 'Evelyn was all over her at the wedding.'

'Jessie was flattered by her offer, I think, but Abbeymead isn't her home. Treleggan is too precious for her to leave.'

'She stayed here plenty of days. I saw her gadding about with Alice Jenner, like neither of them had work to do.'

'They took a holiday together,' Kate said serenely, 'and thoroughly enjoyed themselves. Alice has been saying she might even take a trip to Cornwall.'

Flora was astonished.

'Only might,' Kate warned, seeing her friend's surprise. 'I must go. Tony will be drowning and there's the extra cooking to do for Saturday. But tomorrow, Flora?'

'Yes, I'll be there,' she repeated, wondering why it was so important.

Alone in the shop once more, Flora forgot Friday's meal and thought instead of Harry Barnes. Jack had felt it pointless to speak to Harry, but then he'd thought it a waste of time to go to the Steadfast offices, and look what they'd learned there. When Alice had spoken of a painting of Rillington orphanage, the remark had stayed in Flora's mind and she'd been wondering ever since whether Harry could be another vital link in a chain of clues they were beginning to build. A small clue, she conceded, but one that could matter. Harry Barnes must have some connection to the orphanage to possess the painting. It was hung in the scullery which suggested that either Evelyn didn't like the picture and it had been shuttled far from her gimlet gaze, or Harry's connection to the orphanage was one he wasn't happy about, yet didn't want to disown entirely. Another layer of mystery.

And one she could solve on her own. She would go to see him on Saturday. Kate's news had decided her. Harry wouldn't want to be hanging around Pelham Lodge when Evelyn's friends descended on the house, and where would he go instead? The answer came loud and clear: the Lexington Golf Club. He'd be in the bar, not on the fairway, she was certain, and on Saturday she'd be joining him.

Having waved goodbye to her last customer of the morning, it was high time, Flora decided, to eat the beef and horseradish sandwich she'd brought with her. She had locked the till, turned the shop notice to Closed and put the kettle to boil on the tiny gas ring in what Aunt Violet had insisted was a kitchenette, when the telephone rang. Eager for her lunch, she had half a mind not to answer, but it could be Jack – he was at the college today and perhaps the inspector had telephoned him with news – or the call might involve the promise of a substantial order from another bookshop or from one of her more prolific readers.

'Flora? That is Flora?' She didn't recognise the voice.

'Yes, Flora Stee—' she began.

'Carrington. You're still forgetting!' There was a gurgle of laughter down the phone.

'Roberta?' she queried. It had to be Roberta Raffles.

'That's me. How are you?'

'Fine, thank you. And you?' she remembered to ask, though itching to eat, a hollow space where her stomach should be.

'Also well, but very keen to show you something of Lewes.' Flora didn't immediately respond and her caller said quickly, 'You remember, don't you, I made a promise?'

'Yes, of course, but I'm not sure when I can come over.'

'How about tomorrow? You said you'd given yourself Fridays free.'

Flora was caught. Unthinkingly, she'd mentioned that Rose would be running the All's Well on two days a week and couldn't now disavow it. She'd liked Roberta well enough at their first meeting, but it took time to build a friendship and being rushed felt unsettling. It was clear, however, that this was a lonely woman, her husband away from home the greater part of each day, and Flora felt sympathy. She'd enjoyed Roberta's company at the tearoom, so why not go?

'I'd love to come over,' she said, suppressing her doubts, 'though I can't be in the town before about twelve.'

'Plenty of time for what I'm planning. I want to show you some special places,' Roberta trilled. 'And we must have lunch together. I'll meet you outside the Law Courts – the bus from Brighton stops there, I know. Around twelve then?'

There was no way Flora could refuse the invitation and was reduced to mumbling a weak, 'That would be nice. I'll see you tomorrow.'

She woke to a beautiful autumn morning. The rain that had persisted on and off for several days had at last cleared. It was a day to tackle the garden – the list of tasks seemed to mount daily despite there being two of them to manage a single patch far smaller than Jack's had been at Overlay House.

'Do you really want to do the journey?' he asked, over an

early breakfast. 'I'd give you a lift to Lewes only you'd be hanging around for hours.'

She didn't answer his question directly but jumped up and gave him a hug on her way to the kitchen sink. 'You go. I've chores to do first and I'll be fine on the bus.'

Some time later, as she walked to the bus stop in the high street, a sun, faint and misty, came out to play. Sadly, though, Flora's mood failed to match, her feet seeming to drag, as if keen to retrace every step as she took it. It wasn't so much an eagerness to be busy at home, but more a reluctance to meet Roberta again so soon after their last encounter. She shouldn't have agreed to the visit – it was making her uncomfortable. She had the sense of being taken over, her time commandeered to fill the gaps in another woman's life. But the thought made her feel bad and she shook it away. Roberta had been warm and friendly and she shouldn't begrudge a few hours of her time. She would see her today, Flora promised herself, then gently loosen the tie.

Changing buses proved smoother than previously, and she was very soon bowling along the main thoroughfare from Brighton, the Downs rising steeply to encase the small medieval town in its hold. It was a shorter journey than Flora remembered and she was surprised when the old Victorian prison on the outskirts hove into view. Two immense square towers, crenellated and granite-faced, stared grimly out into the world. From the top of the bus, she gazed across at pairs of arched windows, barred and grilled, that grew smaller and narrower with each ascending floor until at the very top of the building, only the smallest sliver of light would be visible to its unfortunate inmates. The image did nothing to improve her spirits, but she forced herself into a smile when, a few minutes later, the bus pulled up outside the Crown court and she saw Roberta waiting for her.

'How wonderful to see you, my dear.' Flora was enveloped in a hug of patchouli-scented cashmere. 'And how good of you to come. I thought we'd have an early lunch? Sightseeing on an empty stomach is not recommended!'

Without waiting for a response, Roberta took her arm and steered her along a narrow road to their left, followed by a ten-minute climb to the leafy avenue that Roberta called home. Flora guessed the three-storey house had been an expensive purchase. The whole area had the feel of money – wide, tree-lined streets, large houses and even larger gardens – and it was probably necessary for Mr Raffles to spend most of his waking life in the City.

'This is the most beautiful district of Lewes.' Roberta waved an expansive hand at the neighbourhood. 'At least, I think so.'

'It's lovely. Peaceful,' Flora added, hoping she'd said enough.

'It is and we're here!' They'd come to a stop outside one of a row of Edwardian houses. Her hostess walked ahead, up the black-and-white tiled pathway, fumbled for a moment beneath the large terracotta pot at the side of the porch, and opened the front door with a flourish. 'Do come in.'

She came in, to a hall splashed with pools of bright colour, the morning light filtering through the door's decorative glass.

'Come in, come in,' Roberta urged. 'Don't be shy.'

Flora was more preoccupied than shy. Gazing at the succession of tall ceilings and spacious windows ahead, her immediate thought was that her new friend's home could not be more different from her own.

'I thought we'd eat in the kitchen,' Roberta said. 'Much cosier.'

Cosy was not the epithet Flora would have chosen for the wide open space that looked out onto an equally wide open garden. The table was large, seating at least eight people, yet it squatted comfortably in the middle of a continuous run of built-in cupboards.

Roberta had begun to move plates of food from the refrigerator to the table.

'Can I help?' Flora hovered in the doorway.

'Not at all. You're my guest. Come and sit down.' She gestured to one of the wooden chairs, surprisingly quite badly scratched and dented. The chairs, at least, were cosy. 'Now, can I offer you a glass of wine?' she asked. 'I don't drink myself at midday but I know others have a partiality.'

'A cup of tea would be fine.'

'Tea afterwards, perhaps,' Roberta said brightly. 'I'll bring a jug of water.'

Flora had evidently committed a social faux pas. In this section of society, it seemed, you did not drink tea with your lunch. And what a lunch! A plate of cold meats, a plate of cheeses, every kind of salad, and two large baking potatoes, each with a mound of butter. The dessert Flora glimpsed from the corner of her eye, waiting patiently on the counter, was a treacle tart – home-made, she judged, but naturally – accompanied by a jug of cream.

Overwhelmed by the hospitality, Flora took a seat somewhat nervously at one side of the table, her hostess at its head.

'Please, help yourself,' Roberta said. 'We don't stand on ceremony here.'

That was unlikely to be true but the baked potato smelt extraordinarily good and, having woken early, Flora was very hungry.

'So...' Roberta beamed across the table. 'How is your husband getting on at Cleve?'

The way she spoke of the college made Flora feel she must know it better than she'd suggested.

'Jack is still finding his feet,' she said cautiously, 'but he says the job is enjoyable.'

'That's good to hear. Men have to work so many years that finding a job they like is essential. But, of course, you work, too.'

It was as though Flora was a special exhibit. 'Did *you* never work?' she asked.

'Oh yes, in a flower shop. I was the manageress actually.'

'How lovely.' The heavy perfume made sense.

'It was.' There was a small sigh as Roberta cut herself a slice from a cheese that Flora had never seen before. A thick rind with holes – was that the Gruyère she'd heard about? 'But marriage was more important,' her hostess was saying. 'Important for me to support Paul.'

'Has he always worked in the City? The journey from here must be tiring.'

'We could have moved when he got the job, but this is such a lovely house I wanted to stay. And Paul is so good to me that he agreed immediately.'

Flora put down her knife and fork, feeling nicely replete. 'Before, he worked locally? In Brighton?'

'In Lewes,' she said. 'At the college, in fact.'

She had thought Roberta had some connection to Cleve College, but that her husband had actually worked there was a complete surprise. The woman had given the information willingly, there'd been no reluctance on her part, but why hadn't she mentioned it before?

'Was Paul the principal before Professor Dalloway?' Flora prompted, intent on learning as much as she could.

'Nothing like that, my dear. Paul isn't academic in that sense. Figures are his thing. He was the bursar. Now, how about some treacle tart?'

13

Having eaten a large slice of treacle tart, following what had been a substantial first course, Flora was feeling nothing like exploring the places of historic interest that Roberta had promised her. Lewes was built on a succession of hills and the thought of climbing one after another on a very full stomach was not a happy one. But her hostess seemed filled with energy, briskly collecting their empty plates to store in the sink, and showing no sign of abandoning the proposed visit.

It would do her good to walk, Flora told herself and, staggering to her feet, offered her help.

'You are not to do a thing,' Roberta declared. 'You are my guest. The sitting room is just across the hall – make yourself at home while I whisk through the washing up. Oh, and if you need the bathroom it's up the stairs, first on the left.'

'Thank you. I'll find it.'

Leaving Roberta to her kitchen duties, Flora walked out into the light-filled hall, first gazing into a large sitting room, made even larger by the sparseness of furniture, then, about to climb to the first floor, she saw a half-open door to one side of the stairs, and a washbasin beyond. She would use that, her hands uncomfortably sticky from treacle tart.

A wash in heavily scented soap later, she was about to leave when she saw from the image in the oval mirror that her hair, painstakingly wound into what she'd hoped was an elegant topknot, was now in imminent danger of falling to her shoulders. Grabbing hold of the pins she'd used to anchor it, Flora began to wind the recalcitrant waves into something that resembled a loose bun.

For a moment, her glance was distracted by the arrangement of pictures to one side of the washbasin. Photographs of Roberta and a man she presumed was her husband. They stood smiling together – smiling somewhere that looked like Rome, somewhere that looked like the West Country, and that was Paris, Flora was sure. There were several framed commendations, too. Prizes the husband had won and a certificate which Flora presumed was his accountancy qualification. It seemed faded with age and she bent to peer at it.

'Don't use this room, Flora. The bathroom is upstairs.' The figure of her hostess appeared in the mirror behind her.

'Sorry.' She turned to apologise. 'This was nearer.'

'Nearer, but not functioning, I'm afraid. The flush doesn't work and yesterday the plumber let me down again. Best to go upstairs.'

'Yes, of course. I'll be two minutes.'

'I'll be waiting. We've lots to see.'

Roberta's words proved true. During the next two hours, Flora thought she must have walked up every hill and down every twitten in the town. She was shown the plaque commemorating the Protestant martyrs – seventeen in all – burned at the stake outside what had been the Star Inn and was now the town hall. The steps down to the grim cellar where they'd been imprisoned were still clearly visible, but now glassed over and out of bounds. Then it was on to Bull House where Thomas Paine had lived for some years before travelling to America, his political writings helping to inspire the revolutionaries and their declaration of independence.

'He's quite a hero in the town,' Roberta remarked. 'But I have to admit I don't have much sympathy with people who deliberately set the world by the ears. I much prefer to live peacefully.'

'I think all of us do but sometimes, I guess, it's necessary to disrupt – in order to move forward.'

'You're right, of course.' She tucked her arm in Flora's. 'It's just knowing when that's important.'

There followed several small digressions to salute a scattering of literary figures – William Cobbett, Daisy Ashford, Virginia Woolf; how could such a small town boast so many luminaries? – and then finally to St John's churchyard and the seventeen-foot obelisk erected by the Czar to commemorate soldiers of the Russian Army, captured during the Crimean war, who had died in a Lewes prison.

The graveyard had, in parts, been allowed to grow wild. Bushes spread their limbs, a canopy of trees bent their heads in shelter, and the grass, left to its devices, had grown tall and strong.

Standing in this delightful green space, Flora looked around her. 'This is beautiful.'

'I agree. A member of the women's group I attend – my little treat every Monday afternoon – introduced me to the graveyard a few years ago. I sometimes come and just sit. Over there.' She pointed to one of the benches half-hidden in the grass. 'There's an amazing amount of wildlife here.'

'I can imagine. How long have you lived in Lewes?'

'Oh, years,' she said vaguely.

'You came here for Paul's job?'

'That's right. We were just married and Cleve was his first post after he qualified.'

Flora tried to calculate how old Paul Raffles would have been when he began work as an accountant. The cloakroom certificate had been too faded to make out the date.

'Would he know anyone at the college now? The caretaker, Joe Miller, for instance?'

Roberta's mouth tightened. 'I know the name – I think Paul gave him a job. He felt sorry for him. My husband's always been what you'd call a soft touch.'

'You don't approve of Joe Miller?'

'I don't know him,' she said abruptly.

'And Gregory Gilmore?'

'Sorry, never heard the name. Should I have? But why don't we have tea before you leave. You'll have time if I drive you back to Abbeymead.'

Flora began to protest but was cut short. 'You don't want to be catching buses at this time of day.' When Roberta saw her glance at her watch – it was only a few minutes past four o'clock – she pressed Flora's hand. 'I insist. It's the least I can do when you've made the effort to come, but I hope you feel the visit's been worthwhile.'

'It's been fascinating.' And it had, Flora thought, in more ways than one.

They had walked back to Roberta's house to collect keys and car and were now, half an hour later, edging out of Lewes, past the prison, and joining the crowd of other homegoers. With traffic this heavy, Flora calculated, it was unlikely she'd have time to return to the cottage before the traditional supper.

'When we get to Abbeymead, could you drop me at a friend's house?' she asked her hostess, sitting confidently behind the wheel. Roberta appeared an excellent driver. 'I have a

Friday evening supper to go to and it doesn't look as though I'm going to make it home first.'

'Not go home? But what about your husband?' Roberta sounded slightly scandalised.

'I'll phone Jack from Kate's and let him know where I am.'

'But *his* supper?' She still sounded aghast.

'Jack can manage. He's a whizz with poached eggs.'

Roberta stared at her. 'Well, if you're sure.'

Flora nodded cheerfully. 'Absolutely, and thank you so much for the lift. Pure luxury!'

The traffic continued heavy and it took far longer than either of them had expected to cover the twenty-odd miles to Abbeymead. Even so, Flora arrived at Kate's cottage in good time.

'What a wonderful little house,' Roberta enthused, pulling into the kerb. 'And the garden! My goodness, if the front garden looks like this, what must the back be like?'

'The cottage belonged to Kate's father. Cyril Knight was a gardener by trade and he took huge pride in his own patch. Kate has tried to keep it as her father would want, despite all her hours at the Nook – that's the village café. *She* works, too,' Flora added a little cheekily.

'These chrysanthemums are heavenly. All of mine died in the frost.' Roberta stooped to admire the huge pot of golden flowers growing by the front entrance, but bounced quickly up when the door suddenly opened.

Tony Farraday, smart in casual trousers and a new jumper – poshed up would be his expression – stood on the threshold, a cheerful grin on his face. He was ready for his card party, Flora saw.

'Oh, hello.' His gaze scanned them both, but for the first time, he seemed to notice Roberta. 'It's nice to see you.'

Flora was baffled. What a strange thing to say.

'I don't think we've met,' her friend said with a smile.

It was Tony's turn to look confused. 'Tony Farraday.' He held out his hand. 'Sorry, you looked like... but obviously not. Well, must get going.'

'Me, too.' Roberta turned to Flora. 'I have to get back. I've supper to prepare. Paul is always very hungry.'

Whereas Jack will have to go hungry, Flora thought crossly, because he's a man who doesn't have the ability to open the larder door and feed himself.

'Thank you for the lift,' she said aloud. 'And thank you for lunch. For the entire visit. I've enjoyed myself.'

She had. It had been a walk through history, but it wasn't something she wished to repeat too often. Roberta was generous and warm-hearted, but just a little too... what? Enthusiastic? Cloying? Needy? She scolded herself – now, she really was being horrid.

'Flora, come in,' Kate called from the kitchen. 'I'm having trouble with the dumplings. I need your expertise.'

'I doubt it,' she said, waving a final goodbye as the pink-and-white Vauxhall Cresta disappeared towards the Brighton road. If Alice was the best cook in Abbeymead, Kate came a close second.

She walked the few yards into the kitchen and peered into a saucepan of boiling water. 'The dumplings look fine to me.'

'They're a little thin.'

'They're fine,' she assured Kate. After the enormous lunch she'd consumed, plump dumplings would not be her ally. 'If it's OK with you, I'll telephone Jack. I've travelled from Lewes and haven't had time to go home.'

'Really? But wasn't Jack in Lewes, too? He didn't bring you back?'

'No, Roberta... I'll explain later... I'll just ring.'

'Yes, go ahead. Oh, and can you answer the door?' The knocker had sounded loudly. 'It will be Alice.'

Jack had arrived home some time before and sounded glad

to hear from her. Glad but subdued. He wanted to know everything she'd been doing but his replies to how his own day had
gone were brief and muted. Something had happened at the
college, Flora was sure, and she felt an insane urge to rush from
the door and run full speed home to her cottage. But Alice was
already unwrapping a blackberry-and-apple tart and the meal
must take precedence.

In the event, she made a poor fist of the lamb casserole that
Kate brought to the table. Cleve College was playing on Flora's
mind and, when that wasn't bothering her, it was the odd
moment between Tony and Roberta. What had that meant?
Had she reminded him of someone? Had it meant anything?

Kate, she noticed, had eaten even less than she.

'Well, that wasn't much of an effort.' Alice puffed out her
cheeks, looking from one to the other. 'I think mebbe I'll take my
tart home.'

Flora almost hoped she would, although an Alice blackberry-and-apple tart was a wondrous dish.

'Sorry,' Kate apologised, even though she had been the one
to cook. 'I'm not eating much at the moment. The thing is, I'm
feeling a bit...' To Flora's bemusement, her friend's face blazed
excitement.

'You're never...' Alice began, her plump face breaking into
the broadest of smiles.

'I am.' Kate's smile grew as broad.

'Pregnant?' Flora stared at them both, trying to make sense
of the situation. 'You're having a baby?'

'Isn't it wonderful?'

She supposed it was wonderful. Kate certainly seemed
pleased and, if Flora knew anything of Alice, she'd be rushing
off at any moment to fetch her knitting needles. Babies, though,
were something Flora didn't want to think too much about. Her
mother's loss of a child, the sibling Flora had never known, as

well as Sarah Steele's own death, still cut deeply. Childbirth, it seemed, was riven with danger. And with fear.

'Congratulations,' she managed to stutter.

'We'll have the christening party at the Priory,' Alice was saying.

'Not so fast!' Kate exclaimed, but she was laughing.

'You can't be prepared too far ahead. The Priory is that busy these days, rooms booked months in advance. I'll speak to Sally. It's not likely to be a large gathering, is it?... I don't want to give Sal too much extra work. She's on her own managing that big place, but a small party should be fine.'

'It's a shame she can't find someone to share the burden,' Flora said. 'Not necessarily a financial partner, but an assistant manager, that kind of thing.'

'The girl's better on her own,' Alice said definitely. 'After that Dominic.'

'Does she ever hear from him?' Kate looked a little sad. 'I don't think he's ever been back to Abbeymead. I quite liked him.'

'You were the only one who did,' Alice retorted. 'But she's in touch with him. Apparently. Good friends, she says. I have my doubts, I must say. Anyways, he's found a job managing a bar in Brighton. A decent bar, not like the one he had in London and lied about.'

'It's good he's making a life for himself.'

'He doesn't deserve to, not after the terrible trouble he caused Sally. Rents a flat on the seafront, she says, and has joined some swimming club.'

'Really?' Flora was amused at the idea.

'He was always pushing Sal to install a pool at the Priory but it was far too expensive. She won that argument – it would never be used enough to justify the money they'd have to spend. He just wanted it for himself. Now this party...'

Kate gave up, looking expressively at Flora. When Alice began organising, everyone gave up.

'It will give Sally something else to think about,' their friend went on. 'She can help with the planning. It will keep her from mooning around.'

Flora hadn't dared mention Hector Lansdale and neither had Kate. They exchanged another look across the table, as if to judge whether or not they should risk it.

'Let's have the blackberry and apple,' Kate said, evidently deciding they shouldn't.

14

Jack had set off for Cleve College early that Friday morning. Too early for Flora who had seemed happy enough to take the bus. He had only two appointments in his diary, both before ten o'clock, and he was hoping he'd have much of the day and the weekend that followed in which to write.

Driving into the reserved space, he saw the college car park was virtually empty and, instinctively, glanced towards the portico, wondering if Joe Miller would be there. Lurking. Watching. But there was no sign of the caretaker and no sign of him on the staircase to Jack's office.

Billy Parish, his first student, wasn't due until half past eight. Jack had read his protégé's short story with interest – a reinterpretation of *The Turn of the Screw* – but had been left with a strong feeling that he should urge Billy to forget rehashing the old and write something original. Glancing at his watch, he judged he'd have enough time before Billy's arrival – as a student, he was more than likely to be late – to grab a cup of tea.

The staffroom was emptier than the car park, although a tray of cups sat ready for the mid-morning rush. Walking over to the urn, he realised that the steel cylinder was stone cold, despite the switch being clearly on. Jack stood back, seeing from the corner of his eye an electric plug lying useless on the worn carpet. Had someone unplugged the urn last night and forgot to reinstate it?

He bent down to reconnect the electricity and was met with a loud crackle. In an instant, a hot flame had shot from the wall socket, burning Jack's hand and making him leap backwards to safety. It was fortunate the flare died almost immediately, but his hand had not been as lucky. He was binding a handkerchief around the burn when the college matron walked through the door.

'I'm parched,' she announced, marching up to the urn, 'but what happened there?' She was looking at the blackened wall.

'I don't rightly know. The plug was on the floor. I went to reconnect it and bang. It could be a loose wire, perhaps.'

'And your hand.' She had noticed the handkerchief for the first time and came quickly to his side, her white apron crackling with starch. 'Let me look.

'You need that cooled and bound,' she decided, assessing the burnt hand with a professional eye. 'Otherwise it will blister and could get infected. Come down with me to the infirmary. Miller will have to sort out the plug – and the tea – it's his responsibility. I'll leave a note for him on the front desk.'

Once in the large basement room set aside for an infirmary, she insisted that Jack held his hand beneath the cold tap for what seemed an inordinate amount of time. It did, though, give him instant relief from a pain that was hot and searing.

Matron dabbed his hand dry, then smothered it with a cream she'd taken from a well-stocked cupboard, and began wrapping the affected spot in a sterile bandage.

'Can you leave my fingers free? I have to be able to type.'

The typewriter in his college office wasn't a patch on the Remington, but it sufficed. It did the job and it needed to. The thought of a deadline that was coming ever closer brought him out in a sweat.

'Your fingers will be free,' she promised. 'A loose wire, you reckon? What is this place coming to? Falling about our ears, that's what. You should make a complaint. Insist on seeing Professor Dalloway.'

'Am I likely to get to speak to him? Does anyone ever see him?' It was a caustic question, but he was interested in the matron's opinion of their invisible employer.

'He doesn't have much time for his staff, that's for sure.' She banged the tube of cream back into the cupboard. 'Hides away in his office. But if he won't see *you*, he'll see *me*,' she said grimly.

'I understand my predecessor had a fairly difficult time with the professor.' It was as delicately put as Jack could manage.

'You could say that. Gregory Gilmore was a sensitive man. He needed understanding, not bullying.'

Jack nodded. 'Miss Draper mentioned to me that Gregory had been suffering from very low moods before the... before the accident.'

'Mr Gilmore had his problems.'

'At least, he had a friend in Miss Draper,' Jack pursued. The nurse made no comment. 'It's sad she wasn't with him the day he died. Her help might have been crucial.'

'Wasn't with him? What makes you say that?'

What made him say it were Jocelyn's own words, but Jack kept silent on that. 'I'm not sure. I assumed the poor man was alone. I don't suppose there are too many teachers who enjoy an early morning swim.'

'He wasn't alone,' Matron said, her tone definite. 'The girl went swimming with him that day, but even so she couldn't help. In a terrible state she was when they brought him in. Crying and wailing fit to bust. Mind, I could understand it. They were friends, like you said, really good friends.'

'Had Jocelyn tried to save him?'

'I never asked her. Not directly, and she's never wanted to speak of it since. I assumed she'd tried to save him – when she realised what he was doing. It takes quite an effort to drown yourself, you know. Blamed herself, did Miss Draper, though she shouldn't have. She's not a trained lifesaver, after all. *Still* blaming herself, if you ask me. She's the one in need of friends now. She needs a kind voice and not all the staff are sympathetic. Mr Gilmore wasn't best liked, but he meant a lot to her.'

'When you say Gilmore wasn't best liked, why was that?'

Matron cut across the roll of bandage, wrapping Jack's hand securely in its protective wadding. 'People don't understand low spirits,' she said heavily. 'For a time maybe, but as a permanent condition, they get irritated, think the person is pulling a fast one, trying to get out of work, that kind of thing. But Gregory was a decent man. I got to know him a little – he used to come and talk to me when he was really low.'

'Did he ever say why he felt so bad?'

She shook her head, packing away her nursing kit. 'Nothing specific. I got the impression it was something that happened in the past, but isn't it always? We all have our demons to wrestle – it's just that some of us are better at it than others.'

'I don't think Miss Draper had any more success than you at getting him to tell his troubles. She said he was a very private person.'

'He was, but Gregory wouldn't have confided in her anyway. They were good friends, as I said, but Miss Draper was too eager, too demanding for him. Wanted something that wasn't on offer.'

'How do you mean?' Jack's interest in the matron's answer was keen, keen enough to lessen the sting in his hand.

'He wasn't interested, that's what I mean. Poor Jocelyn, all that swimming in the lake, all those early mornings. I think she hated it. And for nothing.'

'I wonder she persisted.'

'She's that kind of woman,' his companion said wisely. 'Doesn't give up, even though it seems hopeless. And it was – a hopeless kind of longing, I suppose you'd say, on her part. Gregory didn't reciprocate, nor was ever likely to. Not with any woman.'

Jack waited.

'Sad, really,' she went on. 'He was someone who... preferred the company of men, if you know what I mean. But Jocelyn was too naive to realise it.'

Too naive for revenge, as well? Why had she insisted that she hadn't been to the lake that morning when it was clear she had? What was she hiding? It looked as though Flora's theory wasn't so tentative after all. Jocelyn, it seemed, had been a woman doubly spurned, her advances rejected, her love dismissed. Jack recalled what Joe Miller had said days ago, though less than eager to give him any credit. *A bit of a man-eater, our Miss Draper... had her claws into Mr Gilmore...* Had she waded into the water, lashed out in frustration, in a spurt of anger that she'd failed? A sudden burst of fury that had gone very wrong. Or had she followed him to the lake with murder in mind – as months later she would go to Abbeymead on the track of Russell Farr?

As if Jack had magicked up the man, Miller banged open the infirmary door and stood in the doorway.

'Don't you knock, Mr Miller?' the matron asked sharply.

'You left me a note.'

'I did. The electrics in the staffroom are dangerous. You need to make them safe before anyone else gets hurt.'

Miller slouched against the doorframe, plainly uninterested in the matron's complaint. Then looked pointedly at Jack's bandaged hand.

'Oh, dear!' he said and scratched his head. 'Have we had a problem?'

.   .   .

It took time to persuade Billy Parish that he should abandon his rewriting of Henry James, but he had the makings of an excellent writer, Jack thought, and it was worth the effort to set him on the right path. An hour's discussion had Billy propose several new ideas, eventually fixing on a ghostly tale, set in the college itself, as his first completely original story. The principal building of Cleve College was old – early eighteenth century – and there was bound to be mileage in finding a ghost or two. The fact that today was Hallowe'en had no doubt prompted the idea, but what Billy would make of it would be his own.

Barely five minutes after Billy had gathered his papers together and left, there was another knock on the door. Jack was surprised to find Reg Easton, the desk porter, waiting for him.

'You've a phone call, Mr Carrington,' the man said. 'You can take it in the hall.'

As a part-time teacher, Jack wasn't permitted the luxury of a telephone in his office. Intrigued, he ran down the single flight of stairs to find that it was Ross Sadler at the other end of the line.

'Sorry to ring you at work, old chap. I did try the cottage, then the All's Well. A Mrs Lawson said you'd be here and gave me this number. The thing is, Jack, I'm going away for a few days and I wanted to pass this on – just in case it's important.'

'That's good of you, whatever it is.'

'You can judge how good of me when you've heard! I've discovered a little more about one of the boys at the orphanage, one of the three you were interested in. Joe Miller. He was a soldier.'

'Thanks for that, Ross, but I did know. I'm not sure it changes things.'

'Did you also know he was dishonourably discharged?' Jack

was silent. 'Court-martialled for theft,' Ross continued. 'Stealing army equipment and flogging it to the highest bidder.'

Why wasn't he surprised? Had Miller, in dogging his footsteps, been hoping to steal from him, rather than the other way round?

'It's no more than I'd expect,' Jack said drily, 'except how on earth did he wangle a job here with a record like that?'

'I'll leave that one to you, my friend. I'm off to the Peak District, a few days' gentle potholing!'

Jack shuddered at the thought. 'Have fun, and thanks again.'

He was replacing the receiver when he heard a sharp, distinctive click on the line. Someone, it was clear, had been listening in.

Flora was back from the friends' evening supper by ten o'clock, a pungent smell floating through the front door as she turned her key. Desperate to hear what might have happened at the college, she walked quickly into the sitting room where Jack was reading a newspaper.

'Did you cook the last of the kippers?' she asked, before starting on her questions.

Looking up, he put his glasses aside. 'Was that OK? They looked a bit sad in the larder. I actually poached them!'

Jack seemed tired, she thought, and felt guilty. Was it the constant driving in an unreliable car? There had already been problems with the battery and this week a knocking sound in the engine had appeared from nowhere. She went over to the sofa and bent to kiss him.

'Congratulations on the poaching. I must tell Roberta.' He looked enquiringly at her. 'Never mind. Once I get this coat off,

I'll make some cocoa.' Her fears could wait a few more minutes, she decided.

But bringing two mugs of the bedtime drink back into the sitting room a short while later, she went straight to what had been bothering her for much of the evening.

'You sounded uneasy on the phone.' Flora made a nest for herself, cuddling up close to him. 'What happened today?'

'This happened.' He showed her the bandage, now slightly ragged and soiled around the edges.

She was startled. 'I didn't notice. I'm sorry. Is it bad?'

'It's been stinging like hell but, no, it's not serious. Matron has creamed and bandaged me. It was a faulty plug in the staffroom.'

'That sounds dangerous. Were you the only one injured?'

He nodded. 'It's what makes me uneasy. The staffroom was empty and it was clear none of the teachers had been there that morning. Too early, I guess. So was the plug left lying on the carpet an accident waiting to happen or was it a deliberate attempt to injure me?'

'And you think it might be... Joe Miller?'

He nodded again.

'But how would he know you'd go to the staffroom before anyone else?'

'He lurks, Flora. Watches everyone. He could have seen me parking the car, going up to my office, then heard me coming down the stairs again. I wouldn't put it past him to slip into the staffroom just before I arrived at the door.'

'Still... he couldn't have known for sure.'

'No, he couldn't but there's something else. Ross telephoned. He got my number from Rose Lawson. You must have written it down somewhere.'

'On my desk pad,' she confirmed. 'What did Ross want?'

'To pass on the news – before he went potholing – that Miller was court-martialled for stealing from the army.'

'That's surely not a surprise.'

'Not much of one, but I *was* surprised by the click on the telephone when I stopped speaking. Someone had been listening in and I can guess who.'

Flora sat thinking for a while, sipping the very hot cocoa with caution. 'Miller is obviously a villain, but is he *our* villain?'

'Whoever he belongs to, why is such a man working at the college? With his record, how did he get the caretaker's job?'

'I've a possible answer, though it's not very satisfactory. I saw Roberta Raffles today. Her husband, apparently, was once bursar at Cleve.'

Jack's mouth fell slightly open.

'I know. Quite a revelation! She didn't think to tell me that when I first mentioned you were working there. But she knew Miller's name. Said her husband was a soft touch and had given Miller the job out of sympathy.'

'It sounds as though you don't believe her.'

'Her husband might be the good-hearted man she claims, but somehow it doesn't ring true.'

'There's a lot in this case that doesn't. God, this cocoa is hot.'

'It's meant to be. Take it slowly. It's intriguing though, isn't it, that she has this connection with the college? With a little more digging, I might find out more. She didn't know Gilmore when I asked, but the third boy in that gang? We've hardly any information on him.'

For a while, they drank in silence, until Flora, thinking back to his earlier remark, asked, 'What else doesn't make sense? What else has happened?'

'Just a few more lies. Jocelyn Draper told me to my face that she wasn't swimming in the lake when Gilmore drowned. Yet Matron is clear that Jocelyn was not only swimming but, in her view, might have tried to save the man and was distraught when she'd failed.'

Flora pulled a face. 'After what we discovered at the insurance company, how true does that ring?'

'I'm uncertain. Jocelyn seems to have been in love with Gilmore, or what passed for love, so maybe she did. On the other hand, I'm thinking that someone trying to save a drowning person might not look that different from someone doing quite the opposite.'

'And succeeding perhaps.' She collected their cups to wash. 'Another puzzle to add to our list, but right now, my dear sweet husband, it's time for bed.'

15

It was just shy of two o'clock when Flora wheeled Betty into the forecourt of the Lexington Golf Club the following day. Crossing her fingers that Harry Barnes would still be holding a glass in his hand rather than a golf club, she left Betty in the cycle rack and walked through the entrance, turning immediately right into the bar she knew from a previous visit. The bloodied image of Raymond Parsons, a former club barman, flashed into her mind and was forcefully shunted away.

The club hadn't changed: the same swirly carpet, the same velveteen chairs, and a bar of polished wood that took up almost the entire side of one wall. Flora was in luck. Harry was lodged precariously on a stool, one elbow on the counter, the other holding a cocktail glass to his lips, a moody expression on his face.

'Mr Barnes!' There was no point in wasting time. 'How good to see you.'

Harry half turned, his face an unhealthy pink, and nodded. 'Miss Steele, no, sorry, Mrs... um...'

'Carrington,' she helped him out.

'Mrs Carrington, that's right. How's it all going?'

'Marriage? Fine. I find I like it.'

'That won't last,' he muttered to himself, his expression glum. Then remembering his manners, 'Can I get you a drink?'

'A lemonade maybe.'

'Easy enough.' He gestured to the barman, then frowned. 'What are you doing here? Taken up golf?'

'I don't think that will ever happen. It would annoy me too much.'

'Me too,' he said gloomily, 'but I keep on keeping on.'

'Mr Barnes.' She leaned towards him confidentially. 'I wanted to tap your memory.'

'Oh, yes.' He was instantly suspicious. Flora's conversations inevitably led to trouble, she could see him thinking.

'It's about the picture you have.'

He relaxed. 'Which one? We've got dozens of 'em. Evelyn buys them by the yard.'

'The one you have of Rillington Orphanage.'

'Have you seen it?' he asked, surprised. 'It's on the scullery wall. Evelyn doesn't like it and what Evelyn doesn't like...'

'But you bought it?' she suggested.

'No, my ducks. That wouldn't have been allowed. It's Evelyn who holds the purse strings. It was a present. A young man I did a good turn painted it for me — especially.'

'What a lovely thought. You must have done something exceptional for him.'

'I think I probably did.' Harry leaned back, looking satisfied. 'He was a bright lad. I knew that as soon as I took him on. That was when I was running the business,' he explained, somewhat needlessly. 'Yes, a bright lad,' he went on, 'and he's done well for himself whereas he could have easily landed on the rubbish heap – that orphanage had a bad name before it closed.'

'You knew the orphanage personally?' she asked, excitement stirring.

'I wouldn't say personally. My company did some of their

catering. We delivered there regularly and I heard from my blokes there was trouble. Trouble with the director. The man wasn't liked, not one bit. Far too strict, brutal with the cane, though Bettina always maintained he was a fair man.'

'Bettina?'

'Bettina Lyons. We used to speak on the phone – orders and so forth – and once or twice she came over to the offices. Nice pair of legs, she had. She was the director's personal assistant, but after his wife hopped it, a bit more than that, if you know what I mean. Leastways, that was the rumour.'

'What happened to Bettina when the orphanage closed?'

'Got another job. I thought she'd be OK – as far as I know she was a good worker. Moved on to a children's home over in Worthing. Mind you, she was heartbroken about what's-his-name's death. It was a nasty business. She told me on the quiet there was a gang of older boys that made her boss's life hell.'

'But not the boy you befriended? He wasn't part of the gang?'

'To be honest, I don't know, but the lad was old enough to leave school when the place closed down and I liked him. Put him to work in the distribution division and he did me proud. I'd see him in the yard sometimes, sitting on a bench or hunched up in a lorry taking a break, and he'd be reading. Always reading,' Harry said wonderingly.

'Reading *and* painting,' she said, trying to work out just where the conversation was heading. 'He sounds creative, an artistic man.'

Harry nodded. 'There was writing, too! You could have knocked me down with a feather when he told me he'd written a book. A whole book! Then Bob's your uncle, it gets published and suddenly he's a best seller. The lad had earned his promotion at work and he deserved it, but when I heard about the book... well, that was something special.'

'Apart from giving him a job in the company, did you help him in other ways?'

'Ah!' Harry rubbed his nose with his forefinger. 'Spot on, I did. It was here, right here at the Lexington. I was playing a round with that old fusspot, Dalloway.'

Flora clasped the cold glass tightly between her hands. Was another part of the puzzle about to fall into place?

'At the time, he was new to the club, new to the area,' Harry went on. 'I reckoned that's why he'd joined, to get to know people, because he was as useless at the game as I am. Joined for the contacts, you see. He'd just taken over at Cleve College – you know the place in Lewes – and he was keen to make changes. It was stagnating, he told me, losing students to colleges in bigger towns, and it was up to him as the new principal to sort it out. He was very enthusiastic.'

'How did he propose to sort it out?'

The conversation had strayed and Flora was beginning to forget why she was here. The painting, she told herself. She must get Harry back on the subject.

'The prof wanted to offer something a bit different. A bit unusual. Make his college stand out from the others. He explained it all as we were walking the course – more talk than golf that day. More talk most days, to be honest. He had this idea of giving his students – they were coming to write, paint, that kind of thing – the chance to work with people actually doing the stuff. Bring in some big names, if he could. He was thinking of having a writer, a painter, maybe even a sculptor, give classes in the college. It would boost enrolments, he said.'

'His plans went ahead,' she remarked. 'Jack is working as a writer at Cleve for several days a week.'

'Well, there you go. Anyway, as he talked, I had a crafty thought. How about my lad? He shouldn't be spending his life humping great boxes around. He was an artist, painting at the weekend and writing – he'd just begun to write a second book –

so I suggested to the prof he might like to use him. And Dalloway agreed.'

Flora said nothing, her mind working at speed. No name had surfaced as yet, but who else could Harry's lad be but Jack's predecessor? Did Harry know his protégé had come to a horrific end in the college lake?

It seemed not because her companion talked on cheerfully. 'The lad was thrilled. He gave up his delivery job and as a thank you he painted me a picture. I'd never had a painting done for me before! Evelyn hated it, naturally. Said it made her want to lie down with a bottle of pills.'

'The orphanage wasn't a happy place, by all accounts. Why do you think he chose to paint it?'

'No idea, my love. Perhaps Rillington wasn't such a bad place for him.'

Or perhaps it was, Flora thought, and painting it was a way of exorcising the demons.

'The man who painted this, who was he?' she asked at last. Did she really need Harry to spell out a name?

'Gregory, that was his name – a bit sissy, I thought, but it fitted him. Gregory Gilmore.'

Jack wasn't home when she unlocked the cottage door, having seen Betty comfortably settled for the rest of the day in her garden shed. Flora was disappointed – she had stuff to tell. Had he gone to the Nook for lunch and she'd missed him? The thought of lunch had her suddenly longing for food. Apart from the lemonade Harry had bought, she'd had nothing since breakfast.

She had her head in the larder when she heard a key in the lock and the front door creak open. As if by a miracle, it was accompanied, bliss of all blisses, by the smell of fish and chips.

'The weekly van came by as I was leaving the post office. I

needed some writing paper and Dilys obliged.' Jack brought a blast of cold air in with him. 'I thought while I was out and about, I'd grab a meal for us both.'

Walking into the kitchen, he kissed both her cheeks, one after another, while holding the precious package high above his head.

'I'll get the plates,' she said swiftly. 'I am ravenous. What wonderful intuition made you buy?'

'A rumbling stomach mainly. I bought for two and reckoned if you didn't want yours, I could manage most of it. A bowl of cornflakes and the tiniest bar of chocolate is all I've had today.'

'Which is more than I've had. And I *can* manage all mine.'

Jack deposited the newspaper-wrapped parcel on the table, shrugging aside his winter coat and throwing it towards the nearest coat hook where it teetered for a moment, then settled in a neat balance. How did he do that? She could try the same manoeuvre a hundred times and fail just as many. But forget the coat, forget the coat hook. In double-quick time, she found knives, forks, salt, pepper and vinegar, and cut and buttered several slices of bread.

'We should really eat it from the newspaper,' she said, restoring the loaf to the bread bin. 'Violet always maintained fish and chips tasted better that way.'

Jack turned from the sink where he'd been washing his hands. 'With all respect to Aunt Violet, I think I prefer china.' He reached into the top cabinet and brought down two dinner plates.

In minutes, the only sound in the kitchen, apart from a quietly ticking clock, was the crackling of paper, followed by sighs of satisfaction as first the battered cod, then the chips, were savoured.

Flora was halfway through her unexpected lunch before she spoke. 'I don't want to spoil this wonderful meal, but we do need to talk – about Russell Farr.'

'Yes, we do,' Jack agreed, scooping up another forkful of soft white fish.

'I went to see Harry Barnes this afternoon about the painting Alice saw. Guess what? It was Gregory Gilmore who painted it as a present, to thank Harry for helping him get the job at Cleve College.'

Jack looked astonished. 'Gilmore was a painter as well as a writer?' He thought for a moment. 'Interesting that he chose to paint Rillington after what must have been a miserable childhood there, though I'm not sure that knowing Gilmore painted the orphanage gets us any further.'

She waved her fork in the air. 'It does, kind of. It highlights the importance of whatever happened there all those years ago. I don't think Gilmore *chose* to paint the orphanage – I think he *had* to paint it. Maybe against his own free will. He was a driven man. He couldn't rid himself of the past or the place.'

'So... we're back to the orphanage as our major clue. Have we forgotten Jocelyn's revenge?'

'Not forgotten,' she said slowly. 'But put aside for the moment. There are all these connections between Gilmore and Miller, the orphanage and the college. And Russell Farr is the main link. We're pretty sure he was the one who came calling at Cleve. The unknown man whose visit sent Gregory Gilmore spiralling downwards. Maybe Gregory had exorcised the ghost, or thought he had, but Russell's visit brought it all back: the director falling from the balcony, the police interviews. Perhaps he knew more about the man's death than he told the police.'

'If he'd been involved in what was a murder, it would explain his wretchedness. Maybe explain his suicide, if it was suicide.'

Flora put down her cutlery with a contented puff. 'That was good. The best ever. But what about Miller's reaction to meeting Russell Farr? According to Jocelyn, he was the one who took Russell up to Gilmore's room and it must be the case that

Russell questioned him, too. Yet if he did, the caretaker doesn't appear to have been affected by whatever was said. Unlike Gilmore.'

'From the police reports, Miller was a hard nut and still is.'

'And he's the person who's been tailing you, breaking into your office and possibly rigging a faulty plug.'

'And I still have no answer as to why he's so keen to dog my footsteps. Is he guilty of something – beyond thieving from the army – and thinks that I know, or suspect, that I'm trying to nail him?'

'Well, if he's our murderer, you are,' she pointed out.

'It's a big if, though. Russell didn't stop his questioning at Cleve College, did he? He went on to Abbeymead as well, and there can't be any reason for his trip here other than he was on the same mission to discover what actually happened to his father. Where does Miller fit into that? Or does he?'

'Harry,' she said suddenly. 'Harry Barnes. I'm sure from talking to him that he knows nothing, but Russell must have come to the village to find him. It may be that Gilmore mentioned to Russell that he'd worked for Barnes when he left the orphanage. Harry's catering firm delivered there.'

'Really?'

'See, something you didn't know!' she said. 'If Russell met a brick wall with either Gilmore or Miller or both, he'd look else-where. And if Harry's name was mentioned on that visit to the college, he might have latched on to it as a real possibility – Harry's men were regularly at the orphanage. Russell must have seen the vans with Harry's firm's name on them.'

'He would have been a young child when his father died.' Jack frowned.

'He still might remember the vans and the name of the village. If he thought Harry might know something about the day his father died, he'd come to Abbeymead to find him. He wouldn't know Harry's address so he'd wander around looking for someone to ask.'

'OK,' Jack said slowly. 'He goes to the church – the vicar might know – but then decides to follow us when we leave. Maybe to ask if *we* know Harry. But why not just ask someone in the high street?'

'It was Saturday afternoon. The shops are closed and there wouldn't have been many people around.'

'That's true. So... we're around, and he follows us along Greenway Lane, until someone who is in Abbeymead that day decides that the looking has gone far enough and Russell has to be stopped in his tracks.'

'Who, though? We saw no one in the village on that walk who shouldn't have been there.'

'It doesn't mean there *was* no one.' Jack collected the plates to take them to the sink. 'Apart from us, who was on Greenway Lane that afternoon? That's the question.'

'There is another. Who sent the anonymous note to Russell in the first place? *They* must know something or they wouldn't have written it.'

'Unless they were out to make mischief.'

She shook her head. 'Someone out there is, at the very least, suspicious of his father's supposed accident and wants the truth revealed. I wonder if Bettina could help.'

'Bettina?'

'Just another snippet of news I discovered,' she said airily.

He jumped up from his chair and, swooping on her, wrapped his arms tightly around her. 'OK, you win. Tell me about Bettina.'

16

It had been a leisurely weekend and, for once, Jack felt happy with his word count. In addition, he'd found time to help Flora in the garden and, on Sunday afternoon, take a walk with her to Abbeymead Farm. The beautiful old farmhouse was under renovation to become a convalescent home, sponsored among others by Piers Neville, Sir Frederick's successor to the estate. It was on the walk that Flora had told him of Kate's surprise announcement, something she must have mulled over since the Friday evening supper. Jack couldn't be sure how she felt about it, but guessed that neither could she. He knew from experience it would take time for Flora to come to terms with what was another big change to her world.

Last night, he'd written well into the evening, leaving her to check the local telephone directory for a list of children's homes in the Worthing area. She'd come up with four addresses and, from the spare bedroom where he was working, he could hear the murmur of phone conversations in the hall below.

'I've found her!' she announced, as he walked down the stairs, feeling a trifle punch drunk from three intense hours. His brain seemed temporarily to have stopped working.

'Bettina Lyons. She's still Miss Lyons and works as a secretary to the director of the Blenheim Road children's home. I actually got to speak to her, even though it's Sunday evening.'

'Perhaps she does shift hours. How did your request go down?'

'Not that well. She was wary, I'd say, unsure if she wanted us to visit. But...' Flora paused. 'When I mentioned it was to do with Benedict Farr and an investigation into his death, her attitude changed completely. It was very noticeable. I think she might have information, Jack.' Flora's voice held a note of excitement and, putting her hands around his waist, she danced him into the kitchen.

'Careful! My writing hand is precious!' He steadied them before they cannoned into the table. 'So, we're going? Tomorrow?'

'We are. She's agreed to see us in the morning, as long as I can prise you from the typewriter.'

'In this instance, I think you can. Bettina seems too good an opportunity to miss. In an odd way, I've begun to think of Russell as *our* dead man. And we're the ones who need to find his killer.'

'Exactly. But food first. I've been cooking as well as phoning and there's a cottage pie in the oven.'

'You are a miracle worker, Flora, as well as a demon sleuth.' He took her hands from around his waist and kissed each of her fingers in turn.

The children's home in Blenheim Road resembled every other house in the street: a mock Tudor style of half-timbering with a steeply pitched roof, latticed windows and a solid oak front door. Unlike many of the others, however, a large extension had been built to one side and the front garden partially paved to take a number of vehicles. Climbing out of the

Austin, Jack could hear the shouts of children from behind the house. Evidently, the home was blessed with a large back garden.

A cleaner answered their ring at the door and, with a wave of her duster, pointed them towards an office at one side of the square entrance hall.

Bettina rose from her desk to greet them as they walked through the door. A pretty woman – and very petite. Jack found himself bending almost double to shake her hand. She gave him a dimpled smile, looking sweetly up at him through her lashes. Quickly, he introduced Flora as his wife, whereupon Bettina became entirely businesslike, gesturing them to take the chairs that sat either side of her desk.

Flora had made her own assessment of the woman, Jack could see. Her first questions were clearly designed to winkle out the details of the relationship Bettina had enjoyed with her former boss.

'You were personal assistant to Benedict Farr, I believe, Miss Lyons?'

Bettina nodded. 'I worked with Benedict for two, maybe three years, before the orphanage closed.'

'During that time, you must have got to know him well, I imagine.'

'I saw him daily and was privy to what was going on in his life, so yes, I did know him well.'

'And afterwards?' Jack asked.

'I found a job here. I've been at Blenheim Road ever since.'

He did a quick calculation. Bettina could have been no more than twenty at the time of Farr's death, he reckoned, and twenty years later she had barely aged.

'Did you know his son – Russell?' Flora leaned slightly forward. It was a crucial question.

She must have, Jack thought, but her response still surprised him.

'I met him, of course, but I wouldn't say I knew the boy. He was at boarding school and rarely came home for holidays.'

'How old would he have been?'

Flora was trying to get a timeline in her head, as he was, too.

'I think he was sent to school when he was about eleven. The same year as I joined the orphanage. His mother abandoned her family a year later.'

Flora frowned. 'Abandoned?'

'Well, what would you call it? She found a new man – and a new life – in Australia, and Russell was a burden she simply shrugged off. Benedict, too.'

'When the orphanage closed, did Russell continue at boarding school?' If so, Jack wondered, who had paid his school fees?

'No,' Bettina said firmly. 'I know that now, though at the time everything was in such chaos I had no idea what had happened to the boy. He would have been around sixteen and simply left school. He found a clerical job in a local insurance company.'

'When you say you know that now, how did you find out what happened to him?' Flora was edging a little closer to what they needed.

'I met the grown-up Russell.'

'Recently?'

'A few months ago, it would be. I still place flowers on his father's grave.' A faint blush appeared. 'I was very fond of Benedict.'

That tallied with what Jack had heard, but from where? It was Harry Barnes, wasn't it, telling Flora that he reckoned Bettina Lyons had had something of a passion for the director.

'I don't go that often,' she was careful to say, 'but this summer, it seemed right. My garden had some beautiful roses and I thought Benedict would appreciate them. He always loved roses. When I walked up to his grave that day, a young man, well, youngish, was standing there. It took me a while to realise that it must be his son.'

'Russell was in the habit of visiting his father's grave?'

'He said so, though I'd never met him there before. Ships that pass in the night, I suppose. He told me he lived in Brighton, in Freshfield Road. He'd moved into a flat there as soon as he started his job. That was with the insurance company, straight from school.'

'Did he talk about his father?' Flora asked.

'Not a great deal. We talked a little about the orphanage, but Russell seemed to have only the haziest recollection of his early life and didn't remember much at all about his father's death. It was such a horrible time that perhaps it's just as well.' She paused for a second, as though deciding how much to say. 'From what Russell said,' she went on, 'it was clear he believed the coroner's verdict – that Benedict died as the result of an accident. He seemed never to have questioned it.'

'But you did?' Flora suggested quietly.

'I never believed it. I always knew the coroner's decision was wrong.' Bettina was vehement. 'Benedict falling from a balcony? Not the man I knew. It was totally out of character. He didn't drink, he was fit and strong, and he was a man who never took chances – he lived his life with what I'd call military precision.'

'Yet the police investigation concluded that it *was* an accident,' Jack reminded her gently.

'The police took the easy way out. They made a show of investigating, but that's all it was. Window dressing. That gang of boys... they interviewed them but briefly, and just the once. The police should have pressured them, kept questioning, then they'd have learned the truth.'

'You believe the boys were responsible?'

'Who else? For months beforehand, their little gang made Benedict's life a misery, or tried to. He wouldn't let them win, though. He had them under control – until they decided to do that dreadful thing.'

'Do you have any proof they were guilty?'

'Of course I don't.' Bettina jumped up and stomped to the window and back. 'If I had proof, don't you think I'd have given it to the police? But I'm as sure as I'm standing here that Benedict was lured to that balcony – it was in the west tower and why otherwise would he have gone there? – and one of them or all of them pushed him to his death.'

'Did you know the boys personally?' Time to calm the mood, Jack thought. Change the questioning a little.

'Miller was an out-and-out thug,' she said without hesitation. 'Benedict refused to be his referee when he applied to join the army. I thought that was a mistake. It would have got the boy out of the orphanage, broken up their gang. And military service might even have disciplined him. But Benedict said it was *his* job to discipline and he wasn't going to land the army with a boy like Joe Miller. Benedict had been a soldier himself.' She smiled at the memory. 'He was very proud of his service.'

'And the other two lads?'

'Paolo could be charming. He had me fooled for a while, but it was surface charm. Beneath the fake politeness, he was as much a thug as Miller. His father had killed his mother and was serving a life sentence. That tells you everything you need to know.'

He saw Flora about to protest but then think better of it.

'And Gregory Gilmore?'

'Greg was rather a sweet child,' she said unexpectedly. 'Quite different from the other two. After the orphanage closed, he was sent here.'

'To Blenheim Road?'

She nodded. 'I had no idea when I took the job that he'd been moved here, but a few days after I arrived, I met him in the corridor. He'd be thirteen, nearly fourteen at the time, and very quiet. Worryingly quiet. I think he'd been badly affected by what happened at the orphanage. He was never a noisy boy, mind. A mild sort of lad, easily bullied. He was only part of that gang, I think, because he was lonely and desperate for friends. His parents had died when he was a small child.'

'And he left Blenheim Road a year later – at fifteen?' Jack hazarded a guess.

'He took a job with the catering company that delivered at the orphanage. In fact, they delivered to Blenheim Road as well and still do, though the business has new owners now. But Harry Barnes – I haven't seen him in an age – it was his company at the time and I suggested he take Greg under his wing, find him a job. And he did. Harry was a nice man.'

'I suppose you never saw Gilmore again, after he left here?'

She shook her head. 'I waved him goodbye and wished him luck for the future. I felt he deserved a better life. I remember now, I gave him a St Christopher to see him on his way.'

A small bell rang somewhere in the back of Jack's mind. 'If you had no further contact, I imagine you wouldn't know he's become a best-selling author.'

'My goodness, has he?' Jack noticed she used the present tense. Bettina hadn't known of Gilmore's success and nor, it seemed, had she known of his death.

'When you said goodbye to Russell at the grave, did you arrange to meet again?' That was a good question, Jack thought. He could see the way Flora's thinking was going.

'He invited me to go for tea. Come by any evening, he called out as he was leaving. Number 82a Freshfield Road. But I don't know how serious he was.'

'You didn't go?'

'It wouldn't have felt right. I can't explain. It was just that Russell was so innocent, so trusting, believing the police had it right, that his father had suffered an accident. I found it difficult to keep quiet about what I believed really happened. Best to leave it as it was, I thought.'

'You didn't leave it, though, did you?' Flora's eyes were sparking. She was onto something, he knew.

'What do you mean?' Bettina had resumed her seat, but now swivelled her office chair in a half circle and sprang to her feet once more.

'You sent him an anonymous note,' Flora went on, 'urging him to investigate his father's death.'

The woman looked defiant. 'Why shouldn't I? No one else was going to. I wanted him to know the truth, and what's wrong with that?'

'You sent the note to his address but without a name.' That fact had always puzzled Jack. Maybe now he'd find the answer.

'I wasn't sure if he still went by the name Farr. There had been such a noise in the papers when his father died, their family name bandied around for weeks, months even. I thought he might have decided to take another name when he started work. I had the address of his flat and that was sufficient.'

'It was. Your anonymous note started Russell off on a quest for the truth, but it also led to his death.' That was brutal, Jack thought, but necessary, and Flora wasn't about to compromise.

Bettina stared at her. 'What do you mean? How can it have done?'

'As soon as Benedict's son began questioning what happened to his father at Rillington orphanage, he had to be got rid of.'

'How, where?' she stuttered.

'In Abbeymead. That's a village—'

'I know where it is,' she interrupted.

'He was run down on a local lane and left in a ditch.' Probably too brutal.

Bettina had turned a horrible shade of grey. 'I saw an article in the local paper,' she stammered. 'About a man found dead in

Abbeymead, that no one knew. That was...?' She looked as if she might be sick.

'That was,' Flora confirmed, 'and if you think of anything that might help the police find his murderer, let us know. A note or telephone call to the All's Well – it's the village bookshop – will find us.'

Bettina continued motionless, her expression fearful.

'We're determined to see Russell get justice.' Flora tried to rally her. 'You must want that as well. And it would mean justice for his father, too. Whoever killed Russell is likely to be the same person who killed the man you admired.'

The secretary ran a distracted hand through her hair. 'I don't know what to think. What to say. Sending that note... it's as though I've killed a man. I feel terrible.'

'You didn't kill anyone, Miss Lyons,' Jack said quietly. 'And it should be some comfort to you that Russell's death has vindicated what you've always claimed – that Benedict Farr's death was no accident and the coroner's verdict should be re-examined.'

They were leaving the last of Worthing behind when Flora said suddenly, 'Was I unkind?'

'A little but she needed to know the part she's played in this drama. If Bettina Lyons hadn't sent that message, Russell would still be alive.'

'As his murderer is. And,' she added gloomily, 'his father's murderer.'

'All true, I'm afraid. And I'm not sure this visit has got us much further, except for filling a few gaps.'

'They're important gaps. You can tell Alan Ridley that we've found the anonymous writer. If *he* questions Bettina, he might get something more from her.'

Flora's hands were folded in her lap, he noticed, and she was studying them intently. 'Jack... I've been thinking.'

'Aren't you always?'

'Not about Bettina or Russell, but about us.'

His own hands slipped on the steering wheel, the car narrowly missing a bulging hedge. 'It's a bit late to have second thoughts.'

She gave him a gentle poke in the ribs. 'Not like that. I've been thinking about where we live.'

His breathing returned to normal. For a moment, he'd felt annihilated. Did it mean that despite a wedding, he was still unsure of Flora's feelings? Silently, he scolded himself. He must stop allowing Helen Milsom's rejection all those years ago to wreak damage on him still.

'I've been thinking about the flat at Cleve College,' Flora went on, blithely unaware of the disquiet she'd caused. 'The one the principal said you could have rent free.'

'What about the flat? I've never bothered to go and see it.'

'Then perhaps you should. Perhaps *we* should.'

He took a while before he answered. 'You can't want to move there. It wouldn't work. How would you manage to run the bookshop?'

'I've been wondering,' she said tentatively, 'if I could ask Rose to change her days. maybe manage the shop mid-week. If we drove to the college on Tuesday morning and stayed until Thursday evening, it would mean you'd have only two journeys a week.'

'You have been thinking!' There was another pause while he digested Flora's suggestion. 'Monday is set aside for workshops or lectures,' he said at length, 'and I do few of those, so that could work well, but individual appointments would need to be restricted to the middle of the week. I guess that would be OK – I was told I could choose whatever times suited me.'

He drove on in what felt an uneasy silence and it was

several miles later before he said abruptly, 'There's more to this than a timetable. How would you feel living in unfamiliar surroundings for half the week?'

'I probably wouldn't like it much,' she said frankly, 'but if it will help you, then I'll do it.'

'You are a lovely woman, Flora.'

'I am!' she said happily. 'Though I'd like to see the flat before we make any drastic decisions.'

'You're right. For all I know, it could be somewhere that neither of us would ever want to live.'

'Wednesday afternoon for our first viewing perhaps?'

He reached over and squeezed her hand. 'It's a date.'

17

Flora had managed a quick sandwich and brought a cup of tea back to her desk when Alice bustled through the door, her mackintosh gleaming wet and her grey curls hanging damply beneath what had proved an inadequate rain hat.

'Alice, you're soaked through!' she exclaimed, taking in fully the bedraggled figure. 'Though it's lovely to see you.'

'I'm on my way up to the Priory, but thought I'd pop in for a minute. I had the morning off. It should have been a whole day – I missed taking my usual Thursday last week – but there's a party comin' in this evenin'. Cocktails, Sally said, and I need to make sure Hector has got them canapés sorted.'

'I'm sure he will have,' Flora said pacifically.

'Well, I'm not. Most of the time, his head's in the clouds. Chasin' my niece, for one thing, or dreamin' about buying some new-fangled sword or other.'

'He's still involved in the re-enactment society?'

'Talks about nothin' else. The latest thing he's on about is Sal goin' with him to one of those stupid battles he fights. This Sunday. You'd think takin' her to the pictures was enough, but now he wants her chargin' round a pretend battlefield.'

If Flora knew anything of Sally Jenner, it seemed highly unlikely she would enjoy battlefields, pretend or otherwise. It would be a sure way of ensuring the girl lost interest in Hector and, if anything, Alice should be encouraging her visits to the re-enactment society. But Flora kept the thought to herself.

'It sounds innocent enough,' was all she said. 'Where's he fighting the next battle?'

Alice tutted. 'Kingston. That's where they're practisin'. At the rec there. It's for a big show next spring, would you believe? They're goin' to enact the battle of Lewes for the umpteenth time. Nearly seven hundred years ago and they're still rememberin' it.' Alice plumped herself down on the window seat. 'I did hear *you've* been gaddin' over to Lewes yourself.'

'Last Friday.'

'Really? You didn't mention anythin' at supper that night,' her friend said, a little piqued.

'It was just a lunch invitation,' she said airily, not wanting to upset Alice with the news of a new friend. 'Not terribly important. Someone I met in a bookshop there asked me over.'

Alice hauled herself to her feet. 'Sally should stick to business. And you should stay in the village,' she said firmly. 'Some people aren't keen on Rose Lawson at the All's Well.'

Flora's eyebrows lifted. 'Really? Who would that be?' It sounded like tittle-tattle, hurtful tittle-tattle at that, and she was surprised that Alice had repeated it.

'Elsie Flowers, for instance. She's not at all struck on Rose serving her.'

Elsie was an avid reader of crime and a regular at the bookshop. 'I expect Rose told her to stop reading books off the shelf and buy one instead.'

'Elsie does buy books,' Alice countered. 'I've seen a shelf of 'em in her cottage.'

'She does,' Flora agreed, 'but she'll read three in the All's

Well for every one she buys. Rose seems to me to be doing an excellent job.'

'We'll see,' her friend said doubtingly. 'It'll be your shop that'll suffer if it doesn't work. What are you goin' to do with all your spare time anyways?'

'Two days a week isn't that much time. And it's nice to have the freedom. I'm going over to Lewes again this afternoon, as a matter of fact. With Jack. We're going to look at the flat the college has offered him.'

She said it as casually as she could, but immediately Alice's figure stiffened and her mouth pursed. 'Why d'you want to do that?'

'I'm thinking of moving into the flat for a few days a week so that Jack doesn't have to drive as much.'

'I knew it! Didn't I say the journey would be too much for him?'

'It's not that it's too much, but the car—'

'Isn't reliable. I said that, too.'

'You did,' she acknowledged, 'but Jack is enjoying the job.' It was only half a lie. 'And I want to support him. In any case, the flat might not be suitable.'

'I don't like it. Everythin's changin'.' Her tone was mournful.

'Not everything, and some changes are good. Kate's baby, for instance.'

Alice brightened. 'I wasn't expecting that, I can tell you. But why not? She's young and she's never had the chance of a family. Not married to that useless Mitchell.'

Flora agreed wholeheartedly, Bernie Mitchell having been in her view the worst husband anyone could possibly have.

'And Tony – well, I didn't like losin' him at the Priory, that's for sure – but he's a decent chap and Kate seems happy.'

'She is happy. Very happy.'

'That's why I came in.' Alice shook her head in irritation. 'I knew there was somethin'. My head's all over the place. The baby. What should we knit, do you think?'

Flora blinked. 'I think I might leave the knitting to you. I'll buy something nice. There's a baby shop in Steyning.'

She was sure she'd seen a pink-and-blue-adorned shopfront a few doors down from the flower shop that had been involved in the very first mystery she and Jack had solved together.

Alice didn't look too convinced by the suggestion of a shop-bought offering, but she had another worry on her mind. 'I thought we should give Kate a small party to celebrate.'

'When she's had the baby?'

'She'll be too busy then – much too busy. I don't know what she's goin' to do about the Nook.' Alice veered off at a tangent. 'There is Charlie, though. He's doin' a couple of days a week at the café, but the rest of the time he's with me at the Priory. Mebbe I can spare him for longer.'

'Perhaps we should leave Kate and Tony to work that out,' Flora said diplomatically.

'Yes, yes, you're right. So the party... it will have to be soon. She's due late March.'

'The village has already planned Christmas activities – there's so much happening in the next few weeks – so maybe January?'

'January...I—' her friend began to say when the Victorian station clock chimed two. Alice almost yelped. 'I got to go,' she said distractedly. 'What am I thinkin'? Standin' here and naggin' when them canapés won't cook themselves.'

'We'll talk about it on Friday,' Flora called after her friend as Alice reached the door. 'It's my turn to cook supper.'

Spotting the small red Austin outside the All's Well a short while later, Flora made haste to collect her coat from its peg in the kitchenette but, before shrugging herself into it, she bent to check the corduroy skirt she'd chosen that morning. It was important she didn't let Jack down. Not too creased, she noted thankfully. It was a rich blue and she'd found a pale blue lamb-swool jumper at the back of her wardrobe, unsure where it had come from but glad to look reasonably smart for her first visit to the college.

The All's Well's notice turned to Closed for the afternoon, she climbed into the car, giving its driver a hug and a kiss.

'Looking forward to it?' he asked.

'Actually, I am!'

'I've been told the flat is situated in what used to be the stable block – owning a string of horses went with a big estate, I guess. It's a five-minute walk from the main building.'

'I think I'll cope.' She grinned. 'Don't forget – *I'm* still in my twenties!'

'Careful, dear Flora. I could make you suffer for that!'

The journey went smoothly with little traffic on the road in the early afternoon but, by the time they drove through the college gates less than an hour later, an unpleasant wind had begun to blow, occasional scurries of rain borne on its wings. Flora waited in the car while Jack walked into the foyer to collect a key from the porter's office.

'He's lent me his whole bunch,' Jack said, as he helped her out of the car. 'The single key to the flat seems to have gone missing for the moment.'

Heads down, they made for the stable block. 'There are four or five flats available, but I'm told only three are occupied. Most members of staff prefer to live off campus.'

'Do you know who the other occupants are?' Flora asked, breathless from the battering wind.

'The head cook is one and the desk porter, another. I think there's a mad sculptor who appears in the college from time to time when he feels the urge to impart his skills. He seems to be the third.'

The walk was slightly longer than the five minutes Jack had promised, but the stables, when they reached them, was an attractive building: long, rectangular and stone-built, it was punctuated by five neat front doors, each dwelling having latticed windows on either side of a main entrance. Once inside, Flora could see that the pattern of windows and door had been replicated at the rear of the house.

She was surprised to walk from the path straight into the sitting room – even her small cottage had a minuscule hall. The room was sparsely furnished with a sideboard and coffee table and two easy chairs, though to Flora's eye they didn't look too easy. A door led from the sitting room into a small kitchen and beyond that to two bedrooms, one with a sagging double bed, a single wardrobe and a tiny chest of drawers, while the fourth room was completely empty.

'That's it.' Jack sounded depressed. 'Somewhat disappointing.'

'The college doesn't charge rent,' she said practically. 'It was never going to be a palace.'

'A palace it certainly isn't. I thought it might have been more... more homely.'

'I guess we could make it more homely.' Flora was trying hard to feel positive. 'You'd need a desk and chair in the spare room, but maybe the college could find them for you. And the kitchen has a cooker and a gas ring.' She paused, scrambling for something good to say. 'And we'd have a bed.'

'We would, but how comfortable? It looks in danger of imminent collapse.'

'Then we'd have to be sure not to forget ourselves!'

'I don't think we're likely to here,' he said drily.

'It's quite pretty at the back of the house, Jack. Come and look.'

A square of unremarkable garden, mainly of lawn that had

been left untreated for years, gave way to a low fence and an open gate which led out into the field beyond.

'There are trees! And a magic gate,' she teased, 'leading to who knows where... quite romantic!'

'If you say so. But could you really live here?'

'I could give it a good try. Let me speak to Rose to see if it's possible. Dilys might have other ideas, of course, if she suspects I'm pinching one of her assistants. She likes them to work extra days if she needs more help.'

'I think I'll leave you to deal with our beloved postmistress.'

'Such a chicken!'

'You're right, I am, if only to save my eyesight from an onslaught of Dilys's magenta. Seriously, though, you can't want to live here.'

'I don't,' Flora said honestly. 'But I'll do it.'

He shook his head. 'I'm not sure, but have you seen enough for now? Not that there's much to see. I'd like to take you over to the main building and maybe introduce you to some of the teachers. I forgot to mention that the college has decided – which means that Professor Dalloway has decided – to hold a bonfire celebration this evening and the staff will be arriving back any time soon. We can stay to watch if you like.'

'And *I'd* completely forgotten that it's November the fifth, though really I shouldn't have. Every time I've passed the village green this last week, I've seen the guy on his pyre.'

'So, we'll stay?'

'Why not? It should be fun.'

On their way back to the main building, they passed Joe Miller making for the field behind the Queen Anne building, planks of wood balanced on his shoulder. Momentarily, he lifted his head, a surly expression on his face.

'Is that...?'

'It is.'

'How did I guess?' she asked laughingly, as they walked

through the front entrance and into the foyer. 'It's very quiet. Are you the only teacher here?'

'Hang on a minute. I'll take a look in the staffroom.'

'Jack.' She called him back. 'Where does that lead?' She pointed to a narrow passage that ran from the foyer to the back of the building.

'Nowhere special. I think Miller has his lair there. I'll—'

But Flora was already halfway down a passageway that came to a halt at an oval-shaped wooden door which reached no higher than her shoulder.

'More magic.' She turned to look at Jack who had just caught up with her. 'The doorway looks as though it could have come out of a fairy tale.'

'Not with Joe Miller behind it.'

'He's not though, is he? Behind it. He's out there, collecting wood for the bonfire.'

Jack's eyes held a wary expression.

'You have a bunch of keys,' she said, 'so...'

'No. Definitely no! I'm not prying into the man's room. It's private.'

'He pried into yours,' she pointed out.

'Yes, but... he could come back at any moment,' Jack said weakly.

'You know you're losing the argument don't you?'

Silently, he handed her the bunch of keys.

'They're nicely labelled,' she decided. 'Mr Easton has done a good job. JM. This must be the one.' Fitting the key into the over-large lock, Flora turned it smoothly. 'And it is,' she announced joyfully.

In a second, she had slipped around the door with Jack following warily.

'Well, well, would you look at this!'

He came to stand by her shoulder and joined her in looking. There was certainly plenty to look at. Instead of a functional desk and chair with perhaps a basic sofa or armchair for comfort, the room radiated luxury. There was a table but it was polished rosewood, there was a chair, though upholstered in the most expensive velvet. The curtains when Flora stroked them were clearly of silk and every available space in the room had been filled with expensive goods: an embroidered footstool, the latest model of wireless, a complicated camera.

'Leica,' Jack murmured.

Porcelain figures decorated mahogany shelves. A bowl, it looked to be Sèvres from Flora's sketchy knowledge of her aunt's forays in auction rooms, was filled with a dozen or more red roses.

'What on earth do you make of this?' she asked.

'He's a thief. Still a thief.'

'But how do you steal a chair, not to mention a table, that looks very like one that Chippendale might have made?'

'You steal money and buy them with it.'

'I suppose.' For some time, she stood looking around the room, trying to absorb the meaning of this Aladdin's cave of riches.

'Or,' she said thoughtfully, 'you blackmail.'

Jack looked startled. 'What made you think of that?'

'I don't know. Making connections, I suppose. Miller is a nasty character, you've experienced that, and Bettina called him an out-and-out thug. Gregory Gilmore was depressed and getting worse. I wondered if the two went together. The two men shared a past, didn't they, and it's not inconceivable that Miller was using that past to blackmail.'

'Gilmore would never have earned enough to pay for this little lot.'

'But over several years?'

'It's possible, I suppose. I don't know how long he was in the job. Flora, we need to go. I really don't want us to get caught here.

'OK. But what should we do next?'

'We can decide that later.' He walked quickly to the door and opened it very slightly. 'The passageway is clear. Come on.'

As they hurried back along the corridor to the foyer, Jack spoke quietly. 'I think I need to talk to Ridley. He should know about this room and about Bettina. While you're having supper on Friday, I could ask him to join me at the pub. The beer should be sufficient enticement.'

They had returned the keys to the porter's office, in their haste almost throwing them onto his counter, when the front door banged open and Joe Miller strode in. He stared hard and, seeing them loitering in the hall, scowled.

'Just in time,' Jack said into her ear. 'The staffroom – let's go.'

'Phew!' she whispered back, as he ushered her through the nearby door.

18

Only some of the teachers had decided to return to college for the evening and it took a while for a group to collect in the staffroom. As they trickled in one by one, Jack had the task of introducing Flora to people he barely knew: Valerie Longstaff, who despite teaching literature seemed to have nothing but scorn for working authors – they had to be dead to count, Jack concluded; Gabriel Donatello, though he doubted it was the man's real name, in charge of oil painting; and Lily Burns, a fresh-faced recent graduate who taught drama.

Jocelyn, along with a trolley of food, appeared in the doorway as Lily was shaking hands. The college kitchen had been prevailed upon to work late today: there were the inevitable sandwiches and sausage rolls, but several more interesting snacks had infiltrated – small baked potatoes with cheese and butter, and wooden skewers threaded with prawns and mushrooms.

'I bring food with me,' Jocelyn announced gaily and, whether it was her entrance or the advent of refreshments, an atmosphere that had felt starchy loosened and everyone began talking about previous November the fifths and their adventures or misadventures at those events.

Flora seemed unfazed by the host of new faces and chatted happily to whoever was close by, even the haughty Valerie, Jack saw. His wife had a knack of getting people to talk. He'd noticed that from the first time he'd met her. She'd got *him* to talk, hadn't she, after years living as a recluse, nursing what he'd thought was a broken heart but that turned out to be no more than broken pride.

Jocelyn, he noticed, was unusually animated this evening, moving between small groups of teachers and talking non-stop, her shrill laugh puncturing the general chatter. Tonight was the first time Jack had seen her since his encounter with Matron – unconsciously, he must have gone out of his way to avoid meeting her. Really, he should take this opportunity to introduce Flora, but the lies Jocelyn had told over Gilmore's drowning, the fact that she had not only known Russell Farr but been his girlfriend, had deepened Jack's suspicions to the point where it seemed impossible to maintain any façade of friendship.

'The bonfire's lit, if anyone's interested.' The head cook for the evening, arms folded, stood in the doorway. 'If you've finished eating, I need to get this room cleared, folks, so if you wouldn't mind...'

There were multiple thanks for the food she and her team had prepared and then an obedient drift to the outside door. They were in the hall when Jocelyn stopped suddenly, a hand to her forehead. 'My handbag! I've left it behind.'

'Leave it,' someone advised. 'You don't want it near a bonfire and it will be safe enough in the staffroom.'

Jocelyn ignored the advice, however, and turned back, leaving Jack and Flora to flow with others out of the building and into the field, Jack feeling a definite niggle as they walked towards the bonfire. Was it Jocelyn's handbag that was bothering him? And what had that to do with another niggle, an elusive memory that had worried at him from the time they'd said goodbye to Bettina Lyons? Something the woman had said. Two itches he couldn't soothe.

It was when the flames had begun to roar skywards that the connection came to him. The open handbag that day in the staffroom... the St Christopher that had spilled out... and Bettina Lyons mentioning she had given Gilmore just such a medallion to speed him on his way. Could it be the same one? And, if it was, how had Jocelyn come by it?

'A penny for them?' Flora said, walking close by his side.

'Not worth even that.' He smiled down at her. It would be best to question Jocelyn first before he said anything, though he couldn't be sure how that particular conversation would go.

'The guy they've built is not too splendid, is he?' Flora wrinkled her nose. 'As a connoisseur of village bonfires, I'd say he'll burn in a trice.'

Jack looked at the figure stuffed with straw. His hat had fallen over what seemed a half-finished face and his coat barely covered a meagre body with stump-like arms, and legs that finished somewhere at the knee. There had been no need for trousers. Whoever had made him – Joe Miller, presumably – had run out of straw and not bothered to find more.

'I guess he's good enough to burn and it will be the fireworks that everyone will want to see. They're just starting. Are you happy to hold a sparkler?'

That was one more thing he didn't know about Flora – they had never spent Guy Fawkes evening together.

'As long as they don't burn too quickly.'

'Here, take this one.'

He handed her one that had been lit by Reg Easton. Along with Miller, the porter had evidently been put in charge of the evening's celebrations. As well as lighting sparklers, the two of them were busy setting up a host of rockets that over the next

half hour provided the gathering with cascades of coloured
stars, only just visible in the cloudy sky. More food arrived in
the shape of roasted chestnuts and mugs of hot soup. More fireworks, too – Roman candles and Catherine wheels took pride of
place. Jack could feel his feet slowly freezing and Flora, in
thinner shoes, must be even colder. His arm around her, he
shuffled them forward, hoping she'd benefit from the warmth of
a fire that had already begun to die.

'Pass me them offcuts, would yer?' It was Joe Miller. The
porter had disappeared and Miller had taken over feeding the
fire. 'These are way too green.' He kicked aside the pile of fallen
tree branches that had been stacked by the pyre.

Jack picked up several long, thin planks of wood that had
been sitting close by and handed them over. Miller shoved
several into the bottom of the bonfire where they immediately
caught fire but, instead of pushing them further in, he pulled
one out again, waving it in the air like a fire eater in a circus.

'Steady on, Miller. That could be dangerous.'

Gabriel Donatello's reproof appeared to have no effect, the
caretaker continuing to swirl the burning wood in large circles
around his head. Several of the women retreated a few paces
back, clearly worried at the man's antics, while Jack pulled
Flora closer to him.

It was when Miller stopped his wild dance and looked
around, that he deliberately and unbelievably threw the flaming
plank at Jack.

'Here, Mr Carrington,' he yelled. 'Catch! Oh dear!
Butterfingers!'

The brand had missed Jack's hand but landed on his overcoat, singing the wool and sending a spurt of fire across the
lapels.

Flora was swift. While the rest of the crowd stood gaping in
amazement, she tore the coat from Jack's shoulders, buttons
popping, and threw it to the ground. Emerging from the tempo-

rary paralysis he'd fallen into, Jack took a boot to the flames, beating them out with the help of Donatello who had finally woken to what was happening.

'Damn fool thing to do, Miller,' the painter said. 'Are you OK, old chap?'

'Just about,' Jack muttered. 'Thanks to my wife.'

'A quick thinker, luckily for you. Sorry, I didn't realise...'

'Why would you? The man is a lunatic. But it's time we left, I think. It's cold and I'm short of an overcoat. Flora?'

She nodded and he noticed how very white her face appeared in the glow of the flames. Without saying their good-byes to the rest of the group, they walked arm in arm back to the car park and the safety of the Austin.

Before he switched on the ignition, Jack turned to her. 'That was quite deliberate.'

She nodded, her mouth tightly shut. Her hands were shaking, he noticed, and he reached over to clasp hold of them. 'I'm all right, Flora. Thanks to you.'

'But you nearly weren't,' she blurted out, and he saw her eyes fill with tears. 'That man wants to hurt you.'

He couldn't disagree. Miller was out to get him, it was clear, to wound or disable or maybe even kill. But why? He shook his head at the unspoken question.

'It makes no sense,' he said aloud. 'What does he think I know? Something of his past, certainly, but nothing of his present – he can't know we saw into his room this afternoon. If we'd found that evidence earlier and taken it to the police... but we haven't. So, why the violence?'

'The man has been watching you, listening in on your conversations, searching your office.' Flora had blinked back the tears. 'It has to be that he believes you know more about him than you actually do. It's the fact that he does that's important; it proves he has something to conceal and is desperate to keep his crime hidden.' She paused for a moment, before saying with conviction, 'For me, that's the murder of Russell Farr – and his father.'

Jack started the car, glad to be making for home. On balance, he thought Flora was almost certainly right, but where was the evidence for Miller as a murderer?

'We have no evidence.' He spoke his thoughts aloud as they drove through the college gates. 'I can't even explain why Miller is so sure I'm a danger.'

'Ross's phone call will have told him you've been digging for information.' Flora nestled into the winter blanket Jack carried in the car. 'But even before that he was watching you. I think he knows it was us who found Russell's body. We haven't read the newspaper reports that Alan Ridley spoke of, but Miller probably has, and if they mentioned a local couple... he knows you live in Abbeymead.'

Jack frowned. 'Too vague. Much too vague.'

'*Someone* was in Greenway Lane when we found Russell. I've thought about it. A mass of birds don't fly out of their nests unless they've been disturbed. If Miller killed Russell that day, and I think he did, he might still have been hanging around. Hiding behind hedges.'

'But why? He'd surely want to get out of the village as quickly as he could.'

'Perhaps he wanted to make certain the man was dead or he was waiting to see if anyone would find the body.'

'And the orphanage when we visited? Are you saying he was there, too?'

'There was someone in that ruined building,' Flora said confidently. 'I knew it at the time.'

'He knows I live in Abbeymead, so your theory is just about feasible, if I'm being generous! But how would Miller have known we'd go to the orphanage?'

'He wouldn't.' She pursed her lips. 'But it doesn't mean he wasn't there, too. It could have been coincidence – maybe he'd returned to the scene of his earlier crime, heard us arrive and found a hiding place.'

This was beginning to sound very like one of Flora's massive leaps of imagination and Jack said so.

She was unrepentant. 'When you see Ridley, you need to tell him everything that's happened,' she said firmly.

'I can tell him what we suspect, but that's all. I only wish we *had* the evidence that Miller obviously fears.'

Driving to Cleve College the following day, Jack made a decision. Before he met the inspector tomorrow, he would seek out Jocelyn Draper and challenge her on the gold pendant she'd secreted in her handbag. Stolen, he felt certain. What else she might be guilty of was likely to remain hidden, but the St Christopher would be a start and if her story began to unravel and the full truth emerge... Whatever he managed to uncover, it was likely to be an uncomfortable exchange, but he'd make himself do it before he left for home today.

He had just two student appointments in his diary, both in the afternoon, and had stayed at the cottage all morning working furiously on the novel which thankfully he was beginning to pull together. Pausing only briefly for a lunchtime sandwich, he set off for Lewes on a day the temperature had barely crept above freezing.

His first mentee was already at his door when he arrived. A budding playwright and a good one, as far as Jack could judge. Drama was not his forte and he felt more of an imposter every time he met with Louise. But the girl seemed happy enough with the discussions they'd had and he could see the play, now in Act 3, was progressing well.

As soon as she'd left his office, Jack walked down the stairs, making for the staffroom, hopeful of seeing Jocelyn at the tea urn. A fair number of teachers had gathered there – the

Thursday afternoon timetable was evidently a busy one – but Jocelyn wasn't among them.

Forgetting tea, he walked through to the other side of the building where a large art studio had been added. Jocelyn was there, as he'd expected, putting easels to rights and tidying paints. He was lucky – she was alone, her last class having left some time before.

'Jack!' she said in welcome, spotting him in the doorway. 'You've come to see where all the work is done!'

He tried to fix his face into a smile. 'I'm sure you're right but actually I've come to see you.'

'That's nice.' Her own smile slipped slightly. 'But how are you after last night? I didn't see what happened – I was on the other side of the bonfire – but I heard Miller threw a plank of burning wood at you.'

'As you see, I survived, unlike my overcoat. It was reduced to a bundle of rags and has been duly buried.'

'That man!' She took off a still remarkably clean linen overall and draped it across a chair. 'Gabriel reported the incident first thing this morning and Dalloway should sack him. Miller isn't even a decent caretaker. The faulty socket in the staffroom was his responsibility. He should never have allowed it to get in that state. Is your hand OK now?'

'I was lucky. Matron was around and she was brilliant. She bandaged me up beautifully. Made sure I wouldn't have blisters. See?' He held out his hand to show her, at the same time taking a deep breath. 'While I was in the infirmary, I spoke to her about the day Gregory Gilmore drowned.'

'Really? Why would you do that?' Jocelyn's tone had subtly changed.

'I suppose because he was my predecessor and a fellow writer. I felt sympathy for him.'

'But you never knew him. You never even met him. If you

don't mind my saying, Jack, your interest seems a little unhealthy.'

'I don't mind at all. I suppose there's also the matter of untruths. I don't like being told lies. According to Matron, you were at the lake that morning. You came back into the college along with the rescue party, very wet and deeply distressed.'

She sat down on the nearest chair with a thud. 'Wouldn't you have been distressed?'

'I would, but why lie about it?'

She took a long time to answer, fiddling with paints that had been left on the desk, wiping the same brush clean over and over. 'I heard a noise and I didn't go to him,' she said at last.

Jack frowned.

'Do you understand?' She almost shouted the words. 'I was angry, upset. Greg... he knew I loved him... knew, but... I followed him to the lake that morning and I heard him drowning. But I left him to it. And you ask me why I lied about it!'

'But if you were at a distance, you couldn't have known he was drowning.'

She hung her head. 'I didn't see anything and he was a very strong swimmer as I told you. But that sound – the thrashing of the water, I must have known... and I can't get it out of my ears, even now.'

Jocelyn buried her head in her hands, tears falling. 'I killed him,' she said despairingly. 'I let him drown. That's killing him.'

'Not in law, I think. Why *would* you suspect he was drowning? He might have been playing around.'

She shook her head. 'No, the sound – I can't describe it, but he wasn't fooling. And I just went on swimming.'

'At the shallow end of the lake?'

She nodded.

'So, you wouldn't have seen if there was anyone else at the far end?'

'As I said, I saw nothing. You think there was someone?' She grabbed hold of what must seem a lifeline. 'You think someone was there and drowned Greg?'

'Why would they?' he asked simply, though it was precisely what he did think. 'It was an accident, like everyone said. But Matron believes you tried to save him – even if it was a little too late.'

'I helped Biddle – he's one of the gardeners – to pull Greg out. That's all.' It would explain Jocelyn's distressed appearance when she reached the infirmary.

'And once you had Gilmore out of the lake, Biddle went for help?'

She nodded again.

'The St Christopher in your handbag. Is it yours?'

The sudden brutal question shocked. She took what seemed a painful breath, sending a shudder through her angular frame. 'No. It's not. It was Greg's.'

'You took it from his dead body when you were alone with him?'

She began to cry again. 'I wanted something, anything, to remember him by.'

'And Russell Farr? Do you have something to remember him by?'

Instantly, Jocelyn jumped to her feet, as though the chair beneath her had caught fire. 'How do you know of Russell?' Her voice was thin, scraping the air. 'Why are you asking me this? Who are you, Jack Carrington?'

'An author and now a teacher,' he answered calmly. 'But Russell Farr – do you remember him?'

She stalked across the room to the wide plate-glass window and stared out at the bleak winter's day. 'How could I not?' she asked, without turning to face him. 'A man who walked out on me!'

'A man who didn't want to know. Another man.' This was

not the time to be gentle. 'You say you let Greg die. Did you also let Russell die?'

She whipped around, her face frozen. 'Russell Farr is dead?'

If that was pretence, she was a very good actress, Jack thought. 'He came here, didn't he? You told me that you didn't know the man Joe Miller took to see Gilmore, but you recognised him, didn't you?'

Her mouth tightened into a hard bud. 'I've no wish to continue this conversation, Mr Carrington, now or later. I thought you were a friend. Instead, you're a... a...'

'A seeker of truth? In the meantime, Miss Draper, you should keep the memento you thieved safe. You might need it.'

For a moment, they glared at each other, then Jack walked to the door.

19

It was rare for Jack to visit the Cross Keys in the evening, but with Flora at the cottage cooking for her friends, it seemed an ideal opportunity. Jack was conscious that in this investigation he hadn't been keeping the inspector up to date – Ridley knew nothing of Jocelyn Draper's involvement, for instance – but in all probability he and his team were way ahead.

Alan Ridley had already made himself comfortable by the time Jack arrived, having finished work for the day and driven straight from Brighton. 'Ordered a steak and kidney,' he said, when Jack found him tucked away in a corner closest to the bar. 'How about you?'

'The same, I guess.' It was said with an inner sigh. He had found the Cross Keys' pork pies inedible, so what horrors would they perpetrate with the steak and kidney?

Jack walked back to the bar to give his order, pushing through the crowd of customers who'd gathered around the dartboard. The pub looked a little less depressing in the evening, a little more mellow, he reflected, picking up the beer the barman had pulled for him. Small lamps had been lit, one at either end of the curved counter and one for each table. Their soft light streaked across the polished woodwork, illuminating the row of glasses that hung face down from the gantry. Only a cloud of smoke massing heavily in the air spoilt the scene.

'How's the Farr investigation going?' Jack asked, as soon as he'd settled in his seat. 'Any developments?'

Alan Ridley stared moodily into his beer. 'I've had my blokes in the village for a couple of weeks talking to the locals – you might have seen them? But you're in Lewes a lot these days, aren't you, so probably not. Anyway, the chaps have been asking around but turned up zero. Farr was killed several weeks ago and if people did notice anything odd, they'll have forgotten it by now.'

The inspector took a long draught of beer, wiping his lips with the back of his hand. 'I interviewed Bettina Lyons, you might be interested to know. After your call. She admitted sending the note to Farr, then took me to town. I got a right scourging. The police hadn't listened to her at the time, hadn't investigated Benedict Farr's death thoroughly enough. An innocent man hadn't received justice, and so on and so on. Did she have some kind of thing for him?'

Jack nodded. 'It seems so. But nothing new emerged from your talk?'

'Not a thing. It's beginning to look like a dead end. We know the man's name. We know where he lived and where he worked. And judging by the letter he was carrying, we can speculate on why he might have been murdered, if indeed he was. But there's no sign of a villain and no proof that the chap's death is linked to his father's. It could simply be a bad coincidence. Maybe Russell Farr was unlucky. He met a mad driver in a narrow lane, a hit-and-run merchant who isn't about to come forward.'

'A hit-and-run from a tractor, Alan?' Jack was sceptical.

'I'm not saying it *was* definitely a tractor. In fact, the farmers we've spoken to swear it couldn't have been one of theirs.

Rather than a tractor, perhaps it was a heavy duty vehicle like a Land Rover or a Jeep.'

'But who in Abbeymead drives such a vehicle?'

'You tell me.'

'No one, as far as I'm aware. Hardly anyone in the village holds a licence and those that do drive saloon cars. Pretty ancient ones, often pre-war.'

'It could have been a vehicle from out of the village.'

'If it was a strange car, it would have been noticed, and that wouldn't be forgotten, believe me.'

'Jack, old chap, we're going round in circles... ah, good, food!'

One of the casual staff who worked the Friday evening shift had arrived with a tray. Two plates of steak and kidney pie, replete with gravy and vegetables piled high, appeared on the table.

'It smells OK.' Jack tried not to sound too surprised. 'Actually, it tastes OK,' he said, taking a cautious bite. He *was* surprised.

'Course it does. So...' The inspector paused between mouthfuls. 'Where was I? Oh, yes, telling you about the dead end we've reached. After you told me that both Miller and Gilmore had worked at your college, I looked again at the list of boys living at the orphanage when Farr senior died – not the tiddlers but the older boys. It would have taken a fair amount of strength to heave a grown man over that balcony. I was looking for a link.'

'And?'

'I didn't find one. None of the names stood out in any way.' Ridley put down his cutlery and opened the briefcase Jack had noticed sitting by his chair. He pulled out several sheets of printed paper. 'Here's the full list of the boys, in case anything strikes you. And a copy of the police interviews and the post-mortem on Farr senior. You'll see the man was in good health.

There was no sign of a heart attack and no evidence he'd been drinking.'

It was as Bettina had claimed.

'I went back to the three lads who were interviewed, seeing as they were prime suspects at the time. Trying to winkle something useful out of my colleagues' reports since it's more or less impossible to find the men they've become and question them. Ruffini has disappeared, Gilmore is dead—'

'Which is suspicious, surely?'

'The coroner's verdict was accidental drowning. A misadventure.'

'Another coroner's verdict. Another accident. Too many, surely.'

'I agree, but once again, there were no witnesses, no one in the vicinity when Gilmore drowned.'

Now, it seemed, was the time to tell Jocelyn's story but, after Jack had briefly recounted her relationship to Russell Farr and her role in Gilmore's drowning, the inspector remained unimpressed.

'The woman heard his death throes – will probably hear them for the rest of her life – but she saw no one. That's not going to be much help.'

'Jocelyn has lied constantly,' he pointed out. 'She could be lying about that. She might be much stronger in the water than she claims. Could have entered the deep end of the lake and taken Gilmore by surprise, especially if he thought her a weak swimmer. And I don't think we should forget her connection with Russell Farr.'

'But you say he ended the relationship a year or so ago. Why would the woman take it into her head to punish him now?'

Jack thought of relaying Flora's theory that Farr's appearance at Cleve College had triggered a desperate need in Jocelyn for revenge, but he knew that Ridley would dismiss it as insubstantial or, worse, judge it 'a woman thing'.

'Jack?'

'Sorry, daydreaming. If you're not interested in Miss Draper, how about Joe Miller?'

'We can talk to him, certainly, but as far as I can see he's gone straight ever since the dishonourable discharge.'

'He was court-martialled for stealing.'

'And that's important, why?' Ridley looked at him with a sudden glint in his eyes. 'You've found something!'

Jack nodded. 'A room filled with expensive, even luxury goods. Miller's room.'

The inspector paused, his knife and fork mid-air. 'And you think the little twister has been stealing again?'

'Either that or he's been getting money from somewhere other than the salary Cleve College pays him.'

'Blackmail,' the inspector said with satisfaction.

'Can you...'

'I certainly can. That is something to get on to. First thing tomorrow we'll be into his finances. Weekend leave cancelled. Right now, I can't see the connection – if he's blackmailing why would he kill his victim? – but any lead is better than what we have at the moment.'

'While you're looking at his finances, can you check Gilmore's as well? Flora has a suspicion that he was the one being blackmailed. The chap was deeply depressed when he died, which is presumably one of the reasons the coroner came to the verdict he did.'

'Gilmore was a teacher? Would he have earned enough to pay up?'

'Small sums could add up,' he said, repeating Flora's contention.

'OK. Worth a look,' Ridley said amiably, and returned to finish his pie.

'About Miller. He's been behind several attacks on me.'

Alan Ridley frowned. 'What kind of attacks?'

Omitting the fact that he'd sensed Miller constantly following him, even to the point of invading his office, Jack detailed the electrical burn he'd received and the near calamity of Wednesday's bonfire. 'The man threw a lighted plank at me,' he finished. 'It was sheer luck that it set fire to my coat and not to me.'

'He could have something to hide and be trying to scare you off, but – he just might not like you, Jack!' The inspector grinned, then seeing Jack's expression, was quick to say, 'Miller's definitely a person of interest. We'll start with his finances, then move on to what he's been up to these last few years, apart from caretaking at the college.'

'And not doing that particularly well.'

Ridley pushed his plate to one side. 'Another beer? The night is young, as they say.'

Jack looked at his watch. 'I think I'll call it a day. Flora...'

'What it is to have a wife waiting for you!'

'Don't mock till you've tried it,' he said as a parting shot. 'Thanks for the company, Alan. Let me know if you have any luck with Miller.'

'You take care. He sounds a bit of a clown, but you never know. Clowns can turn dangerous.'

On Saturday morning, Flora arrived at the bookshop a good half an hour before she needed to open, keen to ensure the All's Well looked its best. It wasn't that she distrusted Rose, rather the need to satisfy herself that every book had been properly reshelved, the front table shuffled to include newly arrived publications, the window display left undisturbed, and every piece of rubbish whisked from sight.

Promptly at nine o'clock, the door chimes rang and, tucking her feather duster out of sight, Flora came forward to greet her first customer of the day. Not a customer, though, but Charlie Teague, looking as flustered as a fifteen-year-old could.

Flora felt a sudden sinking in her stomach – she hadn't checked on Betty this morning. Charlie was still doing her deliveries despite working at both the café and the Priory. With little time to spare, had he rushed his round last night? Betty should have been returned safely to her shelter in the courtyard behind the shop, but had the boy come to confess some hideous accident on his Friday evening delivery? It had happened before.

'Everything all right, Charlie?' she asked brightly.

'Sort of.' He gave her desk an experimental kick.

'Only sort of?'

'Sorry, Miss Steele. Mrs C,' he corrected himself. 'It's the money. That's why I've come.'

'What money?' Flora was mystified.

'My earnin's. For the deliveries.' His face was hopeful.

'But Mrs Lawson will have paid you. She knows to take the money out of the till.'

'Yeah, she does normally.'

'But not yesterday?' Flora remained puzzled. Rose knew the routine. Indeed, had been following it for several weeks.

'She forgot and I didn't like to say anythin'. She wuz upset, see.'

'Upset? Was that you? Did you upset her?' Flora was still struggling to understand.

'Nah, not me. It wuz that woman.'

'You'd better tell me exactly what happened, Charlie. I can't keep guessing like this.'

'I came here from the caff to pick up the books like always. There wuz only four houses on the list so packing the basket didn't take long. Then I came back into the shop to collect my money. Like always.'

'Yes?'

'There wuz a woman. She'd come while I was outside. She wuz arsking lottsa questions. I don't think Mrs Lawson wanted to answer, but she wuz tryin' to be polite and then she got in a right old tangle.'

'What kind of questions?'

'About you,' he said unexpectedly. 'Like where did you live? Where did you go when you weren't in the shop? What had you been doin' this week? Weird stuff like that.'

'Goodness. That is... weird. Did you recognise the woman?'

'Nah. Never seen her before. Posh lady. Spoke very lah-di-dah, you know.'

Flora's stomach suffered another sinking. 'Could you describe her? Was she quite tall with dark hair pulled back into a bun?'

He nodded.

'Wearing a deep green coat?' she asked, with sudden remembrance.

'Yeah, that wuz her. Friend of yours, Mrs C?'

'Not quite,' she said cautiously. 'But thank you for telling me, Charlie. Here, you must have your money.'

The boy's face brightened. 'I got up specially to see you,' he said, stuffing the precious coins into his jacket pocket.

'I thought you might have. It's Saturday morning after all and one when you're not working!'

After she'd seen him to the door, Flora flopped down on her stool. Roberta Raffles, it had to be. Roberta had come to Abbeymead to find her. And not just find her, but to find *out* about her. She had grilled Rose as to Flora's whereabouts, her activities, her daily life. An uncomfortable prickle made its way down her spine. The feeling of being taken over, of being controlled, returned. And returned forcefully.

Flora was beginning to wish she'd never met Mrs Raffles.

20

Concerned for how Rose might be feeling, Flora decided over the weekend that she would call at the bookshop on Monday and apologise for her 'friend's' insistent questioning. She hadn't mentioned the incident to Jack, certain he'd advise her to have nothing more to do with Roberta Raffles. In Flora's mind, though, it wasn't that simple. If she were to live in Lewes for what amounted to half of every week, she would need to make some kind of life for herself. It meant new contacts, new friends maybe, and Roberta was the only person she knew in the town. She was also, Flora guessed, a woman who moved in a good many social circles and it wouldn't be the best idea to be at odds with her. A comment here, a comment there, and Roberta Raffles could easily blight her move to Lewes.

After Jack's supper with Inspector Ridley, there had been plenty of other matters to talk over during the weekend, apart from Roberta. Chief among them was what to do about Joe Miller. In the end, they'd decided to do nothing. Now that Ridley knew everything they had learned and had promised to dig for more, they would leave the investigation hanging, at least for the time being. Both of them were certain they had pinpointed the villain – that was unusual, Flora thought wryly – and it was up to Ridley to find the proof to arrest him. Even if a murder charge wasn't forthcoming, once the inspector began probing Miller's finances, an arrest for blackmail would surely follow.

Monday morning involved an early start for Jack. Last week's lecture on misdirection in crime fiction had been a success and there had been calls to repeat the talk and to offer more. Yesterday, he'd put aside the current novel to work on a second session, this one on characterisation and, with two students needing individual attention as well as the two lectures, he had a busy day ahead.

Having waved him goodbye shortly after eight o'clock, Flora made ready for her meeting with Rose, deciding to leave Betty undisturbed in her garden shed and walk the short distance to the All's Well. At the front door she was taken aback to feel the faintest whispers of snow on her cheek, the very first of this winter. Crossing virtual fingers that it wouldn't turn into a full-blown storm, she tugged a woollen hat down over her ears and began the fifteen-minute tramp along Greenway Lane. She should have known that snow was on the way. For days, the temperature had been steadily falling.

Rose was rearranging the front display table when she walked into the bookshop.

'Flora!' Her assistant looked up, a smile on her face. 'I'm so glad you're here. We've had a double order arrive this morning – the wholesaler must have made a mistake. It's the latest Agatha Christie, *Ordeal by Innocence*. I was wondering if I should send one of the boxes back or whether we might be able to sell them.'

'We'll sell them all,' Flora said immediately. 'Christie flies off the shelves and this one is particularly good, according to the early reviews.' She stood back to gaze at their current display. 'Why don't we clear the table completely and fill it with

Agatha? We could do it for just a few days – I think a whole table of the same book would make a real impact.'

'I like that. It's a brilliant idea. I'll start on it straight away.'

'Rose, before you do... I didn't come by to tell you how to run the shop, but to say sorry. For Mrs Raffles.'

When Rose looked blank, Flora hastened to explain. 'She called here on Friday and according to Charlie almost pinned you to the wall with her questions.'

Rose flushed slightly. 'It was a bit awkward,' she admitted. 'The woman was so insistent. I didn't want to be impolite, but I didn't think it right to give personal information to someone who could be a total stranger. She said she was a friend of yours, but then she started asking me where you lived, who your friends were, and that seemed odd if she really knew you.'

'It must have done. She knows me, but not very well. Thank you for dealing with it – I'll make sure she doesn't come to the shop again when I'm not here. In fact... I'll send her an official invitation. That will make sure she won't visit unannounced!'

'Who is she, Flora?'

'Someone I met by chance – in a bookshop in Lewes. We had a cup of tea together and then she invited me for lunch. That's about the limit of our acquaintance. I have the feeling that she's pretty lonely.'

'Ah!' That seemed to be sufficient explanation for Rose.

'I was also wanting to talk to you about the days you work here.'

'You don't need me any more?' Rose paused from stacking the books she'd taken from the display table, alarm filling her face.

'No, nothing like that. I was hoping that maybe you could change your days – work mid-week instead. It would mean that Jack and I could be in Lewes from Tuesday and I'd be back here on Friday.'

'I could do that.' Rose looked relieved. 'I'd be glad to change.

In fact,' she said in a rush, 'I'd be happy to take over the whole week if you wanted. Dilys has made it clear that I won't be needed at the post office after Christmas. Maggie will be taking on any days I do.'

'How is that?'

'She's leaving the Nook – you know she's been working part-time in the café for a while? She's not happy about taking my days, but she needs the money. A case of "last in, first out".'

'Kate hasn't mentioned Maggie leaving.'

'I think it's only just been agreed. It's Charlie, you see. Since Master Teague left school last term, he's been training at the Nook for two days a week – but you'll know that. I think originally Kate thought of Charlie as an extra, not really part of the staff, but he's proved so good in the kitchen that she doesn't really need another person.'

'I didn't realise how Charlie might change things at the Nook,' she admitted. 'I suppose I'm still seeing him as a school-boy. But thank you for your offer – it's something to think about.'

With her recent inheritance lodged securely at the bank, she could afford to pay Rose's wages for the week, but the prospect of even more leisure time scared Flora. What would she do with herself? And how could she bear to be separated from her beloved bookshop for days on end? But if Jack continued at Cleve, it was a possibility she'd have to consider. He wasn't entirely happy at the college and his contract was a temporary one, but he seemed invested in his students and things could change, particularly if Miller were safe behind bars.

Leaving Rose to find a home for the books she'd cleared, Flora delved into her desk. 'While I remember, I'll write that card to Roberta. There are stamps in the till and I can post it on the way home.'

The missive – a promotional postcard for the All's Well –

was soon written, an invitation for Roberta to telephone her at the shop and arrange a date to visit.

'I must go,' she said. 'You've work to finish and I'm getting in the way!' Rose had already begun to pack the contents of the display table into several cardboard boxes.

Opening the All's Well's wide front door, Flora felt the whoosh of cold snow in her face. The earlier whispers had become thick flakes and, since she'd been in the shop, had begun lying fast.

'If it keeps snowing, you must close,' she told Rose from the doorway. 'I can't imagine we'll have too many customers in this weather and you need to be home before it gets really bad.'

Rose smiled. 'Once I've sorted this table, I'll be sure to check what's going on outside.'

By the time Flora reached her garden gate, it was an entirely white landscape, a thick blanket of snow smothering her front garden and climbing the fence. Her immediate thought was for Jack. Would he cancel his lectures? But then it might not be as bad in the east. Sussex was such a long county that the weather could be quite different from one end to the other.

By lunchtime, though, her worries had increased. An anxious look through the kitchen window offered no reassurance, the snow seeming to fall more thickly than ever and the blanket of white rapidly becoming a feather mattress. What should she do? Ring the college? No, she couldn't do that. It would smack too much of the nervous wife. Well, she *was* a nervous wife. The Austin was not a car you'd want to take through a snowdrift.

Picking up the phone, she dialled the number Jack had scrawled on the nearby pad, but it was silence that greeted her. No buzz, no static. Just silence. The telephone lines must be down. Nothing to do then but keep calm – and carry on, she added, smiling to herself. Those wartime days now seemed far away.

Around teatime, a knock on her front door had her rushing to open it. Jack was home! He must have forgotten his key. But it was Tony Farraday on the threshold, wearing an outsize yellow plastic raincoat and knee-high wellingtons.

'Kate sent me.' He grinned from beneath a matching plastic rainhat. 'I called at the shop, but it was closed.' Thank goodness, Flora thought. Rose had had the good sense to lock up and leave.

'Kate wanted to check that you were OK,' Tony said, his breath forming a spiral in the air. 'We've closed the Nook and Alice is back home from the Priory.'

'Then it's just Jack who's not home,' she said forlornly. 'And I can't contact him – my phone line is down.'

'Ours, too. The radio's working, though, and it looks pretty bad everywhere. Kent, in particular.'

'Which means the east of the county will be even worse than here.'

'Maybe not,' he said, though he didn't sound confident. 'But you shouldn't worry. Jack won't try to drive in this. He's got a warm building to shelter in and they're bound to have food. They've a kitchen and a refectory, haven't they? He'll sit it out until he can move the Austin.'

'I suppose.'

'If there's nothing I can do...'

'Nothing, Tony,' she began to say, when he bobbed down and picked up a pint bottle of milk that she hadn't noticed.

'You forgot to take this in,' he said, handing her ice-cold glass.

'Wilfred hadn't delivered by the time I left this morning. I imagine the weather is making life difficult for him.' She took the bottle. 'And he's left me gold top. Perhaps that's all he was carrying today, but it's far too creamy. It will have to do, though. I'm not walking back to the village for a silver.'

'You wouldn't be lucky anyway.' Tony pulled a small face.

'The shutters are down everywhere. We'll be in touch, Flora, as soon as the phone comes back on. Otherwise, I'll call by tomorrow.' He turned to walk back to the front gate, the imprint of his boots like a giant's footsteps on the path.

At least I can have a cup of tea, she thought, taking the bottle into the kitchen and storing it in the larder. It won't taste as nice with gold top, but a smidgen of milk should be OK. But Jack...

She stood staring out of the window, anxiously watching the still falling snow, then scolded herself. Tony was right. Jack would be safe. He'd find shelter at the college.

21

Both his talks today had been well received and, in good spirits, Jack walked back up the stairs to his office. Writing was a solitary pursuit and being able to pass on the knowledge he'd gained felt rewarding. It satisfied him that he could share the highs and the lows, the successes and the pitfalls, of the career he'd adopted since handing in his military uniform. He was beginning to enjoy being a mentor – and enjoy the company of the students who consulted him. This afternoon's appointments were particularly interesting: one with an aspiring crime writer and the other with a student writing romance. It was a genre new to Jack and, on the surface, seemingly disconnected from anything he'd written himself. But when you analysed the fundamentals, he thought, really it was not. Stories were stories. Henry James had been right: *There are bad novels and good novels... that is the only distinction...*

Both appointments lasted longer than he had bargained for and, by the time he'd gathered his papers together, donned an overcoat and collected his car keys, he found the college completely snowbound. Partially opening the huge oak front door, he stood looking despairingly out at the monochrome scene in front of him.

'You'll not get home today.' Reg Easton had come out of his porter's office – it was little more than a cubicle in one corner of the foyer – and was shaking his head.

'I doubt I'd even get the Austin to spark in this cold,' Jack responded, closing the door on an icy draught that was cutting through his legs.

'You're well and truly stuck, Mr Carrington. The radio says it's worst in the east of the county – you'd not make it out of the grounds. You can walk round to the flat you've been given, if you like. I'm just off to mine. I can let you have the key – we found it, by the way. Though on second thoughts, there's no heating there so you'd be best to stay in the main building. The kitchen will have stuff. You won't go hungry.'

'Let's hope it won't be a prolonged stay.' There'd been no offer from the porter, Jack noticed, to share his own accommodation.

'The Highways Department have been informed,' Reg Easton went on. 'They know we need help. Managed to ring them before the line went down. They'll send a snowplough when they can, but it might not be until morning.'

'There's no phone?'

The porter gave another sad shake of his head. No call to Flora then. Jack hoped she was at home and not worrying too much.

'Am I the only member of staff left in the building?'

'Miss Longstaff's still around, I think. I saw her half an hour ago.' Reg shut his office door with a click that echoed around the empty building. 'I'll wish you a good night then.'

Some hope of that, Jack thought. He should have cancelled that last appointment and left while he could. Snowed in with only Valerie Longstaff for company and no way of checking that Flora was OK. Could it get much worse?

Once the porter's figure had disappeared into the haze of snow, still falling fast, Jack made his way along the passage to the refectory and the kitchen beyond. At the doorway, he gave an inaudible groan. Miss Longstaff was already there. She'd evidently been busy in the cupboards, several doors stood open, and now she was burying deep into the huge refrigerator that stood against one wall.

She looked around when he walked in. 'You're stuck, too? Ah well, you can make yourself useful now you're here. I reckon you're tall enough to see to the top shelf. Is there anything worth having up there?'

Jack walked over to the refrigerator and peered. 'Two slabs of butter,' he reported, 'and what looks like a round of Cheddar cheese.'

'We can have that. I've found a jar of pickle in one of the cupboards and there's bound to be bread.'

'There's also half a ham.'

'Getting better all the time. Do you drink tea? There's nothing stronger. I checked that, too.'

'Tea will be fine.'

'Poor show this, isn't it?' Valerie muttered, once they were seated at the table, her mouth full of bread and cheese.

'The snow?'

'Yes, of course the snow. You'd think someone would have warned us. Told us to go home. I bet Dalloway is back at his house, safe and sound.'

'Does he live nearby?' Jack wasn't that interested but some conversation seemed necessary.

'A grace and favour house, a few miles down the road. What else?' she muttered, giving her attention to a second large chunk of Cheddar.

A long silence followed until it came to Jack that this could be an opportunity to probe. To hear from a teacher who, he guessed, had been at the college a fair number of years. Certainly at the time Paul Raffles had been bursar.

'What do you make of the professor?' he asked casually.

'He's a money man, through and through,' Valerie said dismissively. It was much the same as Jocelyn had said. 'Where he got his professorship, God knows. I wouldn't be surprised if he'd bought it from some made-up university.'

'A money man who can't seem to manage the college's accounts!' Jack tried a joke, hoping it might lead to Raffles.

Valerie took his words seriously. 'He employs a bursar. Always has. To take in the money and pay it out – very different from managing the accounts. Dalloway gets a slice of the profits and the bursar doesn't.'

'You're sure that's the arrangement?'

She shrugged. 'Common knowledge, Mr Carrington. It's why Dalloway is desperate to sign up students. More students, more profit for him. He recruits far more than any of us can reasonably teach. Haven't you noticed your timetable has become busier since you've been here?'

'Now you mention it, yes.'

'And it will get a whole lot busier. He starts newcomers with what looks an easy schedule then, gradually, they'll have more and more dumped on them. You'll be inundated soon,' she said with a grim satisfaction.

'The previous bursar. Did you know him?'

'Paul Raffles? Not a bad chap for someone who spends his life totting up figures. I was sorry when he left. Surprised, too. He always seemed happy enough, but then suddenly he was gone.'

'He was the one who employed Joe Miller, I believe.'

'One of the few mistakes he made and a gross one at that. I can't understand why he did it. There must have been far worthier applicants. More tea, or shall I throw?' She picked up the huge stainless steel pot and waved it at him.

'I've had enough, thanks.'

'In that case, I'll be off. I've a settee in my office so I'm more or less OK. How about you?'

'There's a chair.'

Valerie pulled a face. 'That's too bad. Sorry, but I won't be sharing my settee.'

A lucky escape, Jack congratulated himself, walking back up the stairs to his office. The chair was at least large with a removable seat and back cushions. He pulled them to the floor, lining them up to form a makeshift bed. His overcoat would be his blanket. He'd read for a while and then try to sleep. It was hardly comfortable, but he'd slept in worse conditions. A particularly noisome pigsty in northern France flashed across his mind.

'Luxury,' he murmured, stretching himself as flat as he could, his lower legs drooping from the furthest cushion.

For a long time, it seemed, he fidgeted from one side to another, on cushions more lumpy by the minute but, finally, weariness overcame discomfort and Jack drifted into an uneasy sleep. How long he slept he wasn't sure. Grabbing the watch he'd laid beside the narrow bed, he tried to make out the time in the hazy light filtering through the window. Only two o'clock?

Something must have woken him, something more than aching limbs. A noise? He listened intently, but the building was quiet except for the odd creaking of old timbers, hardly loud enough to have woken him. Suddenly, he knew. It was smell, the last of the senses to come alive. It was the smell of burning!

Scrambling to his feet, he staggered over to the window and looked out. A moon, drifting from behind cloud cover, shed a small pool of light, but otherwise all was darkness. Smoke without fire then, but was it coming from within the building?

The kitchen was his immediate thought. An appliance left switched on that had overheated. He tried to remember what they had used. No cooker, just the kettle, and Valerie Longstaff had been the tea-maker. It must be the kettle. She wouldn't be getting up to check, he could guarantee. He was the one who would have to stumble down the stairs.

But when Jack opened his door and walked out onto the landing, he was confused. The smell was stronger here, but he could swear it wasn't emanating from the floor below. From where though? He looked along the corridor to the flight of stairs leading to the upper floor. As far as Jack knew, there were only attics above, unoccupied and used as a dumping ground for anything for which the college no longer had a use.

Feeling some alarm – if there was a fire in one of the attics and no telephone line to call for help, it could become a desperate situation – he tried to think as coolly as he could. Realistically, how likely was it that a fire could have started? Perhaps it was his nose playing tricks, but he dare not rely on that. Sighing aloud, he stumped along the corridor to the stair-case at the far end and began to climb, fervently hoping he was mistaken.

At the top of the stairs, he was faced with another corridor, this time a good deal narrower, with a row of doors along one side, most of them shut and, for all Jack knew, locked fast. The final door, however, *was* open and, trying to keep himself awake – his eyelids were heavy with sleep – he peered along the passageway and saw what he thought was a wisp of smoke floating in the air.

As soon as he walked into the room, he saw the fire. It made him want to laugh. A tiny circle of screwed up paper intermingled with one or two small pieces of wood, like the fires he had tried to light with his fellow cubs on their childhood expeditions. A fire, but a puny one, and almost welcome in the freezing temperature. He could deal with that, he decided. A few minutes stamping with his boots should extinguish it. But Jack was puzzled. Someone had set this fire, it was clear, but who and why?

Before he thought too much about it, he needed to shut the double glass doors which had been left open to the balcony beyond. The breeze blowing into the room had begun to fan the fire, causing the flames to leap and endanger the several cast-offs that had been abandoned close by: a Chesterfield sofa, its seat badly split, a tea trolley with three wheels and a guitar minus most of its strings.

Striding across to the glass doors – Jack was beginning to wake up – he reached for one of the door handles, but never made it. His hand fell back, limp and useless at his side, as an almighty blow to his neck caused him to crumple. Dazed, he tried to stagger upright, tried to turn to face his antagonist, to confront this new danger, but was felled by a second, even heavier blow. His legs gave way, his body thudding to the floor. On his way down, he narrowly missed the campfire burning merrily through the rough floorboards.

22

Flora went to bed that night worrying, despite her determination not to. Would the telephone lines be repaired by tomorrow? Would Jack be able to drive the Austin home? What if he'd tried already, and was stuck in a snowdrift?

This is stupid, she told herself crossly, throwing on pyjamas in double-quick time – the cottage was freezing tonight even though she'd banked the sitting room fire as high as she could. There was nothing she could do to help Jack and she must sleep. She needed sleep or she'd be good for nothing tomorrow and she was due at the All's Well before nine. Punching her pillows into shape, she tried to relax. But telling herself to sleep was one thing, actually managing quite another. Eventually, though, she fell into a deep slumber, the thick snow on all sides of the house muffling any sound that might have disturbed her.

It was around two o'clock when she woke. Abruptly. An intimation of danger? Of course there was no danger. She was being foolish again. She snuggled down beneath the counterpane, hoping to drift back to sleep, but suddenly felt very sick. A scramble from the bed, a dash to the bathroom and Flora was only just in time before she was violently ill. The vomiting left her shivering and her hands, as she sank down onto the bathroom stool, had begun to shake.

Where had that come from? She wiped the wetness from her forehead with a towel. She was rarely sick and she'd had a plain supper – ham and eggs. Had the ham been suspect? But it had tasted fine. Or the eggs? Hardly, they were fresh from the local farm. Giving up the quest to find a reason, she put her sickness down to bad luck. Maybe an excess of worry could make you ill. She would go back to bed, go back to sleep, and wake up tomorrow as right as rain.

She had regained her bed for only a few minutes, however, before her stomach began heaving and another dash to the bathroom proved essential. It left her limp and shuddering. And so it went on for the rest of the night. It was when she found herself slipping from the bathroom stool, having in desperation fallen into a doze, that she realised morning had arrived. A thin dawn light was coming through the window. Hugging her dressing gown close, she made her way down to the kitchen and put the kettle on to boil. At last, her stomach seemed to have settled and a cup of tea should help to keep her awake. Somehow, she had to get through the day ahead.

Pouring the smallest amount of milk into the cup of tea – it was too creamy to use much – her hand stopped mid-air. The milk? She hadn't thought of it before, but could it have been that? She sniffed the bottle and it smelt like... well, milk. There had been a late delivery, she remembered, the bottle left outside for some hours. But it had been so cold that the milk should have been preserved rather than soured. When had it been delivered?

Her mind was tired and confused, but step by step she tried to recall what had happened yesterday. She had walked back from the All's Well after seeing Rose – she was certain the bottle hadn't been on her doorstep then. It had been Tony who'd found it when he called by some hours later. That was around teatime, so had Wilfred delivered it in the interim? She hadn't heard the milk float arrive, but perhaps she wouldn't in snow that had been falling fast. But then how had the milkman navigated Greenway Lane? The snow would surely have been too thick for an electric float. She hadn't thought of that before.

Flora studied the milk intently, wondering who had actually left it on her doorstep. It was certainly something to investigate. Picking up the bottle, she tucked it out of reach and out of sight. It would be black tea for her this morning.

Jack regained consciousness as the cold air hit him squarely in the face. His head was throbbing, his mind a haze, but it took him only seconds to realise he was on the third floor of the building and being thrust through the glass doors and out onto the balcony. He tried to twist so that he could see his adversary, though he knew without looking. It would be Miller. And Miller, having previously failed to set him alight, had used fire tonight to lure him to the attic, to a balcony three floors above the flagstoned terrace.

Jack went slack, an old trick he'd learned in his fighting days. His shoulders slumped, his torso sagged, his legs dragged, and suddenly he was a dead weight again for the man pushing him forward. But Miller wasn't giving up. He'd been a soldier, too, albeit a disgraced one, and he was strong. With his arms around Jack's chest, he carried on dragging him over the threshold of the double doors and onto the parapet.

In an instant, Jack came to life, no longer dragging his legs but kicking out viciously and catching the caretaker somewhere he hoped was very, very painful. There was a momentary slackening of Miller's hold, but then he was back, manhandling his captive closer to the waist-high wall. Jack's elbow thrust backwards and jabbed hard, producing a grunt from his attacker but no diminution of force. Miller's arms were tight around his chest and inch by inch he was being dragged forward until his body was jammed against the parapet. With an enormous heave, his attacker made to hike him up onto the wall, intent on pushing him to almost certain death on the paving way below.

Waiting for his moment, Jack allowed himself to be half-hoisted onto the wall, then using the last of his tricks, suddenly twisted his body, this time kicking out with both legs, his feet hitting Miller in the chest and sending the man staggering backwards into the room. Jack was off the wall and on his feet, swinging a fist at Miller's jaw but missing as the caretaker ducked. His enemy launched himself forward, hands out, scrabbling to grab Jack by the throat.

It was to be strangulation now rather than death from a catastrophic fall. Choking, Jack managed to fasten his hands on the man's arms and force them down and away, but over and over Miller attempted to grab at him, to clutch at his throat. Two figures, like creatures from the underworld, locked in a ghastly dance, circling the flames ceaselessly, their shadows on the wall bloated and grotesque.

Both men were almost spent but, with a final, massive effort, Jack managed to force Miller's hands far enough from his body to head butt his adversary in the chest. Once more, the man staggered back, this time badly winded. Miller teetered on his heels, seeming about to renew the fight, but then, as though he'd had enough, or was too weak to withstand a further attack, he turned tail and ran out of the door. Jack heard his stumbling footsteps as he took the stairs two at a time.

For several minutes after he'd gone, Jack remained slumped against the wall, his breathing harsh and uneven. Every part of his body screamed pain, but he was alive. Miller had been determined to kill, but somehow he'd survived. Why the man wanted him dead was still unclear. Almost from the moment Jack had joined the college, the caretaker had mounted a campaign of intimidation against him – dogging his footsteps, breaking into his office, the faulty plug, the lighted plank on bonfire evening. And tonight? Tonight surely had to be Miller's last act.

Jack stamped a weary foot to extinguish the last of a fire that had now dwindled to little, and walked cautiously down the stairs to his office. There was no sign of his would-be murderer. How Miller had left the college, how he would get through knee-deep snow and where he'd gone, if in fact he had, was a mystery. At this moment, Jack didn't much care. He almost fell into his office, turning the lock behind him and, with what little strength he had left, pushing the desk hard against the door.

His body wrung out and hurting in every conceivable place, he was no longer conscious of the discomfort of his makeshift bed. In minutes, he'd fallen into a deep slumber and stayed sleeping until woken by a smudge of winter sun shining directly into his eyes and the noise of something large and mechanical beneath his window. With difficulty, he rolled himself off the chair cushions and, creaking, blundered to the window. Looking down on the scene below, he felt a surge of relief. A snow-plough had arrived and Valerie Longstaff was talking to its driver. Was she offering him tea or complaining about the noise? Probably the latter.

Jack picked up his overcoat from the floor and, shifting the desk back to its usual position, walked out of his office and down the stairs. The snowplough had already cut a clear path along the driveway as far as the college gates. Hopefully, beyond those, the road would be at least partially cleared.

The porter was unlocking the door to his cubicle when Jack walked into the foyer. 'Morning, Mr Carrington. Sleep OK?' he asked cheerfully.

'Pretty well, considering.'

It wasn't far from the truth. Once he'd stopped fighting for his life, he'd slept like the dead, though the phrase made him wince. 'I don't suppose you have a spade handy?'

'This do?' The porter shuffled around at the back of his small space and brought out a flat-faced shovel.

'Perfect. I'll dig the Austin out and return it straight away. In case Miss Longstaff needs to use it.' It was unchivalrous of him, but he really hoped she would.

Dig the Austin out and get home, he muttered to himself, stamping his feet to wake up his toes. Get home and get to Flora.

23

It was a dangerous drive. The county transport department had done what they could, but the smaller roads were impassable and Jack had to make a roundabout journey to reach Abbeymead. He parked in the high street – there was no chance the car would manage Greenway Lane.

Flora was at the sitting room window as he opened the garden gate and came flying to the door to greet him.

'Thank goodness, you're here. I've been so worried. How are you? The phone's still not working.'

'The lines must be down just about everywhere.' He put his arms around her, hugging her tight. 'But I'm fine,' he lied. There would be time later for the truth.

He walked back with her into the house and, for a moment, held her at arm's length. In the brighter light of the sitting room, there were blue smudges beneath her eyes, and her complexion, usually warm and healthy, was a sickly white.

'Something's happened.' He scrutinised her face. 'You look really ill, Flora.'

'I have been ill,' she confessed. 'Actually, quite sick. It was something I ate, I think, or something I drank. Milk perhaps.'

'Milk doesn't sound very likely. Do you still have it?'

He followed her into the kitchen and saw her pull out a bottle from what looked like a hiding place. 'Here,' she offered it to him.

Jack took a sniff. 'It doesn't smell sour.'

'It didn't taste sour either and there may be nothing wrong with it, but it's the only thing I can think that could have made me ill. I only used a tiny amount. It's gold top – you know I don't like it in my tea,' she explained.

'The milkman made a mistake?'

Flora sank into the kitchen chair, as though whatever energy she'd begun the day with had trickled away. 'I'm not sure it was Wilfred who delivered it. The bottle didn't arrive on the doorstep at the usual time.'

Jack sat down opposite, a small fear beginning to form in the back of his mind. 'Who else would have left it? It could have been the milkman running late, couldn't it? Quite likely after yesterday, but then... how would he have driven the float along the lane? I've had to leave the Austin in the high street.'

She said nothing and he pushed the bottle to one side. 'Do you still have the foil top?'

'I threw it in the bin.'

'You screwed it up?'

She nodded. 'What are you getting at, Jack? Why is the foil top important?'

'I'm thinking you may have been deliberately poisoned and it would be helpful if we had the whole item. We shouldn't touch the bottle again – it should go to the police lab for analysis.'

'Really?'

'It's lucky you hate cream in your tea. How much of the milk did you drink?'

'Very little. About this.' Flora held up her finger and thumb to illustrate.

Jack's expression was grave. 'Think what might have happened if you'd used more.'

'I have thought.' She stared at the tabletop. 'I guess I'd be dead or very nearly.'

'Someone tried to kill *me* last night, too,' he said conversationally. There was no point now in holding back.

'What!'

'My surly friend, Joe Miller. He set a fire going in the room above my office. The smoke lured me up to the attic, making me a perfect target. After knocking me out – I had no idea anyone was in the room – he tried to hurl me over the balcony.'

Flora's mouth fell open, her eyes staring into the distance. 'I can't believe... both of us... you were in danger, too. When?'

'When?'

'What time did he attack you?'

'Well, being hit over the head, I didn't have the chance to check precisely, but it was around two o'clock that I walked up those stairs.'

'That's when I woke. When I was first sick. Jack, we nearly died together.'

'It's a romantic idea, but I think I'd prefer that we both went on living.'

'At least *you* know who attacked you. Where is Miller now?'

'I've no idea. He gave up the fight, thank God, and ran off.'

'Did no one come to your aid?'

'There was no one to come. Reg Easton, the porter, had trotted off to his flat earlier in the evening and the only other member of staff trapped in college was Miss Longstaff. Her office is on the other side of the building. She would have heard nothing and, in any case, I doubt she'd have come to help.'

Flora leaned across the table and grasped his hands. 'The man tried to murder you – again.'

'And failed again.'

'But why does he want you dead? It can't only be that he suspects you know more than you do.'

'You would think, but other than that, I've no idea why he's fixated on my leaving this world.'

They sat in silence for some minutes, their hands still locked together. 'Do you think he suspects that *I* know more, too?' she said, at last. 'That you passed on whatever you're supposed to have discovered. He must know you're married and he'll know where you live. Could *he* have tried to poison me?'

Jack shook his head. 'On a purely practical level I'm not sure he could. The roads to Abbeymead have been choked with snow for hours. He has a car, I know, but I doubt he could make it here, leave you the milk and then get back to Cleve before the snow closed in. When was it you discovered the bottle?'

'I didn't. It was Tony. He came by around teatime, but the milk could have been sitting outside for hours. Miller *could* have done it. He could know that we're together in this. He could have seen me with you. In the lane, when we walked back from Overlay House that Saturday. Like I said, he could have been hanging around still and seen us discover the body.'

'How would that make him so suspicious that he has to kill us both? We were just two people who made a horrible discovery and reported it.'

'What if he knows that afterwards we went to Farr's house? What if he knows we've talked to Bettina Lyons? You're sure he's been following you.'

'In college, yes, but he'd have to be on roller skates to get around that much *and* do his job.'

Flora jumped up and stood, arms crossed. She was wearing her 'let's get things done' expression, he saw. 'Someone knows we're investigating or we wouldn't have been threatened and who else is there? Miller kills Farr – he's probably already killed Gregory Gilmore – and now he wants to kill us.'

'We still haven't discovered why he'd want to kill Farr. And why Gregory if he was blackmailing him? It would have meant an end to the money for Miller.'

'Gregory could have spelt danger. If he felt so guilty after talking to Russell Farr about his father that he decided to go to the police and confess what had happened at the orphanage, it would have meant the end for Miller,' she pointed out. 'That would be reason enough.'

'Unless, of course, Gregory's death *is* unconnected. The coroner recorded a verdict of suicide and that might well be correct – the man was deeply depressed. But there's also Jocelyn Draper to consider. She was emotionally involved with both men. She's told a string of lies. And she was definitely at the lake when Gilmore drowned.'

Flora's expression became even more determined. 'We shouldn't get sidetracked. We need to stick with Miller. You're proof he's a dangerous man. The inspector needs to find him and arrest him for attempted murder. And do it before he tries again.'

'As soon as the phone line is restored, I'll ring Alan,' he promised. 'As long as Miller is still in the country, his men will find him. Until then, we're stuck, unless I try the drive to Brighton police station to report my near-death in person.'

She walked behind his chair, wrapping her arms around his shoulders. 'I don't want you driving anywhere. I don't want you even to leave the cottage – until that man is caught. Have you had any breakfast?'

'Not yet. I need a bath. But first *I'm* going to make *you* toast and tea. You look in need of bolstering.'

'Tea? Really?'

'Black, of course.'

It was almost lunchtime before Flora opened the All's Well's door, considering it unlikely she would have many customers and certainly not at nine o'clock in the morning. She had left Jack, fortified by a bacon and egg breakfast. clearing snow from the front path and from the lane beyond. Walking to the bookshop through what was still thick snow took a long time and a lot of effort, but the last twenty-four hours had been ones she'd rather forget and to be in familiar surroundings again, ticking off her daily list of chores, was a comfort.

It was very slightly warmer today and, though she'd worn the thickest coat in her wardrobe, she'd risked a bare head, her one woolly hat tending to make her ears burn. With luck, and as long as they were spared a second blizzard, a good deal of the snow would have melted by tomorrow.

As she expected, she'd spent a lonely hour or so in the shop before, surprisingly, Sally Jenner walked in just as she was finishing the daily dusting.

'You walked down from the Priory?' she asked.

It was a silly question. Sally must have done, since the Abbeymead roads were still largely impassable for even a bicycle.

'I needed a quiet half hour.' Sally let out a loud breath which hung faintly in the air. The All's Well was not the warmest of shops. 'The hotel was driving me to distraction so I thought, why not walk down to Flora? Treat myself – buy a new book for when or if I manage any time free.'

'Are you still run off your feet? I imagine the Christmas rush is just beginning.'

Sally gave a wan smile. 'I shouldn't complain, should I? A year ago I was desperate for customers. And it's not so much the work, but...'

'But?'

'Can you talk to her?' she burst out.

Flora had an idea but still asked, 'Talk to who?'

'Auntie, of course. She is slowly driving me insane.'

'Hector?' It was a good guess.

Sally took up a perch on the edge of the front display table. 'She's either berating me for going out with him or pursed up and cold and not talking at all. How do I deal with it?'

'She loves you, Sally. She worries for you.' It wasn't exactly a solution, but the two of them had been at loggerheads for so long that nothing Flora suggested was likely to work.

'Don't you think I know that? But is it always going to be the same with every man I meet? It was painful with Dominic and now it's Hector she doesn't like.'

'Alice has this thing about not mixing with business with pleasure, and in a way it's good advice.'

Sally snorted. 'I've come to the conclusion that that's just an excuse. Really, it's the man she doesn't like. Any man. Just because she never married...' She left the sentence unfinished.

'Your aunt was right about Dominic Lister, you have to admit.' Dominic had turned out to be an untrustworthy partner, lying shamelessly and plunging Sally into serious financial trouble.

'OK. I agree. Dom wasn't a good choice, but Hector is different.'

'You thought Dominic was different, too,' she pointed out.

'That's not very helpful, Flora.'

'Sorry, all I'm saying is that Alice has your best interests at heart and she doesn't want to see you so desperately upset again.'

Both Sally and her aunt were entrenched and nothing Flora said was likely to make a difference. It was time to change the conversation. 'Have you seen Dominic lately?'

'Actually, yes. He invited me over to view his flat. It's just across from the promenade with a stunning view of the sea. I might have told you. And it's near the swimming club he's joined, so perfect.'

'He's still swimming?' Flora was surprised. In her judgement, Dominic Lister was the kind of person who developed sudden enthusiasms and just as suddenly forgot them.

'He seems really committed. Apparently the club he's joined is the best in Brighton for sea swimming. Maybe the best in the country. They've produced some amazing athletes – Channel swimmers. Dom was boasting that was going to be his next project!'

'To swim the Channel?'

Flora's tone had Sally gurgle with laughter. 'I know! Can you imagine? But he's perfectly serious. One member of the club tried a few years ago and almost made it before she had to give up. Actually...' Sally got up from her improvised seat. 'Dominic told me something that might interest you. Well, interest Jack. She was a teacher at Jack's college. I don't know if she's still there, but she became something of a celebrity in Brighton. Interviewed by the local paper, asked to open a new swimming pool, that kind of thing.'

Flora's mind began to hum. 'That is interesting. Do you remember her name? I could tell Jack.'

'I don't.' Creases appeared on Sally's forehead. 'It was something to do with clothes.'

'Clothes?'

'Taylor? Singer? The sewing machines,' she explained. 'No, Draper. That was it, Draper.'

'Jocelyn Draper.' Flora's voice was neutral.

'Yes! Have you met her?'

'Yes,' she said, still speaking carefully, 'the other evening at the college bonfire. She teaches art.'

'Nice. When she's not covered in grease and powering through the waves, I suppose!' Sally gave a grin. 'Now, what can

you offer me?' Ignoring the Christie display she'd been warm-
ing, she walked over to the bookcase in which Rose had shelved
the former occupants of the front table. '*Our Man in Havana,
Breakfast at Tiffany's, The Witch of Blackbird Pond*... I like the
sound of that one. Wrap me up a copy!'

24

The news of Jocelyn's attempt to swim the Channel had Jack fall silent. The lying shouldn't be a surprise – she had lied several times before – but now, it seemed, she was not only at the scene of Gilmore's death that day, but was more than capable of diving into the deepest part of the lake. And physically strong enough, Jack guessed, to succeed in drowning the man. A man who had rejected whatever advances Jocelyn had made. Motive and opportunity, the key facts in any murder case, were shining brightly.

'We shouldn't let Gilmore's death be a distraction.' Flora repeated her earlier warning, seeming worried he was about to lose focus and swerve direction. 'As you said, his drowning could have been the suicide of a depressed man. And even if it weren't, even if it were a deliberate killing, it doesn't have to be connected to Russell Farr's death.'

'Maybe, but two murders within months of each other, linked to the same college – *and* the same woman?'

'If Jocelyn killed, it was for love,' Flora argued. 'Rejection is a textbook motive for murder. It can happen any time and in any place.'

'You're saying it's a coincidence that Jocelyn, if she is a murderer, has a connection to the college?'

'Why not? It's coincidence, isn't it, that Russell went to the college? If Bettina hadn't sent that note... and a coincidence that Jocelyn saw him there and decided to wreak her revenge. Otherwise, there'd be no connection. Whereas Miller—'

'Relax. I'm primed to ring the inspector. Dilys knocked on the door while you were at the shop. The phone line should be restored tomorrow.'

'Dilys actually walked here?' Flora was temporarily distracted.

'She did, puffing loudly and wrapped in some kind of knitted blanket – a lurid orange. Dark glasses would have helped. She's been tramping through the village, calling on everyone she thinks might be desperate to use their phone. "Community spirit," she insisted, then glared at me for clearly lacking it.'

'Her community spirit didn't quite reach the All's Well.'

'Naturally, I had to be told first. For Dilys, a writer is a rare beast!'

'Did you phone Alan Ridley?' was Flora's first question when she returned from work the next day, having shut the All's Well for the afternoon.

'I did – as promised – but he was in a meeting. Something too important to interrupt. The desk sergeant gave me his word that he'd pass on my message. We'll have to wait for his call.'

It wasn't long coming and, when it did, it wasn't a call that either Jack or Flora was expecting.

'Joe Miller again,' Ridley said meditatively, after Jack had told him he had news of the man, news that could be urgent.

'I know you're looking into his finances, Alan, but something happened on Monday night that makes an immediate arrest possible once you find him.'

There was a puzzling silence at the other end of the telephone.

'Are you free this afternoon, Jack?' the inspector asked finally. 'If you are, meet me at Rillington Orphanage. I think you might be interested.'

'I guess I could make time to come...' Flora, who'd been listening at his shoulder, looked meaningfully at him. 'And Flora will probably be with me,' he added quickly, replacing the receiver before the inspector could protest.

'You're coming?' he asked, flicking the curtain of hair back from her face.

'How could I not?' She squeezed him round the waist. 'Intrigue! I want to be there!'

It was a very different day from the last time they'd driven to Rillington. Then, the trees had still been in leaf, a bounty of autumn gold. The long grass had been dampened by morning dew and a sun, mild and hazy, had tried to warm an otherwise bleak world. Today, the sky was grey, darkening as the hours passed, and the air cold enough for a new blizzard. The wilderness that comprised the orphanage grounds appeared starker than ever: trees stripped of their modesty, bushes weighed to the ground by heavy snow, and grass thick with sharp frost.

Jolting along the rough driveway, Flora saw the outline of the orphanage slowly appear against the horizon. Gaunt and Gothic, it seemed more desolate than ever.

'The building...' she muttered, half to herself, leaning forward to stare through the windscreen.

Jack, concentrating on guiding the Austin safely over a surface that was now more holes than gravel, made no response.

'Jack, look!' she said urgently.

For a moment, he took his eye off the road and his hands slipped from the steering wheel. 'My God! It's a ruin?'

'It was always a ruin but now...'

A façade of blackened brickwork greeted them, a roof open to the sky and rows of windows that were shattered and sightless. Charred fragments of wood began littering the driveway as they drew closer.

'A fire,' she exclaimed. 'There's been a fire.'

'Miller,' Jack said in a quiet voice. 'Miller and fire are inseparable.'

Several police vehicles were drawn up outside the front entrance and a group of men, the inspector among them, stood talking on the forecourt.

As Jack parked the Austin neatly behind the second police car, Alan Ridley came towards them.

'Jack!' he greeted him cheerfully. 'Good to see you. And you, Mrs Carrington.' He didn't sound quite as enthusiastic. 'Welcome to what's left of Rillington Orphanage. The fire brigade has been and gone.' He turned his head to look at the destruction behind him. 'Nothing more they can do. It's a demolition job, I'm afraid.'

'But how—' Jack began.

'Walk round with me to the rear of the building. I've something to show you, although Mrs Carrington might not—'

'I'm coming,' Flora announced, bouncing out of the car. She was feeling so much better now that it was difficult to remember how near death she'd felt during that long Monday night.

Glad to have worn her second-best coat – it was by far the warmest garment she possessed – Flora hurried to keep up with the men as they walked swiftly around the perimeter to the rear of the building, a virtual facsimile of the front façade. A smaller main door, but the same barred windows, the same iron-railed balconies.

Balconies, as well as fire, had become quite the thing in this case. Benedict Farr, Jack and now...

She looked to where the inspector was pointing. Some

distance away, a body lay sprawled across the weed-strewn paving stones. The man's head was twisted at an odd angle, his legs splayed, his arms outstretched. Flora looked up. Immediately above, yes, a balcony, with the iron railings only slightly contorted by the fire.

'Who is he?' Jack asked.

'You're allowed one guess.' The inspector's tone was dry.

'Not... not Miller?'

'The very same. Mr Miller of the dubious finances and the predilection for fire.'

'The predilection for murder, too.'

Alan Ridley's eyebrows rose slightly. 'Is that why you wanted to see me?'

'Miller,' Jack nodded towards the inert figure, 'tried to kill me on Monday night. At Cleve College. Tried to throw me off a balcony onto the flagstones below.'

The inspector looked across at the body and shook his head. 'He must have thought you were on his trail. That you knew more than you should. But poetic justice, eh?'

'Someone threw him over the balcony?'

'Unless he decided to end it all after setting fire to the building, and I guess he could have done. Once you refused to die, he might have reckoned the game was up and couldn't face the music. Tell me what happened – after you survived his murderous attack?' Ridley was unable to suppress a smile.

Flora, watching him closely, was incensed. Jack had nearly died and here was the man, who should be protecting them, making a joke of it. So far, she'd said nothing, but she soon would.

'He ran off,' Jack said mildly. 'But where to, I'd no idea.'

'Then he may have come here. To hide, to shelter? Perhaps to jump. Fearful for the consequences of what he'd just done.'

Jack shook his head. 'Not Miller. He's a man without a conscience, a man without fear. If he jumped, it would have been to escape the fire. I would bet my life – a stupid thing to say in the circumstances – but I'd bet heavily that someone decided it was time for Miller to depart. It would have taken some strength to get him over that balcony, so a man? A colleague? A boy from the orphanage, now fully grown?'

All three looked up at the still sturdy railings guarding the balcony. 'You're right. It wouldn't have been easy,' Ridley said. 'It's the fire that bothers me most, though. Did Miller set it? Did someone else? And when? We'll have to wait for the post-mortem to know more, but I'll let you know the results as soon as I have them.'

'But why here?' Flora asked suddenly. The two men swivelled to look at her. 'If Miller was murdered, why choose to kill him here?'

'It's a lonely place,' Jack offered.

'But difficult to get to,' she countered. 'Particularly in this weather.' She turned to the inspector. 'On the way here, we had to change our route several times, so many roads were impassable.'

'It's a good point,' he agreed. 'And a reason why I thought it could be suicide. The orphanage has strong associations for Miller. Particularly if he was more involved in Benedict Farr's death than he admitted at the time. It might have been worth the struggle to get here. He sets the fire and then jumps. It could have felt to him like the perfect place to end it all.'

'Poetic justice rearing its head again?' Jack sounded sceptical. 'It seems to me far more likely that someone arranged to meet him here, having decided it was time for Joe to leave this earth.'

'You find me that someone, Jack, and I'll be delighted to have the handcuffs ready.'

'Actually, we've made something of a start. Brought you something that could help.'

'Really?'

'It's a bottle of milk.'

The inspector looked blank. 'Is it April the first and I've missed it? Milk?'

'I think your lab will find it's poisoned milk. The bottle was left on our doorstep and drunk – thankfully a very little of it – by Flora. And Flora has been very ill.'

Alan Ridley's face changed. 'You think it was deliberate? You're being threatened?'

'Of course we're being threatened,' Flora said impatiently. 'Both of us. Jack was nearly killed and I was poisoned on the same night.'

'But why? What exactly have you been doing to stir things up like this?'

Flora was rapidly tiring of the inspector's stream of questions, but tried not to show her irritation. It was essential to keep him close if they were ever to get to the truth.

'We were hoping *you* might tell us why we've become such a target. We've discovered hardly anything that might be damaging. We found Russell Farr's identity and the link with Harry Barnes. And we spoke to Bettina Lyons, but it's hardly the stuff that warrants sending us to our deaths.'

Ridley stroked the moustache he was still attempting to grow. 'It depends, doesn't it, on how desperate this person is? How threatened they feel. The clues you've come up with seem unimportant, but it's possible they're a red flag to our killer, if he or she is feeling cornered.'

'Joe Miller isn't our villain, at any rate,' Jack said glumly. 'He seemed a racing certainty, too.'

'He still could be,' the inspector counselled. 'Wait for the post-mortem and the lab results on this very special bottle of milk. I hope you've brought it with you.'

'We have.' Flora opened the car door, reaching into the well of the Austin and presenting him with a glass medicine bottle.

'We had to decant the milk, but we've brought the empty bottle with us.'

'What about the foil top?'

She shook her head.

'Pity. It might have told us something. There won't be prints on the bottle – the poisoner will almost certainly have worn gloves – but to replace the bottle top with a gloved hand so tightly and so precisely that it looked genuine? Not impossible, but difficult.'

'I'm sorry you won't get your fingerprints, Inspector, but let's hope you're grateful. Our medicine bottle should keep the milk safe – no accidental poisoning – and you're sure to reach the station unharmed!' She spoke tongue-in-cheek.

The inspector glowered at her and, having stowed the rogue liquid in the boot of one of the police cars, bid them both a clipped farewell.

'He doesn't like being teased, does he?' Flora observed, as they climbed back into the Austin, ready to leave.

25

On their way home, Jack insisted they stop at the fish and chip shop opposite the Cross Keys to buy their supper.

'But it's not Friday.'

'Defy tradition, Flora! Live dangerously! You need building up and fish is good for you, that's what you're always telling me.' Flora's spirits had made a good recovery, but to Jack's eyes she still looked pale and drawn and it made him anxious. 'In any case, Friday is your friends' night and you'll be eating Alice's cooking.'

'I'm not sure I'll go.'

Jack brought the car to a halt outside the shop, and slewed around to look at her. That any of the three friends should voluntarily miss a Friday supper was unheard of.

'What's going on?'

'Nothing desperate. I'm just tired, I think. Tired of the arguments over Sally and Hector, tired of all the talk there'll be about Kate's baby and what to knit, what to buy, what to bring to the baby party. I'd rather be at home – with you.'

'Once the fish has done its job, you'll be raring to go,' he prophesied. 'I'll be back in a trice and bearing chunky cod and even chunkier chips.'

He was as good as his word, clambering back into the car only minutes later with two warmly wrapped packages.

'It smells good,' she said more cheerfully.

'I told you.'

Once in the cottage, Flora bundled the fish and chips, still in their wrappings, into the oven while Jack closed curtains and relit the sitting room fire, stacking it with more coal.

'This will be a cosy night in and with no talking shop,' he said firmly.

'Until later. We have to talk things through.' Flora grabbed knives and forks from the cutlery drawer. 'Too much has happened not to.'

'If we must then. What else do we need? Salt, vinegar?'

For a while, there was silence while they tackled the two large fillets of cod, Jack glad to see that Flora ate hungrily.

'I can't manage all the chips, though,' she said, giving up halfway through, 'so...'

'Say no more. Pass your plate.'

Their conversation over supper had centred on whatever news was making its way around the village. Jack had made sure there had been no mention of Miller or the investigation. They both needed a break from what had become a dangerous case, but he recognised that Flora was right – they had talking to do. The dishes washed and dried, he turned down her offer of tea to suggest instead that they try a brandy.

'More bolstering?' She smiled slightly.

'Why not?' He poured a generous shot of amber liquid into the two balloon glasses that Flora's Aunt Violet had absent-mindedly bought at a local sale. 'It will help us to think. And we need to.'

Settled together on Flora's squashy sofa, they ran through an unwritten list of all they knew so far.

'Benedict Farr was almost certainly murdered,' Flora began. 'The coroner's verdict of accidental death was a mistake. And the man has to have been murdered by someone within the orphanage, either a member of staff or one of the boys. The police reports mention no other names – no strangers called at the orphanage, there were no meetings between Farr and any outsider.'

'An inside job.' Jack took his first sip and a fiery warmth trickled deep. 'Given the police focused their major inter-viewing on three particular boys—'

'Boys that were older and stronger,' she put in. 'It's likely to have been one of the three who, at least, knew something about Farr's death.'

'Leaving aside which one for the moment, the assumption at the time was that Farr had fallen from the balcony by accident and the coroner conveniently confirmed it. Farr was buried, life went on undisturbed for the next twenty years, until his son, Russell, has a chance meeting with Bettina Lyons. She's a woman who not only worked for his father but was personally attached to him, and is convinced his death was not an accident. The anonymous note she sends Russell spurs him into ques-tioning the verdict, and a new murder spree begins.'

'Russell, we think, was killed in Abbeymead to stop him from asking more questions.' Flora continued the story. 'I know we can't know that for sure, but he was in the village for a reason and the only one that's come to light is his vague connec-tion to Harry Barnes. First question, Jack: Who knew Russell would be in Abbeymead? Who knew there was a connection between Harry and the orphanage?'

'The killer doesn't need to have known the connection. They wouldn't need to know that Harry's firm delivered at the orphanage. If he or she had been watching Russell, they could simply have followed him to the village that day.'

'They must have had some intimation of where he'd be

heading or they'd have to have watched him twenty-four hours a day,' she protested. 'I feel sure that Gilmore will have mentioned Harry when Russell came to the college to question him. Probably told Russell how he'd come by the job at Cleve, how Harry had sponsored him and, more importantly, that Harry's firm had delivered regularly to the orphanage and he might know something that could help.'

'It would be a way of getting rid of Russell,' Jack conceded. 'Directing him elsewhere. If Gilmore had something to do with Benedict Farr's death, he'd have every reason to divert Russell Farr. But perhaps it was just that he felt sorry for him – he might have remembered Russell as a small boy – and he *was* just trying to help.'

Flora considered this for a moment, sipping the brandy very slowly, something she'd learned to do. 'If that's what happened, Gilmore could have told the killer that he'd sent Russell off to Abbeymead. Maybe said they didn't need to worry – Harry would know nothing and Russell's mission would fizzle out.' Her hand wavered and the brandy lurched slightly in the glass. 'Maybe,' she said excitedly, 'Gilmore even told the killer when Russell planned to visit.'

'So... let's imagine that the killer knows where his victim will be, or at least hopes he knows. Even if Gilmore knew nothing of Russell's plans or he didn't pass them on, the killer is likely to have been watching Freshfield Road – and he wouldn't need to watch twenty-four hours a day. He would know Russell's working hours and soon realise he was a creature of habit.'

'It wouldn't have been too difficult to follow him here,' she agreed.

'If we're focusing on Miller as Farr's murderer, he must already have drowned Gregory Gilmore. *His* death occurred several months before I took the job at Cleve.'

'Drowned him for what?'

'Maybe Gilmore wasn't able to shake off Russell's visit, to lose their meeting from his mind. Jocelyn may have been speaking the truth for once when she said that Greg went downhill after the supposedly unknown man called at the college. Perhaps, after speaking to Russell, Gilmore was so badly upset that he could no longer bear the guilt. So, he decides to go to the police – you suggested that once – and confess what happened twenty years before. If he had gone to the police, he'd implicate Miller. Gilmore might have been willing to suffer his punishment, but Miller certainly wouldn't be. And if it was *Miller*, out of the boys, who'd actually pushed Benedict Farr to his death, his punishment would be to hang. He'd have no option then but to get rid of Gilmore.'

'If that's the true story, Jocelyn Draper has no part in it, despite lying through her teeth and having the opportunity. And a really strong motive.'

'*If* it's the story. The alternative is that she was the one who killed Gilmore, but killed for a completely different reason.'

'Or a possibility that we shouldn't forget – he killed himself.'

'Or, he killed himself,' he agreed. 'He was a man in deep trouble and desperately depressed.'

'Whether he killed Gilmore or Russell or Benedict Farr or all three, Miller was on the loose, and a danger. You could have been victim number four. He knew it was us who found Russell's body – I'm absolutely certain we were being watched – and I reckon he knew that we'd found where Farr lived. He could still have been watching the house when we knocked on the door.'

'Even though Russell was dead?'

'In case of trouble, maybe. He'd need to make sure that nothing and no one could harm him.'

'Except he didn't quite manage it,' Jack added. 'He well and truly came to harm.'

Flora took a last large mouthful of brandy, choking slightly. 'After all this talk, I'm not sure we're any further forward.'

'The post-mortem, when it comes, could be crucial. If Miller's death was suicide, he's likely to be our villain. He died, consumed by guilt!'

'Somehow, I don't think you believe that.'

'I don't. I think he was killed and that means we need to keep looking.'

It was two days later that the inspector telephoned. The snow had partially melted, but the lane was still ridged with ice and too dangerous for Flora to attempt a ride on Betty. Jack had made sure he left the college early enough that afternoon to collect her from the All's Well, arriving in the cottage's tiny square of a hall just as the telephone began its shrill.

'I don't suppose you've anything for me?' Ridley asked, evidently without much hope of a breakthrough.

'Nothing at this end. Sorry, Alan. But the post-mortem results? You have them?'

'Arsenic,' the inspector said succinctly. 'Tasteless, colourless, and lacking any smell. The perfect poison. There was enough arsenic in Miller's body to render him unconscious and, after that, the fall from three storeys up did the rest. It explains why there were no signs of struggle on his body. No defensive wounds. He hadn't a clue what was happening.'

'It also explains why a man of that size and strength could be thrown over the balcony railings. Presumably, he died before the fire caught hold.'

'His clothes stank of smoke and were pitted here and there by falling embers, but not a mark on Miller himself. Someone else set fire to the building after Miller died. Want something even more interesting?'

'You know I do.' It was Jack's turn to sound impatient.

'The milk you gave me. The lab analysed it and guess what – arsenic again. Not a huge amount, but then you only need a small fraction to kill. If Mrs Carrington had drunk more, she would have died a very unpleasant death.'

Jack was struck silent.

'What's happening?' It was Flora, ducking out of the kitchen and standing by his shoulder. 'Who's on the phone?'

Ridley, Jack mouthed. 'We're looking for a poisoner then,' he said, still trying to recover from news that was shocking. He saw Flora's eyebrows waggling ferociously, but kept talking. 'That's very different from running someone down on the road.' Or drowning someone, he added silently to himself.

'I reckon we're talking about two killers here, Jack. Be careful, eh. And that lovely wife of yours.'

Flora was bobbing up and down in frustration when he replaced the receiver.

'I was poisoned by arsenic?' She'd heard enough to add two and two together.

'It looks like it. But—'

'But? Is there a but? I was deliberately poisoned!'

'Poisoning doesn't fit with driving at someone to kill or drowning them in a lake.'

'Miller was thrown off a balcony – the poisoning was simply a means – and twenty years ago so was Benedict Farr. That does fit. It's the twenty years that's important. Whatever is happening now, the truth lies in the past.'

If only the past wasn't so oblique, he thought, though he shared Flora's certainty.

'We more or less know what happened to Gilmore and Miller after they left the orphanage,' she went on, 'but what about the third boy the police interviewed? We've hardly mentioned him. Is he alive? Is he even in this country? I don't remember his name but he was Italian, wasn't he?'

'He had Italian grandparents, that's different.'

'Let's check anyway. Do you have the list of boys that Alan Ridley gave you?'

'Stuffed among my papers, I think. I'll do the search if you put the kettle on.'

Jack ran up the stairs to the second bedroom, now commandeered for his writing. Did that list hold more importance than he'd given it so far? Was it possible they were closer to the truth than they thought? Miller's death might not be the blow he'd first believed, if the man's demise led them finally to uncover what had happened at Rillington all those years ago.

Rifling through the papers on his desk – notes from several of his students, some roughly sketched plan for the remainder of his current novel, a statement from the bank – he managed to uncover the list. It was a long one.

'There must be two hundred names here,' he said to Flora, walking back into the kitchen.

'Let's take a look.'

He handed her the several sheets of paper and, sinking into a kitchen chair, she spread them across the table, running a finger down the first column of names.

'The boys are listed in order of their ages and which classes they were in. We can forget the very young ones, but even the older age groups have around thirty or forty names each.'

Her finger continued to move down the list looking, Jack knew, for any link, any reference, to someone or something either of them might know.

'I've found the third boy! His name was Paolo Ruffini, wasn't it?'

Jack nodded. 'As far as I remember from Ridley, but he'll be almost impossible to trace. I'm sure the inspector will have tried.'

Flora bit her lip, a sure sign her mind was busy. Very busy.

'There's something you're remembering?' he said.

She nodded and tapped a teaspoon idly against the tabletop. 'It's the certificate,' she said at last.

'What?'

'In Roberta's house. A certificate saying her husband had passed his exams and that he was now a qualified accountant.'

Jack was used to Flora's leaps of imagination but, even so, she often left him struggling. And he was struggling now. 'What about it?'

'The name on it was barely legible. It was hazy. The letters seemed to have faded.'

'It was an old certificate,' he suggested.

'Maybe, but the other words were sharp and easily read. It was as though that line of the certificate wasn't part of the original.'

'You think it was altered in some way?'

'I think... I think the name was changed!' Jack could hear the rising excitement in her voice. 'Ruffini? Raffles?'

'Fairly close, I grant you, but it's a pretty big leap... though he *was* bursar at the college.'

'He was, and that might mean that every one of the three boys the police questioned when Benedict Farr died have all worked at Cleve College – and for a period, they were working there at exactly the same time.'

She turned to him, her hazel eyes large and sparkling. 'I think we've got it, Jack!'

'I'm not sure—'

'I am. Roberta's husband is called Paul and Ruffini was—'

'Paolo.'

26

Flora went to bed that night undecided on their next move. Jack, too. Switching their focus to the third boy in the Benedict Farr case had opened a whole new raft of possibilities. Should he ring Alan Ridley in the morning? With two likely murder investigations on his shoulders, the inspector was sure to be at work this weekend. But would he take their suggestion seriously?

Flora doubted it. Paul Raffles was a professional man. He held down an important job in the City and to suggest he was one and the same as a boy involved in a twenty-year-old murder case would be too much of a leap.

'It's the old problem,' Flora said, while cleaning her teeth. 'The inspector will need cast-iron proof before he makes any move.'

'And what proof would that be?' Jack lounged against the bathroom door.

'The accountancy certificate – what else?'

'Even if we managed to get hold of it – and how would we do that? – it won't prove Raffles is a killer.'

'It proves that he deliberately changed his name, and why would he do that if he didn't have something to hide?'

'He could simply have been trying to escape his past. The orphanage was notorious for a while – Farr's death was widely publicised. If Raffles, or whatever his real name is, aimed to establish himself as a professional man, changing his name would be the best move he could make.'

'He *is* a professional man and has been for years, so why does he need to hide the truth? He wants to show off what he's achieved – he hung the certificate on the wall, granted in a downstairs cloakroom, but still a wall – yet he hasn't the courage to display it in his real name. He has something to hide,' she repeated.

'It won't be enough for the inspector,' Jack prophesied.

They were still undecided on a course of action when Flora opened the All's Well's door on Saturday morning. She had barely hung her coat and scarf in the kitchenette and unlocked the till when a pink-and-white car drew up outside. She knew that car. Roberta? Surely not. The postcard she'd sent had suggested a telephone call.

But it was Roberta.

'Flora!' Her friend burst through the door. 'So sorry to bother you at work, really I am, but I couldn't just phone. I had to come. I have such news!'

'It's good to see you,' Flora stammered. 'But if you'd called, I could have arranged something. Shown you around the village. Cooked you a nice lunch.'

'Sorry again. I knew you'd be in the shop today and I really needed to see you. Tell you face-to-face as soon as possible. And never mind the lunch – it's not important.'

'If you had some shopping to do this morning,' Flora said a

little desperately, 'we could have an early meal at the Nook. It's the village café,' she reminded her.

'The one your friends run?'

'That's right. You dropped me off at their house after my visit to Lewes.'

'I remember. But no... it's kind of you... but I have to get back. There's so much to do at home.'

'And your news?' Flora came from behind her desk and gestured to the window seat. 'Come and tell me. I'm not likely to have customers for a while. My aunt always insisted on opening well before nine and I've carried on the tradition. She liked to be ready.'

'How quaint.' Roberta allowed herself to be led to the cushioned seat. 'I'm moving,' she announced, once she'd made herself comfortable, gloved hands clasped in her lap.

'Moving from Lewes?'

'Moving from England, my dear. We're going to New York, would you believe?'

Flora stared at her, hardly believing what she'd heard.

'I know!' Roberta exclaimed, studying her companion's face. 'It's exactly how I reacted when Paul told me of the new job. At first, I said I couldn't possibly leave our beautiful home, then how could I live in a foreign country, where would we live, how would we get on in a very different society? My dear, the questions.'

'You evidently found the answers.'

'Paul has been wonderful.' Roberta tugged off her gloves and made a token effort at patting her bun into place. It was as immaculate as the last time Flora had seen her. 'He calmed me down and made everything easy. The financial corporation that's offered him the job will arrange accommodation for us – at least, initially. Then when we've found our feet, we can look for something for ourselves. All our expenses will be paid, Flora, and the salary – well, I don't like to tell you how much that is!'

'Congratulations,' she said weakly, thinking they should ring the inspector immediately. Could the police stop people from leaving at the airport? 'But... how did it all happen?'

'Paul was headhunted. I think that's what it's called. The corporation wanted him to fill a vacancy they had, thought he was the perfect person, and offered this amazing deal.'

'It is amazing. Almost a fairy tale.'

'I know. I was dubious at first – and I can see you have your doubts – but Paul has explained everything and now I'm raring to go.'

Flora was plunged into confusion. How could this have happened so suddenly?

'Well, congratulations again—' she managed to say, before breaking off as the doorbell clanged.

'Flora? Oh, there you are.'

Alice Jenner, weighed down by a bulging shopping basket, trotted towards her, then seeing Flora was not alone, came to an abrupt stop.

Flora jumped to her feet. 'Alice, let me introduce you to Roberta. Mrs Roberta Raffles. Roberta, this is Alice Jenner, a very old friend and the best cook in Abbeymead – and for miles beyond.'

Roberta remained seated and, after a brief nod in her direction, Alice made no attempt to offer a handshake.

'Was there something...' Flora tailed off, feeling extremely uncomfortable.

'I just dropped in to show you what I've bought – for Kate – before it goes home with me. But it will do another day. Is Mrs Raffles staying long?'

Roberta rose from the window seat, a glacial smile on her face. 'Mrs Raffles will be going very shortly.'

'Oh, and I cooked you and Jack a chocolate sponge,' Alice said, unperturbed. 'Thought you might need a pick-me-up.

Flora hasn't been well,' she said, turning towards the unwel-come visitor.

'My dear, why didn't you mention it? I'm so sorry. And, surely, you shouldn't be working.'

'Some of us have to work whether we feel like it or not.' Alice's tone was caustic.

'Let's hope then that the chocolate sponge does the trick.' Roberta's expression suggested it was highly unlikely. 'I don't eat cake myself. So bad for the figure.' She smoothed the pencil skirt over her slim hips and looked pointedly at Alice's plump form. 'But I must be going. Do come to Lewes, Flora, before I go. Just to say goodbye.'

'Why don't *you* come to Abbeymead and bring your husband? I could do lunch. Jack will be home.'

'That's so sweet of you, but Paul is in New York for the week – imagine! – and when he gets back, he'll be working right up until we leave.'

'Come one weekend then. Or come for an evening.'

'So sweet,' she repeated vaguely. 'But I'm afraid we'll be too busy. You see, it's only a matter of weeks before we leave. It may only be days. I'll telephone instead.'

A kiss on Flora's cheek, a nod to Alice, and she drifted to the door, reaching into her handbag for her car keys. 'I mustn't block the high street for too long.' She jingled her keys in the air. 'I suppose it *is* called the high street even in a village!'

'I suppose it *is* called the high street,' Alice mocked, as the bookshop door closed behind Roberta. 'Another one who's all fur and no knickers, I'll be bound.'

Remembering the meagre furnishings in Roberta's house, Flora wondered if Alice was right, but felt impelled to offer some defence of the woman who'd befriended her and was in danger very soon of having her life turned upside down. 'Roberta's not a bad person when you get to know her.'

'I wouldn't want to, thanks. I didn't like her one bit.'

Flora sighed at this statement of the obvious.

'And where's that husband of hers?' Alice went on. 'Have you ever seen him?'

'What do you mean?'

'She didn't want to bring him here, did she?'

'They're busy. They're bound to be. It's a huge move they're making.' Unless Ridley gets to them first, she added to herself.

Alice sniffed. 'Or maybe there's no husband. Maybe he doesn't exist. You've never seen him.'

'Of course he exists. He works in the City – that's why I've never met him.'

Alice sniffed again. 'If you say so. Now, where do I put this cake? In the kitchenette?'

'Thank you. It's such a kind thought and Jack will love it.'

'I'm more than happy to cook for you both, you know that. But just remember who your friends are.'

With her parting shot, Alice was out of the door, leaving Flora prey to a tangle of emotions.

The notion that Roberta had lied about a husband was silly, but nevertheless it was an idea that recurred to Flora throughout the morning as she advised customers, wrapped books and answered the telephone. Paul Raffles was a real person – he'd been a bursar at the college and presumably must be Roberta's husband – why would the woman pretend to be married if she were not? But had she deliberately kept him hidden from view? She might have done so, if she knew something discreditable about him. Knew he was a killer, for instance. In all her conversations with Roberta, the woman had seemed extremely protective of him.

And had he really been offered a job in New York? The more Flora thought of it, the more extraordinary it seemed. It had to be an escape. Had Paul Raffles been plotting it for months? He must have been, she thought – it was only three days ago that Miller had died. There was no way in that short time that Raffles could have been offered and accepted a job so far away.

The bursar's role at the college, too. There were questions now over that. Had Paul really relinquished it to go to a better job in the City or had he had no option? Had he been forced to leave when he found his past catching up with him? As it was doing now. Whatever the answers, he couldn't be allowed to escape. She must make sure of it, she and Jack together.

27

By the time she returned from her morning in the bookshop, Flora had decided what they should do. Opening the front door, she could hear Jack hammering at the Remington's keys on the floor above and, without bothering to lose coat and scarf and kicking her boots to one side, she ran up the stairs to the spare bedroom.

'We have to get that certificate,' she announced. 'Paul Raffles is leaving the country very soon and once he's gone, we've lost our villain.'

Jack swivelled round, a blank expression on his face, his mind clearly elsewhere.

'Sorry,' she apologised belatedly, nodding towards the typewriter. 'I know you're chasing your murderer, but we need to chase ours and that certificate is the first step.' She sounded as agitated as she felt.

'You're in a pucker. Why?'

'Roberta Raffles called at the shop this morning. Her husband has a job in New York. He's escaping, Jack! That's what this job is about. I was confused when she first told me but after she'd gone, I worked it out.'

'So it seems,' he said wryly.

'I know you don't believe the certificate is that important, but if we get hold of it, take it to Ridley, he will at least have to start asking questions. How did Paul Raffles get the job as the college bursar under a false name? Why did he give Miller the caretaker's job? What did he have to do with Gregory Gilmore? And why is he suddenly decamping halfway round the world? Until he answers those questions, the police can stop him from leaving the country.'

'OK. Slow down. It might get Alan on the case, I suppose. We could ask him to check official sources for a change of name. Raffles must have done it by deed poll – otherwise he'd have had difficulty applying for a passport. But there's no way for us to get hold of that certificate.'

'I've been thinking.' Flora plumped herself down on the upright chair that Jack occasionally used when his back was giving him problems.

He groaned. 'I'm not breaking into their house, if that's your idea.'

'It wouldn't be exactly breaking in. I know where the key is hidden.'

'So we pinch the key, let ourselves in and say, "Hello, Roberta. We thought you might like a visit today?"'

'No, we don't because Roberta won't be there. Not on Monday afternoon. She goes to a women's group which sounds ghastly but which I'm sure she loves. She's bound to be their queen bee.'

'Every week?'

Flora nodded. 'She won't be home, Jack. And neither will her husband. He's in New York the whole week – and there's no reason she'd lie about that. We let ourselves in, walk a few paces to the downstairs cloakroom, snaffle the certificate from the wall and off we trot. Of course, there would be other rooms we could look at. For more evidence?'

'Flora!' This time, the groan was louder.

She jumped up and walked over to him, putting her arms around him and holding him tight. She stared at the half-filled sheet of paper dangling from the roller. 'Are you stuck?'

'A little,' he admitted. 'I don't like what I've just written.'

'Then take action. Get unstuck.'

'How does breaking in to someone's house – and it is breaking in – help move my plot along?'

'It will, you'll see. Let's go Monday. I can make ham sandwiches for lunch.'

'Bribery, Flora.'

'You know it always works.'

Jack was surprised at how easy it was. He'd been careful to park a few roads away from the tree-lined avenue in which the Raffles house was situated and, walking casually up to its front door, he could see they were unlikely to be observed. The houses were spaced well apart with wide front gardens and overgrown hedges obscuring the view from the street. Added to which, there were few pedestrians and the one or two cars that had passed them as they'd walked from the Austin were travelling too fast for their drivers to be aware of strangers in the district.

The key was where Flora had promised.

'You'd think people would be aware by now that flower pots are the most obvious hiding place,' he commented.

'Roberta is a traditionalist.'

'Even to hiding her key?'

'I reckon so. Come on. We're wasting time.'

'It's a women's group she's attending,' he teased. 'We should be safe all afternoon.'

Flora poked him gently in the ribs. 'Any more comments like that and worse will follow,' she threatened.

Once inside the front door, she went straight to the downstairs cloakroom while Jack wandered into the kitchen. 'The place looks a tad shabby to me,' he called out. 'And Raffles is some City bigwig who's been headhunted? There's not much food in the fridge either.'

Wandering back into the hall, he was met by Flora. 'It's not there,' she said flatly.

'How do you mean, not there?'

'Come and see.'

He followed her into the cloakroom and she pointed at a blank space on the wall, a dark outline on the paintwork suggesting that something had hung there in the very near past. Jack walked up to the spot, brushing his fingers against the wall.

'It looks as though someone has tried to scrub out the marks the frame left behind, but not quite managed it.'

'We need to look for the certificate,' she said determinedly. 'It has to be in the house.'

'A quick reminder – you said we'd be here five minutes.'

'That was before it vanished. I didn't expect Roberta to take the certificate down – she was obviously trying to cover for her husband. Or perhaps it was Paul himself who did it. Either way, it proves he has something to hide.'

'Maybe, but we can't start turning the house upside down.'

'Just a couple of rooms, Jack,' she pleaded. 'I'll take the main bedroom if you take the kitchen.'

'Why those rooms?'

'Because that's where people hide things,' she said with confidence. When he looked doubtful, she carried on persuading. 'There's hardly any furniture in the sitting room, so practically nothing to search, but the kitchen and the bedroom have cupboards and drawers. Hiding places.'

'OK, but we set a time limit. No more than fifteen minutes.'

'We'd better be swift then.' She reached up and kissed him on the cheek before disappearing rapidly up the stairs.

Poking her head around several of the bedroom doors, Flora was surprised to find even less furniture than on the ground floor. Had the Raffles already shifted much of their household into storage? Or did they prefer to live in a minimalist fashion? It seemed unlikely, given the smart clothes Roberta always wore, but they were questions Flora didn't need to answer. She was here to search.

The tallboy – that's where she'd start – a masculine affair which, as she whisked through its drawers, revealed only a small pile of shirts and a couple of silk ties. Roberta's dressing table was similarly unforthcoming, containing nothing more sinister than a small pile of underclothes and, in the top drawer, a surprisingly large collection of cheap make-up.

Padding across the room, Flora flung open the doors of the solitary wardrobe and immediately saw why there was no need for a second cupboard. She could count the number of hangers on one hand. It was a shock and she stood for a moment trying to order her thoughts. What she'd seen in this house was at odds with the impression she'd carried of Roberta since their first meeting. A shabby kitchen, an almost bare sitting room, bedrooms hardly furnished and now a wardrobe and chest with few clothes. If you were earning huge sums of money, which presumably was the case for Paul Raffles, why on earth ...?

Blackmail! It had to be. Joe Miller had been blackmailing Raffles! Stripping the man and his wife bare of their possessions while accruing more and more for himself. Was blackmail the reason the bursar had given him the job of caretaker? Miller must have had something on Paul Raffles, something with which he could threaten. And that something was the evidence they needed. She must talk to Jack – urgently – but first the certificate, she reminded herself. It was why they were in the house.

There had been nothing in any of the drawers and the few clothes hanging in front of her had to be innocent. No hiding place there for a framed certificate. Crouching down on the floor, her hands inched hopefully around the base of the wardrobe, pulling out two pairs of shoes but nothing more. Flora was stumped. And annoyed she'd been beaten. Getting to her feet, she looked up. The wardrobe's top shelf, most usually a repository for hats, was her one last chance. Standing on tiptoes, however, she scanned a shelf that looked empty. Perhaps at the very back...?

She grabbed the one chair the bedroom hosted – it was wicker and she prayed it would hold her weight – and reached up to begin sweeping her hand back and forth.

Ah! She had felt something. Something hard-edged. Gradually manoeuvring it forward, she felt a wooden frame and then a sheet of glass. She'd found the certificate!

'Jack,' she went to call out, but not a squeak emerged. The chair was pulled from beneath her, sending her flying onto the hard flooring, her shoulders and back crunching horribly. From her prone position, she looked up at a vengeful Roberta.

'What a clever little girl you are, Mrs Carrington,' she sneered. 'Though not clever enough to know my meeting was cancelled this afternoon. And no key beneath the flowerpot when I looked, but the front door open. Now why would that be unless I had a visitor? An uninvited visitor.'

Flora tried to scramble to her feet, but was pushed back to the floor by a hefty blow to her face and a kick to her legs.

The woman's eyes burnt with anger, her hair unravelling from its tight bun as though abandoning all restraint. She bent over Flora, her hands reaching for the girl's throat.

'I'm sorry to have to do this. No... on second thoughts, I really am not. It's entirely your fault. You should have stayed the ignorant friend.'

Flora kicked out wildly, hoping to bring her adversary to her knees, but Roberta evaded the blows. She balled her fists and punched at the woman's ribs, but Roberta had her hands locked around her throat. Twisting this way and that, Flora jack-knifed her body in a struggle to free herself from the iron grip, but all it did was exhaust her. Her attacker was slowly tightening her hands around her throat. Flora was losing the battle.

Until, suddenly, the pressure eased, Roberta fell back and crumpled to the floor.

It was Jack. He had dived for Roberta's legs and was now pulling her arms behind her back and holding them fast. 'I heard a noise and crept up the stairs. The chair,' he explained. 'Any chance of something with which to tie up this wretched woman?'

Flora staggered groggily to her feet, gazed vacantly around the room and then made for a curtain. It was easy enough to yank from its rail, old and thin as it was. She wondered if it would even bind Roberta securely, but several long strips torn from the bottom did the trick. Once her adversary was suitably trussed, Jack looked across at her, his eyes anxious.

'Are you OK?'

Flora rubbed at her throat. 'I thought you would never ask.'

'I'll look after you once we're home, promise, but if you've got your voice back, can you telephone Ridley? I saw a phone in the hall. I'll stay here and sit on Mrs Raffles until the police arrive.'

Roberta muttered. A muffled and unintelligible protest.

'Sorry,' Jack said, 'I didn't quite catch that.'

28

Inspector Ridley called at the cottage on Wednesday afternoon. He'd telephoned earlier to make sure they would both be at home and, though Jack had been due at Cleve College that day, he'd immediately rebooked the one student appointment in his diary. Ridley's information was too important to miss.

The inspector's bulk filled their tiny hall, his tweed suit seeming several sizes too large. He was looking particularly cheerful, Jack noted, a sign that his current investigation must be going well. His officers had arrived at the Raffles' house within ten minutes of Flora's telephone call, Ridley having galvanised the local police station. Roberta, handcuffed but still spitting venom, had been escorted to a police car and whisked to Brighton. As far as he was aware, she was still there, occupying a well-deserved cell.

'Hello, Mrs Carrington.'

Ridley had spotted Flora lingering in the kitchen doorway. She had hung back from greeting him, uncharacteristically quiet. It was two days ago that she'd suffered Roberta's brutal attack and, though her throat was on the mend, Jack knew the shock, the fury, of her supposed friend still resonated.

The inspector chewed at his moustache. 'By rights,' he said ponderously, fixing them with a stare, 'I should be charging you both with breaking and entering, instead of coming here to fill you in on the case.'

Quickly, Jack ushered their visitor into the sitting room. 'Tea?'

'I won't, thanks. Only just downed a mug at the station.'

Jack felt himself gag slightly, remembering the brew he'd been served by the Brighton police sergeant. It was no wonder that Ridley preferred his beer.

Since Flora showed no sign of speaking, he was the one to ask the first question. 'Do you have Roberta Raffles in custody still?'

'We certainly do. In one of our best cells. And that's where she'll be staying. Her husband is back from New York—'

'There really was a job?' Flora had found her voice – just.

'There was, orchestrated by his wife, though that's gone down the Swanee. Mr Raffles is back in Sussex and employing some smart alec lawyer from London. Whatever money he's paid, it hasn't worked – the judge has refused her bail. Attempted murder is a serious charge and I think the beak was worried she'd skip the country if she was on the loose.'

'Or worse,' Jack put in. 'She'd be out for revenge.'

'Attempted murder?' Flora was beginning to come out of her shell. 'What about actual murder? What about *Paul* Raffles and what he has done? Why is he still free and booking lawyers?'

'One thing at a time, Mrs Carrington. Your statement on the attack you endured, plus the toxicology report on the milk, is sufficient to convict Roberta for attempted murder. A murder charge, two charges of murder, in fact, are on their way. My chaps are working flat out, putting together a watertight case.'

'Are you saying then that *she's* the killer, not her husband?'

Jack looked across at Flora and saw his surprise mirrored in her face.

'I am. Paul Raffles professes his innocence and I believe him.' Ridley stroked a moustache that was slowly becoming more luxuriant. 'The man seemed genuinely appalled when he realised what his wife had been up to. Not that he believed us, not at first. But I reckon he's got the full picture now, though he has to maintain the pretence that she's innocent.'

'And what is the full picture?' Flora's interest had returned in full, it seemed, and Jack was glad.

'Roberta Raffles killed to protect her husband, that would seem to be the motive. Or more likely to protect her own life-style. When Russell Farr visited Cleve College with his questions, she must have foreseen that the world she'd built for herself was about to be destroyed by an old scandal. Farr had to die before he probed further and caused irreparable damage to her life.'

'She followed him to Abbeymead that day?'

'It seems so. She knew where he lived and had been watching him. From what I can surmise, Russell left his address with Gregory Gilmore when he visited Cleve College.'

'I found Russell's address in my desk,' Jack confirmed. 'In what had been Gilmore's desk. I thought at first that was why Miller had been searching my office, but by that time Russell was dead and Miller would already have known his address. Or he didn't need it. Now, I'm fairly sure he was looking for anything incriminating that Gilmore might have left.'

'Interesting. Every small fact, you know, is a help in completing the jigsaw. And this is one jigsaw I'd say that's pretty mind-boggling.' The inspector stretched out a pair of tweed-covered legs. Mind-boggling or not, he seemed pleased with results. 'I guess Russell Farr felt Gilmore was a sympathetic ear and left his address in case the chap thought of anything that might help him discover what happened to his father.'

'But how did *Roberta* know the address? How did she know about Freshfield Road? You said she'd been watching Russell Farr.'

'She had. Gilmore must have mentioned it to Joe Miller, perhaps to warn him that Farr was serious in his quest. Or perhaps because he'd been spooked by Farr's visit and needed to talk to a man who'd been a fellow inmate of the orphanage. So... Miller knew the address and almost certainly passed the information on to Roberta.'

Flora leaned forward. She looked bemused. 'Why would Miller have gone to Roberta?'

'I guess he needed to alert her that danger lay ahead,' the inspector said. 'And if Gilmore had mentioned as well that Harry Barnes and Abbeymead had come up in his conversation with Russell, then Miller could well have passed that on, too. Roberta wouldn't have been surprised then when she realised Farr was on his way to the village. She'd have been half expecting it.'

'But why tell Roberta?' Flora pursued. 'Why didn't he go to Paul Raffles and warn him?'

'If nothing else, Miller seems to have been a good judge of character. He must have reckoned that Roberta had more to lose and that she'd be the one willing to watch Farr *and* take action. Of course, she had the time and the opportunity – her old man was slaving away in the City all day, every day.'

'She might have had time but she couldn't have watched him every minute of the day,' Flora protested.

'She learnt his routine. Russell Farr was a methodical man. He worked set hours and was at home the rest of the time. He had no friends, apparently, and very few interests. The evenings at this time of the year are dark – he wouldn't be venturing out then, she must have decided, so when? It had to be at weekends.

She's admitted as much, though she continues to deny she had anything to do with Farr's death.'

'Her husband would be home at weekends.' It was another protest from Flora. 'He would have known what she was doing or at least questioned where she was.'

'Golf,' the inspector offered, as though that was sufficient explanation. 'Spent most of his weekend up at Chapel Hill. The Lewes Golf Club.'

'Was Roberta following Russell when he met Bettina Lyons at the cemetery, do you think?'

'It's possible. She's insisting she never followed him anywhere, but she definitely knew Miss Lyons – we have Bettina's statement that Roberta Raffles called on her. Used the pretext of representing some charity or other, but Miss Lyons recognised the photograph we showed her. She'd been puzzled at the questions Roberta asked – though not any more!'

'So it's likely that Roberta witnessed the meeting in the cemetery?'

'It's a red herring, Flora,' Jack put in. 'She might eventually confess to having been there, but it doesn't matter one way or the other. The most important fact is that she was watching Russell Farr constantly and she must have followed him to Abbeymead that day.'

The inspector beamed. He had a prize to deliver. 'This is where it gets interesting. Roberta struck lucky and Mr Farr got very unlucky. She pinched a Land Rover that had been parked near the church, just off Fern Hill.'

Flora leaned forward. 'She was at the church when we were rehearsing for the wedding?'

'Farr certainly was,' Jack said. 'I saw the man, though I'd no idea at the time who he was.'

'Mrs Raffles was there, too, I reckon. Hanging around, still watching.'

'We think Russell must have followed us along Greenway Lane,' Flora said.

The inspector nodded. 'I think that, too. He followed you, and she followed him. When she saw him leave the church, it was her chance to strike. We haven't yet pieced together the full story, but my guess is that she saw the Land Rover parked in Church Row, saw that the key had been stupidly left in the ignition, and suddenly this wonderful plan unfurled in her mind. She could get rid of Farr once and for all, stop his infernal questions and get her life back.'

'You have fingerprints?' Flora asked hopefully.

'Oh yes, more than enough. The owner runs a garden centre a few miles out of the village. Do you know it? The Garden Gnome?'

'It's fairly new. I've never been there.'

'He's a careless chap, the owner, but his sloppiness has served us well. He's not cleaned the Land Rover for I don't know how long and Roberta Raffles' fingerprints on the steering wheel are still beautifully clear. Forensics have come up trumps as well. They've confirmed the Land Rover *was* the vehicle that killed Farr.'

'And afterwards? After she'd run him down, she simply returned the vehicle to where she'd found it?'

'She's a cool customer, that's for sure.'

'Even cooler than you might think,' Jack said. 'We reckon she went back to Greenway Lane and hung around, watching to see if anyone found his body.'

'And saw you both?'

'And saw us both,' Jack agreed. 'But if it was Roberta who killed Farr, where does Miller come into it?'

'For starters, he was blackmailing the Raffles.'

Flora and Jack nodded at each other.

'Hence his warning to Roberta about Russell Farr. He didn't want the past to come to light any more than she did –

though for different reasons. He'd more or less been a bystander at the elder Farr's death, a very young bystander, and, if caught and tried, his punishment was likely to be light. More important for Miller was to protect a lucrative source of income. If Raffles went down, the money stopped.'

'And you know all this because?' Jack queried.

'Mr Raffles. He's been very helpful, filled in a lot of gaps for us. And that will count in his favour. He'll be charged, of course. It was he, or rather the boy he used to be, Paolo Ruffini, who gave the fatal heave-ho to Benedict Farr. Gilmore and Miller helped lure the director to the attic, but it was Ruffini – he was the strongest lad at the time – who did the deed.'

'How *did* they lure him to that tower? Was it fire?' Jack asked.

'Got it in one, old chap. They set a small fire—'

'Miller's idea?'

'Miller's idea,' the inspector confirmed. 'The smell of smoke had Benedict Farr climb the stairs to investigate. And Paolo did the rest.'

'Is he in custody along with his wife?'

The inspector shook his head. 'Paul Raffles isn't going anywhere. Shell-shocked, I think you'd say. He'll be charged in due course and his case should come up after Christmas. In all probability, he'll be spared prison. He was around fifteen, at the time of the murder. His barrister will lay it on thick how repressive the orphanage was, how the director had a down on Paolo. In fact, having talked to Raffles at length, I believe that. He was half Italian, a foreigner in Farr's universe and therefore suspicious. It was well known that his mother had been killed by a father who was serving time for manslaughter. Young Paolo did not have a good pedigree. Add to that the fact that he was extremely bright and a very well-built fifteen-year-old who stood up to Farr's bullying, and you have a likely disaster.'

'If the court believes in the bullying, it should help,' Jack suggested.

'I hope so,' Ridley confessed. 'Myself, I'm rooting for a suspended sentence.'

'But he'll lose his job.'

'Already lost it. That's the least of his worries right now.'

'He's also going to lose his wife,' Flora said slowly.

The inspector grimaced. 'Permanently, I reckon. Paolo made something of his life after he left the orphanage. He got a clerk's job in a firm of accountants and studied at night to pass a raft of exams. That took some doing. When he married Roberta, he confessed apparently. Told her everything about his background, including Benedict Farr's death. It was she who persuaded him to change his name. She claims it was so that he could make a new start.'

'Hence the certificate.'

'Exhibit A in our evidence file. He now had an English name, a top class qualification, and an invented background. It was enough to win him the bursar's job at Cleve College.'

'And then Miller turned up, I'm guessing,' Flora said.

29

The inspector returned to stroking his moustache. 'You guess right, Mrs Carrington. The timeline is a little uncertain but, according to Paul Raffles, Gilmore was already working at the college when he joined as bursar. Not by many months, but it made Raffles pause before deciding the job was too precious to allow it to slip.'

'I'm not surprised he took the chance. It must have been a struggle for him to make it that far.' Flora jumped up and looked from one to the other. 'I don't want to miss a thing, but I do need that tea. Anyone else?'

There was a murmur of agreement from the two men, Ridley following her into the kitchen while he continued his story.

'Raffles says that he and Gilmore had little to do with each other – Gilmore appears to have been a decent man – and it seems it was a case of heads down, we hardly know each other and we certainly don't share any knowledge of a murder. It wasn't until Miller landed on his doorstep that Raffles began to have problems.'

'He was blackmailed into giving him the caretaker's job?'

'According to Raffles, yes. Miller had been thrown out of the army, was unemployed and, with that history, probably unemployable, but he was cunning. Somehow he heard that Raffles had fallen on his feet and decided he'd do well to find him. His old buddy would come to his rescue.'

'Here, let me take that.' The inspector picked up the loaded tray and carried it into the sitting room. 'Refreshments, Jack. A plate of shortbread, too!'

'I'm guessing that was only the start of the blackmailing.' Flora poured three cups of tea. 'Judging by the goods in Miller's office and the shabby state of the Raffles' house.'

'Bled him dry, according to Raffles. He wanted to go to the police a year or so ago, but Roberta persuaded him to keep paying. If he reported Miller, she told him, he'd be forced to confess his crime and would lose everything.'

'Meaning she would lose everything,' Flora said tartly.

'Pretty much.'

'In the end, Raffles felt too stressed to continue at the college and left for a far better paid job in the City. By then, he couldn't stand the sight of Miller and believed – erroneously – that his increase in salary would help him keep up with Miller's demands. The sole result, though, was that the demands got heavier. The more Raffles earned, the more he had to pay.'

'So Roberta killed him.' It was a simple statement of fact.

'Miller was demanding more and more and, once Russell Farr appeared on the horizon, the price for him to keep his mouth shut over what he'd seen that night twenty years ago went even higher. For Roberta, he was an obstacle that had to be got rid of. Just like Farr.'

'How did she do it?' Flora sounded intrigued.

'Arranged to meet him at the orphanage. She denies it, of course, but the arsenic almost certainly came from a tin of rat poison that we found tucked away in the Raffles' garden shed. We don't know – though I'll get it out of her eventually, I'm sure – what pretext she used to get him to the orphanage. Maybe no pretext. By then, Miller had landed himself in a desperate situation. He'd run off from the college, having failed to kill Jack, but knew the police would be hunting for him very soon. He needed money to get clear away and, in the circumstances, none of his illegally gained possessions at the college would be much use. Roberta was the one he would turn to. We found a flask in the Raffles' house. It had been washed out fairly thoroughly, but arsenic clings and forensics found traces mixed with what must have been tea.'

'She took a picnic to the orphanage!'

'Offered him a cup as a sign of friendship, maybe. Then when he fell unconscious – she must have really laced that drink – she heaved him over the balcony to finish the job.'

'And the fire?' Having been on the receiving end of Miller's fascination with fire, Jack was interested.

'She has to have been the one who struck the match. An empty can of petrol suggests so. And who else could it be? Miller was already dead when the fire took hold, and no one else was within miles of the building.'

'But why would she do that?' Jack was puzzled. 'Fire was Miller's thing.'

'That's why,' Flora said suddenly. 'Twenty years ago, it was Miller who used fire to start a chain of events that ruined Roberta's life. She's a spiteful woman, I think... so, as payback, she decided she'd use fire against *him*. Perhaps she hoped his body would burn and leave no evidence. Or maybe setting that building ablaze was a symbol of victory for her.'

The inspector gave the ghost of a smirk. 'More prosaically, it's possible she hoped it would look as though Miller had set fire to the place himself, a place he hated, and then jumped.'

Jack shook his head. 'She must have known a post-mortem was likely to tell a different story.'

'What came later was incidental,' Flora put in. 'She was

drunk with success at murdering Miller. She'd erased him – finally – along with a whole chapter of her husband's life that she never wanted to think of again.'

'She's certainly a strong woman,' Ridley said.

A visible shudder passed across Flora's face.

'A cold-blooded woman,' Jack said.

'Everything about her is cold-blooded, I'd say.' The inspector brushed shortbread crumbs from his chin. 'At the moment, she's tight-lipped and won't talk, but once she realises the evidence we have, once she sees the rope dangling... she'll be desperate to save herself. We're certain to be regaled with stories of Miller as the real villain, the puppet master who pulled her strings. Miller launching an attack on her at the orphanage, no doubt, the flask she took there purely a precaution, and his death? Self-defence, I'm sure.'

'And Gilmore's drowning?' Jack asked. 'Was that Roberta? Or Jocelyn Draper's revenge on an unsatisfactory man? Or even suicide?'

'How about Miller protecting himself?' Flora put in.

'That's the one,' Ridley confirmed. 'Mrs Raffles is very happy to implicate Miller, of course. As I say, she'll soon be doubling down on the strategy. But what she has said of Gilmore's death – and she's spoken quite freely about it – I actually believe. The chap panicked after Farr's visit to Cleve College and became a liability that Miller could do without. Russell Farr's appearance must have had a huge effect on Gilmore and he could no longer live with the guilt. Matron, when we spoke to her, told us that he had come to her with a confession that he'd done something very bad in his youth and was planning to go to the police.'

'Matron told me nothing of that when I asked her about Gilmore,' Jack said ruefully.

'She wouldn't, old chap. It was said in confidence.

According to Roberta Raffles, Gilmore actually warned Miller that he was about to go to the police.'

'And thereby signed his death warrant.' Jack felt sad. His fellow writer had been more naive than wicked. Gregory should have lived. He deserved to have lived.

'Miller's nice little earner would disappear out of the window if Gilmore confessed,' the inspector went on. 'What's more, he'd be charged for being an accessory to murder and, though his youth would likely spare him a custodial sentence, it's doubtful he would have kept his job at the college. He simply couldn't let Gilmore go to the police.'

'Miller must have followed Gilmore to the lake,' Jack said slowly, absent-mindedly refilling their teacups, 'but where was Jocelyn when the man she supposedly cared for was being drowned?'

'We've interviewed Miss Draper about the incident. It took some time to get the truth but she did eventually confess to seeing Miller on his way to the lake that morning. She says, though, that she stayed at the shallow end and saw nothing.'

'She knew what was happening. She told me she heard noises but didn't intervene.'

'I'm fairly sure that when she found Gilmore floating life-less, she guessed it was Miller who'd attacked him. She denies it, of course. Says that when she went to investigate, there was no sign of the man. With the help of one of the gardeners, she dragged Gilmore out of the lake and tried to revive him, but it was too late.'

'At least Gilmore is one person Roberta didn't kill. Miller was as much a murderer – and would have killed again if he'd succeeded in wrestling me over that balcony.'

'History repeating itself,' the inspector said grimly.

'It's not surprising we took an age to work it out.' Flora pulled a face. 'With two killers so closely entwined and with Miller seeming the obvious villain.'

'Which he was,' Jack said feelingly. 'He hated me from the moment I joined the college, but I never understood his suspicions. Any clues, Alan?'

'It's pure speculation, but maybe it was because you'd stepped into Gregory Gilmore's shoes. He'd had to kill Gilmore to get rid of him and now there was another man in his office who might prove a problem. You were a fellow writer. Had you known Gilmore before? What had you known about him? Had Gilmore left behind anything incriminating that you might find? Hence his search of your office. Miller probably told himself you were worth keeping an eye on. And when you were named in the local paper – did you know that? – as the people who discovered Farr's body...'

They both looked blank. 'We didn't,' they said together.

'I'm guessing that Miller read that article – he would have been scanning the papers for anything to do with Farr, once Roberta had done the deed. When he realised that it was you, Jack, who'd found the dead man, it was bound to lead to his being extra vigilant.'

There was a long silence, all three of them slowly absorbing the morning's revelations. It was Flora who broke the silence, fixing the inspector with an unsmiling face.

'When you spoke of how cold-blooded Roberta was, did you discover why she made friends with me? Was it on purpose?' she asked in a small voice. 'She would have seen me in Greenway Lane walking back to the cottage the day she killed Farr. Maybe saw us find his body. Perhaps she even watched as we discovered the cigarette case and, if she was monitoring Freshfield Road as you believe, she would know we went there. Did she decide deliberately to seek me out?'

The inspector nodded. 'She probably wanted to, but I think it was luck that she saw you in the Lewes bookshop and recognised you as the person she was interested in.'

'It wasn't lucky for me.'

'The way she's spoken of you in interview, Mrs Carrington,' suggests that she liked you a lot,' Ridley said warmly. 'She seems genuinely to have wanted to be good friends, but you were just too curious.'

'Hah! Wanted to be good friends but then decided to kill me.'

'You were both getting to be too dangerous. Miller had tried to warn Jack off a number of times with his penchant for fire – before he went for broke.'

'It wasn't by chance that we were both attacked the same night?'

'I'm not sure. I don't think they were actually working together – they seem to have hated one another. It was probably a shared danger that had them act when they did. The stakes had become very, very high. The likelihood of discovery far greater. I don't believe, though, that either of them knew what the other had been up to, not until it became evident – Miller's attack on you, Jack, during that snowstorm. Roberta's poisoning your milk, Mrs Carrington. Until Mrs Raffles loses the Trappist silence, it's all guesswork, I'm afraid.'

The inspector helped himself to another shortbread. 'They may not have been working in tandem, but they were necessary to each other. Until they weren't. If Miller, as I believe, contacted Roberta after his bodged attempt to kill Jack, it would have been to issue a threat. A threat to tell everything unless she paid up again, only this time demanding an even heftier price – he'd be hoping to escape the country and that would cost. I reckon that was when she invited him to meet her at the orphanage, probably assuring Miller that they'd come up with a plan together that would save him.'

'And from that moment his death was inevitable.'

'With someone like Roberta Raffles, issuing an ultimatum wouldn't be a wise move. Miller must have been blinded by fear and allowed it to affect his usual canny judgement of people. And he paid the price.'

Another long silence followed before the inspector reluctantly got to his feet. 'Thanks for the tea, both. It's been good to talk.'

At the front door, he turned to say, 'There's no need for either of you to come to the station. One of my chaps will call round for your statements. In the meantime' – his gaze fell on Flora – 'try and keep out of trouble.'

30

It had been a hectic few days. Decisions as to what to take with them to Cleve and the packing of boxes and suitcases; there'd been a removal van to find, and a garden to plunder for several baskets of fresh vegetables. But now, Flora looked around the college flat and felt satisfied. The place was never going to be cosy – it was too institutional for that – but she had made the small space as welcoming as she could, bringing a number of home comforts from the cottage and making several visits with Jack to the second-hand furniture shop they'd found tucked away in one of the town's hidden corners.

This afternoon they were holding a housewarming, hopeful of persuading their Abbeymead friends that a partial move to the college was a sensible solution. Alice had a free weekend and, with Sunday always a quieter day, Sally had promised to take time off from managing the Priory. Tony and Kate were driving them both to the college while Jack had left earlier to collect Charlie and his mother. At the last moment, Flora had thought she should invite Rose. If her new assistant hadn't agreed to change her bookshop days, they wouldn't be moving to Lewes for a part of each week – and there would have been no housewarming.

Charlie Teague bounced out of the Austin and was charging through the front door before Flora had time to realise that Jack had arrived with his passengers.

'This is a good place, Mrs C,' he greeted her. 'All them fields to play footer in.' He turned to look through the doorway at the expanse of grass on either side of the stables.

'I'm not sure I'll be doing that,' she said. 'And neither will you, by all accounts. I hear you've been training hard at the Nook and the Priory.'

'Yeah, it's great. I get lotsa time off, though.'

'At the moment, Charlie, but it's likely to change very soon,' she warned, 'and then your football will have to take second place.'

'That's OK. Once I'm trained, I'm going to be the vegetable chef at the Priory,' he said proudly. 'Mrs Jenner is giving me the job specially.'

It was probably safer than sending him to help with the desserts, Flora thought.

'Is your mum here?' Charlie appeared to have come on his own.

'Nah, she's got a cold and doesn't want to give you her germs. She sent these though.'

He handed her the bag he was carrying and Flora saw three large bottles of elderberry wine. 'Do thank your Mum, Charlie. They'll do nicely, but perhaps not all this afternoon.' Or they would be under the table in no time.

'Rose. How lovely to see you.' Rose Lawson had appeared in the doorway, also carrying a bag. Not elderberry wine, Flora saw thankfully, but a beautifully iced sponge cake. 'How are you?'

'I'm well and thank you so much for inviting me.' The woman seemed inordinately grateful and Flora immediately felt guilty. Despite living and working in Abbeymead for months, Rose continued very much an outsider in the village. She should do something about that, Flora thought distractedly, but what?

At that moment, Jack staggered in with a hamper in one hand and a bag of rattling bottles in the other. 'I'll put this little lot in what we laughingly call a kitchen.'

More bottles! They could wait until Christmas to be opened, she decided.

'I'll help set the food out, if you like,' Rose offered.

'Me, too.'

'No eating, Charlie, until everyone is here.'

'Everyone *is* here,' he said, pointing through the sitting room window at Tony's van which had just pulled up outside.

Flora gave up. There would be plenty to eat for everyone and if she knew Alice Jenner, her friend would have brought more.

Alice had, but didn't look too happy about it. Stomping through the sitting room, she banged the two baskets she carried down onto the kitchen counter.

Flora looked questioningly at Tony who had followed her in. 'Hector,' he said quietly.

Hector?

And there he was, replete in chain mail and wielding a very large sword in one hand and a mace in the other.

'Cor, Mr Lansdale, do you use 'em?' Charlie had his hands outstretched, ready to be a warrior.

'Only when vegetable chefs get out of hand,' Hector joked.

Sally was at his shoulder, looking radiant. How was this going to work? Flora thought, turning wordlessly to Jack. He shook his head. 'Don't ask me,' he murmured, as though he'd heard her thoughts.

'Sorry about the outfit,' Hector apologised. 'I've come straight from a practice fight. A last-minute thing, you know.'

Flora didn't and hadn't counted on his presence, but was very aware of an atmosphere that had dropped to frigid. 'Shall we open some of Mrs Teague's elderberry?' she asked brightly.

Once a bottle had been opened and drunk, the mood warmed considerably and plates were soon being happily passed around the motley collection of furniture that filled the sitting room. The college had provided a sofa and a pair of fire-side chairs, and their visits to the second-hand shop had added two more – occasional chairs, they were called – and you *would* only want to sit on them occasionally, Flora thought.

Seven seats for nine people. Charlie had immediately sprawled on the floor and Hector, seeing the problem, waved Rose to the seat he'd been about to take.

'I'm happy to join Charlie, but I'll take off this breastplate first. It sticks in the ribs,' he explained.

'Thank you,' Rose said, stammering a little. She smiled up at him, a dimple clearly evident.

Flora had never realised before that Rose had a dimple. Sally's cheeks had pinked, she noticed, and she didn't look too pleased.

'I don't know why the pair of you are here,' Alice muttered, buttering a scone for herself. 'This place, I mean, when you have a perfectly comfortable home in the village.'

'So...' Tony stepped into the breach. 'Tell us what happened with that chap you found in the ditch.'

'Russell Farr? He was eventually identified and the woman who ran him down is now in custody, awaiting trial for murder.' Jack's summary was masterful, skating smoothly over the hours they'd spent in getting justice for Russell and the dangers they'd faced along the way.

'I'd wager you both had a lot to do with it.' Tony grinned at them.

'We helped things along,' Flora said diplomatically.

'Helped things? I don't know what's wrong with that

inspector of yours, Jack,' Alice said through mouthfuls of scone. 'Turns up at your wedding – your wedding, I ask you! – badgering you to get involved, then turns a blind eye when you're both nearly killed.'

'It wasn't quite like that,' Jack protested.

'As good as. *You* were nearly set on fire – I heard about that, common gossip in the village – and don't forget I saw Flora the day after that dreadful woman had poisoned her. I knew right away *she* was a wrong'un. And there's more we don't know about, I'm sure. If she's in custody, you'll have had something to do with it.'

She fixed them both with a severe glance, but neither were willing to volunteer anything further. Telling Alice that Flora had been half choked to death by a woman who'd already poisoned her was not the best idea.

'That Roberta,' Alice continued. 'I told you she was no good. I knew it immediately I met her.'

'How could you, Auntie?' Sally challenged, clearly still bristling from her aunt's hostility to Hector. 'Flora liked her and she's a good judge of character.'

'The woman looked the part, I'll give her that,' Tony said. 'Genteel, I thought. Quite posh. I was sure I'd seen her round the village when she came to our door, but then she looked blank and I reckoned I'd been mistaken. She was peering in at the bookshop when I saw her. Snooping, I guess.'

'I was completely taken in by Roberta,' Flora confessed. 'Initially, at least. She could be charming.'

'Charmin' is as charmin' does.' Alice wasn't to be placated.

'You've come from a re-enactment today?' Jack turned to Hector. More breech-stepping had been required and Flora silently thanked him.

'It was a splendid battle.' Hector's face lit up. 'I was a royalist today and we almost beat Simon de Montfort's men.'

'But de Montfort won, didn't he? That's what all the history books say.'

'Oh, yes, of course he did. It wasn't for real this morning. When we do the exhibition fight in May – it will be the 695th anniversary of the battle – we'll do it right and be thoroughly beaten!'

Flora was mystified. 'Why not wait until the 700th anniversary?'

Hector screwed up his face. 'You see, it's Colonel Jenkins – actually he's Tom Jenkins, he owns the jewellery shop in Station Street – he's retiring next year, and we wanted to give him a proper send-off. He'll love the battle.'

'Play-acting.' Alice helped herself to a second scone.

'Yes, it is,' Hector said equably. 'But good fun. You should come and see for yourself, Alice. Maybe even join. We need more ladies, particularly old... more mature ladies.'

'That's a great idea, Auntie. I've joined. I'm going to be a maiden for the celebrations. I'm working on my costume already.' Sally's spiky blonde curls did a small bounce while everyone politely hid their smiles.

'Rose.' Hector turned his head to smile up at her. 'I wonder... does the All's Well have any books on the Battle of Lewes? I've been thinking I should read more. Understand the barons' quarrel with King Henry better.'

Rose looked flustered. 'I don't think so...' She looked to Flora for guidance.

'Probably not,' Flora said, 'but we can always order a book if you know the title.'

'Ah, that's where I'd come unstuck. I'm not really a bookish person.'

'I can look a few out for you,' Rose offered, 'and you can order the one you think best.'

'That's very kind.' He gave her another warm smile and the dimple reappeared.

Oh dear, Flora thought, seeing Sally's expression turn thunderous.

'No more of those fudge fingers, Master Teague,' Alice warned, providing a welcome interruption, 'or you'll be sick.'

'Nah, Mrs Jenner, I'm OK. I got room for a few more.'

Flora certainly hoped so. A sick boy in the middle of a party that wasn't going too well was hardly ideal.

'What are you going to be doing in Lewes?' Kate asked her. It was the first time her friend had spoken this afternoon and she seemed concerned. 'You'll be here' – she gave the rather desolate room an expressive sweep of her hands – 'for what, two, three days a week, but Jack will be working. It could be quite lonely for you.'

Flora looked down at hands that she'd instinctively clasped. It was a problem she'd been wrestling with for days.

'I thought I might volunteer,' she said quietly.

Everyone's heads swivelled in her direction, while Jack looked startled. 'You've never said anything about volunteering.'

'No, sorry, Jack. It's taken me time to work things out. I thought at first that I might try to find a job in Lewes, but it could only be part-time and it seems foolish when I'll be working in my own bookshop for half the week.'

'The whole thing is foolish,' Alice said. 'You should be in the village.' She looked across at Rose, her mouth pinched slightly. 'I'm sure Mrs Lawson does a good job, but the All's Well is *your* shop and that's where you should be.'

'Rose does an excellent job,' she said warmly, 'and while Jack is here at Cleve, I need to be with him. At the moment, there are days when we hardly see each other.'

'Volunteer?' Kate had returned to what interested her most, her mild blue eyes holding puzzlement. 'But how? Where?'

'In a school, I decided. Assisting children with their reading. Schools always need that kind of help.'

'You're a good girl, Flora. A real kind girl, and it's a worthwhile cause, that's for sure.' Surprisingly, Alice nodded her approval while everyone else subsided into a bemused silence.

'I think so,' she said brightly, though uncertainty had gripped her. It didn't help that out of the blue she'd sprung the idea on Jack and now his face, along with those of her friends, wore the same blank expression.

To Flora, the silence felt overwhelming, unbroken even by Charlie's slurping of lemonade, until Sally said cheerfully, 'Any more sandwiches needed, or shall I start taking this little lot back to the kitchen?'

Some hours later when Jack returned from his drive to Abbeymead, he found Flora surrounded by a stack of clean china and a kitchen table half covered in plates of uneaten food.

'What do we do with all of this?' she asked a trifle helplessly. 'We've no refrigerator here and, in any case, the cakes will go stale in no time.'

'That's simple enough. I'll take it to the staffroom tomorrow. Every last morsel will be gone in a flash, I promise.'

Flora padded into the hall and fetched several of the cardboard boxes they'd used for the move. 'You can carry it over in these, but where we put all this crockery...' She pointed to the row of clean cups, plates and saucers currently piled on the tiny kitchen table.

Jack looked aimlessly around a kitchen that boasted very few cupboards, his mind distracted. It was Flora's new start that was bothering him. She'd made no mention of her plans before today's announcement and, coming suddenly as it had, he'd been shocked, wholly unaware that she'd been working her way through ideas of how best to fill her time. That worried him. It spoke of a selfishness on his part; he'd been too intent on his own writing and teaching to think deeply of how this move would affect Flora.

Unsure how best to tackle the subject, he stood silently watching her pack away the food and leave the boxes by the front door, ready for the morning.

'Are you sure about this volunteering?' he asked, eventually deciding a direct approach would be best.

'Why not?' She hung up a very wet tea towel and grabbed a broom that had been propped against one wall. 'It involves books and children. It should be fun.'

Walking over to her, he took the broom from her hands before turning her to face him. 'You're staying here for me, Flora, and I'm not happy. You should be in the village. Alice says so and I think she's right. It's where you belong. You're a fish out of water in a town like this, casting around for some-thing to fill your hours when all you really want is to be back at the All's Well.'

'Don't think of it like that. Think of it positively. It will do me a lot of good to get out of the village. To meet new people. Spread my wings. It's different for you, Jack. You've spent much of your life travelling the world. Apart from the three years I was at college, my world as long as I can remember has been this small circle of people and this one small part of a county. I love Abbeymead, love the villagers, love my friends. And particu-larly love my bookshop. But sometimes, just sometimes, I feel stifled.'

'Really?'

She nodded, her lips forming a gentle smile. 'I'm not that certain about the teaching, I admit, but I need to give it a go. I need to... breathe, I suppose. Breathe more freely, at least.'

'And helping children to read will allow you to?'

'It's a start. This is going to be a new life for both of us, so why not?'

He wasn't entirely convinced but Flora had come to a decision and, when that happened, it was best to accept it.

'All I can do then is wish you well, but if it doesn't work out...'

'Then I'll try something else. A new life, Jack!'

'Still... I hope we can keep some of the old life.' He pulled her into his arms, hugging her close and kissing her several times over. Flora reached up to kiss him back. Then kissed him again.

'I'm all for that,' she said. 'How about right now? The china can wait.'

A LETTER FROM MERRYN

Dear Reader

I want to say a huge thank you for choosing to read *Murder at Cleve College*. If you enjoyed the book and want to keep up to date with all my latest releases, just sign up at the following link. Your email address will never be shared, and you can unsubscribe at any time.

www.bookouture.com/merryn-allingham

The 1950s is a fascinating period, outwardly conformist but beneath the surface there's rebellion brewing, women stirring into action, even in the rural heartlands of southern England! It's a beautiful part of the world and I hope Flora's and Jack's exploits have entertained you. If so, you can follow their fortunes in the next Flora Steele Mystery or discover their earlier adventures, beginning with *The Bookshop Murder*.

If you enjoyed *Murder at Cleve College*, I would love a short review. Getting feedback from readers is amazing and it helps new readers to discover one of my books for the first time. And do get in touch on social media or my website – I love to chat.

Thank you for reading,

Merryn x

KEEP IN TOUCH WITH MERRYN

www.merrynallingham.com

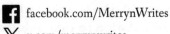 facebook.com/MerrynWrites

X x.com/merrynwrites

PUBLISHING TEAM

Turning a manuscript into a book requires the efforts of many people. The publishing team at Bookouture would like to acknowledge everyone who contributed to this publication.

Audio
Alba Proko
Melissa Tran
Sinead O'Connor

Commercial
Lauren Morrissette
Hannah Richmond
Imogen Allport

Cover design
The Brewster Project

Data and analysis
Mark Alder
Mohamed Bussuri

Editorial
Jayne Osborne
Imogen Allport

Milton Keynes UK
Ingram Content Group UK Ltd.
UKHW031653170724
445742UK00004B/134